Seal of Confession
Jon Brownridge

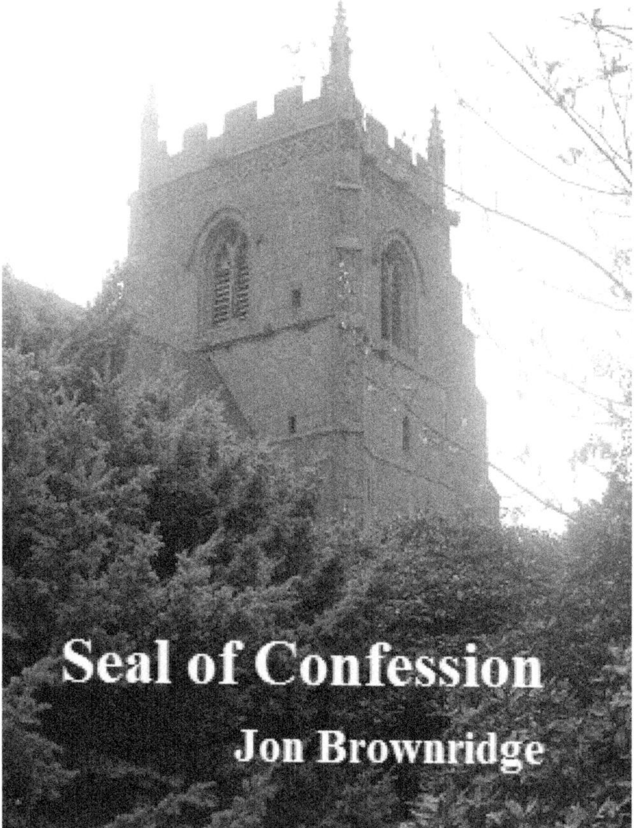

Other books by Jon Brownridge

A Skylark in Blue Yonder

Seal of Confession

Jon Brownridge

Copyright © Jon Brownridge 2012

The author asserts his moral right to be identified as the author of this work

All rights reserved. No part of this publication may be reproduced, stored in a retrieval system, or transmitted in any form or by any means electronic, mechanical, photocopying, recording, or otherwise without the prior permission of the author.

Cover: St. Swithun's Church, Cheswardine, Shropshire

An inexperienced priest must decide whether the Seal of Confession can take precedence over his legal and moral duty to report a serious crime.

*After the death of his young wife, **Marcel Dion** trains for the priesthood and is assigned as Pastor to Maplewood Creek, a small, isolated village on the banks of the St. Croix River. His new life seems to be idyllic, but his euphoria is shattered when his very first penitent confesses to murder.*

After seeking advice from a colleague and then from his bishop, Marcel finds that all is not as it seems, and he is thrust into a tangle of mystery and intrigue. A bizarre act of vandalism in the churchyard seems to be a warning. Unsure of whom to trust, the priest finds himself at the centre of a dramatic arrest and rescue attempt in the St. Croix River.

As new evidence comes to light, Marcel knows he must decide for himself whether the Seal of Confession can take precedence over his moral and legal obligation to report a serious crime.

For Keinan and Willow

One

Maplewood Creek was a small settlement on the southwest corner of New Brunswick, looking across the St. Croix River to the state of Maine. It was remote and secluded, and it was hard to imagine that anyone, apart from the local population of about 250 residents, would actually want to go there. But Marcel Dion was in high spirits as he made his way to the village for the first time on this blustery March day. This was his first assignment, and he was looking forward to his new life as village pastor with a great deal of enthusiasm.

The newly-ordained priest looked around at his fellow travellers in the cramped railway compartment. He would have attempted some friendly conversation but the other passengers seemed to be fully occupied with their own concerns. A heavy-set man in oil-stained blue jeans and loud lumber jacket occupied more than his fair share of the seat to Marcel's left. He was obviously a blue-collar worker, a mechanic probably, judging by his peculiar odour. He exuded a strange smell of oil and grease, flavoured by the distinctive tang of cheap alcohol. The man was engrossed in his magazine and clearly not interested in any small talk.

The well-dressed gentleman facing Marcel seemed to be the exact opposite. He was a professional of some type, perhaps a lawyer or a university academic. He was only in his mid thirties, about Marcel's age, but he looked tired, overworked, and a bit stressed out. He seemed to be uneasy in himself too, pretending to read and studiously avoiding eye contact with anyone else in the compartment.

Marcel assumed his fellow travellers would be headed for Saint Stephen or one of the many stops along the way. He'd be the only one going on to Maplewood Creek—he had no doubt about that. He smiled and closed his eyes as he pondered the assignment he'd been given and the challenging new life it offered.

Marcel could still hardly believe he was a priest. Clara would have been so proud of him, he thought, and not a little surprised that he'd chosen the priesthood after her untimely death. It was an old dream that had resurfaced—a follow up from his brief encounter with a priestly vocation in his late teens. Meeting Clara had put a stop to any plans for seminary training then, of course. One date with her and Marcel knew that she'd be his wife, and any thoughts of the priesthood had evaporated into the clear blue skies of that memorable spring day. But now Clara was gone—claimed by cancer at the age of 29—and to Marcel's surprise, the old dream had returned.

'I've picked you specially for this job, Marcel,' Bishop Giguère had told him in the private interview at the end of the retreat. 'It's unusual for a newly-ordained priest to be given his own parish, but you have an unusual background. Your experience as a banker and administrator has provided you with some very useful skills that most priests don't have. Not only that, but at 35, you're ten years older than the typical seminary graduate. You're more mature after your years as a married man, and you are well able to do this job. I've had nothing but positive reports about you and I know you'll be very well accepted in Maplewood Creek. It's a village that needs you.'

Marcel wondered if his bishop had been too kind and optimistic. Certainly the banking background would be useful, but being a priest involved a lot more than administrative and organizational skills. It's the pastoral skills that really matter, he thought. That's why he had insisted on spending two full years as a deacon, rather than the usual six months. He'd wanted to gain as much experience as possible in pastoral care, and his year in a large Montreal parish had enabled him to do that. He'd done everything there—marriages, funerals, baptisms—to the point that he felt completely at ease with them. He'd become quite a liberal thinker too. After spending the previous summer at St. Francis parish in Fredericton with his friend and mentor, Gérard Rousseau, Marcel had become totally convinced that the focus of attention must always be the people.

There was one thing that Marcel still found a little disconcerting—the issue of hearing confessions. He'd never done that, of course. Only ordained priests could hear confessions, and although Marcel hated to admit it, he wasn't looking forward to that particular duty in his new role as pastor and parish priest. He'd expressed his concerns to Gérard and received advice that was quite typical from the liberal priest. 'Don't worry,' he'd told him. 'You'll have to provide the opportunity, of course, but you'll find it's not that much of a problem.'

The train stopped suddenly with an annoying squeal of brakes, rousing Marcel from his reverie. He opened his eyes with a start, wondering where he was for a moment, and then cleared a patch of fogged-up window with his bare hand. Several passengers were hurrying from the train and heading for the exits of the small station, and the portly mechanic on his left moved over to create some extra room. This allowed Marcel to spread out a little and make himself more comfortable. He caught the eye of the lawyer facing him and smiled. 'These old trains, eh? They don't get any better.'

The lawyer perked up a little, pleased perhaps that someone had broken the uncomfortable silence, but still not anxious to be involved in any on-going conversation. 'Not much further to go, Father,' he said. 'We should be in Saint Stephen within half an hour.' He glanced at the mechanic and then quickly looked down at his book to resume his fake reading.

Marcel sensed an uneasy connection between the two men. Lawyers and mechanics probably don't have a great deal in common, he thought, but there's much more than that going on here. These two guys don't like each other for some reason. They know each other but they're not speaking and there's a definite air of hostility between them. That's very clear. Marcel recalled being the last one to enter the compartment before the train left Fredericton and the uncomfortable silence he'd encountered as he squeezed into his seat. Maybe there'd been some disagreement or altercation between them before his arrival, he thought. Perhaps an argument over a seat or the luggage rack, or some such minor problem. Whatever it was, they were both quite content with their phoney reading, and there was no sign that they were going to change that before they reached their destination.

Over the following half hour, lulled by the rhythm of the moving train, the new priest found himself falling into a dreamy reflective mood once again. What would life in a small village be like, he wondered. The current pastor, Father Lemieux, insisted that his years in Maplewood Creek had been the happiest of his life, yet he couldn't wait to retire and move on to pastures new. It was understandable that he'd want to retire after so many years in service, but there was a hint of bitterness in his voice too—an impatience that might be seen as cynicism and disappointment.

Marcel had met his predecessor on only one or two occasions before at the annual retreats, but he'd talked to him on the phone several times recently about the new appointment. The old priest had seemed pleasant enough but he wasn't very helpful. 'I can't pick you up at the station,' he'd said abruptly. 'My old car can't be trusted. But anyway, it's only a fifteen-minute walk up to the church. Just turn left at the main exit and follow the main road. I'll be waiting for you at the residence.'

The train came to a squeaky halt at the central railway station in Saint Stephen and the remaining passengers hurried from the stuffy compartment leaving Marcel and the lawyer alone. The priest watched the bustle of activity through the dirty window as the last passengers alighted from the train and made their way through the turnstile. His companion seemed to be making no effort to leave, and Marcel wondered what was keeping him. 'This is Saint Stephen station, you know,' he told him helpfully. 'This must be it for you.'

The lawyer looked up from his book. 'Pardon?' he mumbled. 'Oh, no. I'm going on to Maplewood Creek. It's about ten miles down the line. How about you?'

Marcel was taken aback at this news. 'Are you really?' he said. 'I'm going to Maplewood Creek myself. I thought you were probably some high-flying lawyer headed to the bright lights of Saint Stephen.'

His companion closed his book and placed it on the seat beside him. He seemed relieved that the mechanic and had gone. 'Lawyer?' he said, now grinning broadly. 'Not me.' He extended a friendly hand to Marcel. 'I guess it's time I introduced myself. I'm Dr. Pierre Bouchard. I'm new to Maplewood Creek. I'm taking over a small medical practice there.'

Marcel leaned forward and shook the offered hand with some enthusiasm. 'I'm Marcel Dion,' he said. 'I've never been to Maplewood Creek either. I'm taking over the parish of St. Jude's. I'm the new pastor. Now isn't that a coincidence?'

As the train moved slowly from the station, the atmosphere in the carriage lightened up and the two men laughed over the unlikely twist of fate. They chatted amiably, each taking comfort in the fact that he wouldn't be the only newcomer to a small village where it might take time to be accepted by long-time residents.

Dr. Bouchard, it seemed was to run the clinic in place of an elderly doctor who had finally accepted that retirement was his only option. Father Dion was replacing an even more elderly priest who was quite happy to accept his bishop's strict instructions to retire.

By the time they emerged from the train at Maplewood Creek, Marcel Dion and Pierre Bouchard were acting like old friends. They shook hands, delighted to have at least one acquaintance in the village as they began their slightly fearful new lives. 'You and I are in the same business, Father,' the doctor joked. 'I'll be looking after their bodies while you take care of their souls.'

This seemed to be a good way of summing up their respective roles. 'Well, good luck with your new life as a village doctor,' Marcel said as they reached the exit and prepared to get on their way. 'No doubt we'll be in touch.'

Pierre looked up and down the quiet main street. 'In a village this size?' he laughed. 'How can we avoid it?'

Two

Marcel paused for a moment and took a deep breath of fresh air. It was a wonderful feeling to be free of the stuffy train compartment, and he felt a sense of exhilaration and excitement as he stood there on the threshold of his new career. Village life would be such a welcome change after the years he'd spent in big cities, and he looked forward to being involved in an active and vibrant community.

So this is Maplewood Creek, he told himself as he absorbed his first view of the village. An assortment of small, wooden-framed houses lined the main street, all neat and tidy, and painted with an unusual array of bright colours. Beyond the houses in one direction he could see a small service station with a tiny shop attached, and then the road wandered off into glorious countryside. In the other direction the road gradually became a long, winding hill, shaded by a plethora of tall evergreens and maple trees.

Marcel could see the steeple of a large church rising from behind the trees in the distance and he grimaced a little as he realized he'd have to climb the hill to get to it. That has to be the place, he thought. That must be St.Jude's.

It was a long pull up the road with his heavy suitcase, but with a few strategic stops along the way the eager new pastor made steady progress until he was level with the main entrance to the church. He was struck by the size of the impressive stone building. It's incredible, he thought, how past generations believed it was appropriate to build such an enormous edifice to serve the spiritual needs of a small community—almost big enough to be a cathedral, and so typical of the small towns and villages of New Brunswick.

A large board attached to the stone pilaster at the gates gave all the information necessary: St. Jude's Catholic Church. Sunday Mass 11 a.m. Not much going on here, Marcel thought, amused at the apparent meagre range of parish activity. That will surely have to change.

Attached to the church and extending from the back was a striking stone house, reminiscent of a protestant manse or vicarage. It was obviously the priest's residence though, and Marcel followed the paved pathway that led to the large front entrance. He dragged his heavy suitcase up the three steps to the covered porch and was about to ring the bell when the door was suddenly flung open. A cheerful, matronly woman in her mid-sixties stood there bright and breezy, as if she'd been expecting a houseful of guests.

'Oh, Father,' she exclaimed apologetically. 'Do come in. We've been expecting you. You must be the new priest—Father Dion, I believe.'

'Indeed I am. Quite out of breath too after walking up that hill.' Marcel grinned, happy to have finally reached his destination.

'Welcome to the village, Father. I'm so sorry. I would have arranged a taxi for you if I'd known. Father Lemieux said you were making your own way to the residence but I had no idea you'd be coming on foot.'

The bustling woman picked up Marcel's suitcase with some difficulty and dragged it into the spacious hallway. 'I'm Mme Louise Poirier,' she said, offering a welcome hand. 'I'm the housekeeper here. I'm so glad to meet you, and I'm very much looking forward to helping you any way I can.' She turned around and waved the newcomer in with a wide sweep of her arm. 'Please follow me, Father.'

Marcel looked around his new surroundings as Mme Poirier led him through the hallway to the lounge. It was a large, roomy house with panelled walls and high ceilings everywhere, giving the impression of a university building or a gentlemen's club rather than a comfortable home. But the lounge itself was pleasant enough. It was well carpeted and a large attractive fireplace on one wall provided a focal point for the room. The housekeeper pointed to a cosy-looking leather chair in front of the hearth. 'Make yourself comfortable,' she said. 'I'll let Father Lemieux know you've arrived.'

It was a strange feeling. Marcel felt like a visitor as he sat down in front of the empty fireplace, but he reminded himself that this was his new home. From this moment on he would be the one making the decisions and directing all activities relating to parish life. Father

Lemieux's only function now was to show him around and apprise him of everything that was going on at St. Jude's. So far he had the impression that this was very little.

Some five minutes passed before the squeaky floorboards in the hallway indicated someone's approach, and the door slowly opened. Father Lemieux's face appeared round the door. 'So there you are, young man.' The old priest shuffled into the lounge and extended a hand of welcome to his younger colleague. 'You found us all right, then? Welcome to St. Jude's.'

Marcel stood up respectfully and responded with a firm handshake. 'Father Lemieux,' he said, 'so nice to see you again. We missed you at the retreat this year. Everyone was asking about you.' Marcel wondered if this might sound like a criticism and hastily added, 'You must be busy of course. I suppose you'll be anxious to get on with your retirement.'

The old man chuckled at this observation. 'Absolutely,' he said. 'It's taken me a while to pack after being here so long but it's all arranged now. I'll be leaving for Bangor, Maine on Monday morning and this place will be all yours.'

'Bangor? You're leaving the country then?'

'That's right. I was born in the USA you know. My younger sister has invited me to move in with her. She never married and I think she's a bit apprehensive about looking after me, but I'm hopeful that it's all going to work out.'

'I'm sure it will, Father. You certainly deserve a pleasant retirement after working for so long.'

It was an awkward half hour that followed, but slowly the two men began to feel at ease with each other, despite their wildly different personal backgrounds and an age difference of forty years. Most of the talking was done by the older priest as he reminisced about his twenty years in the village. He obviously cared for his people a great deal and he knew all the intimate details about their troubles, their successes and failures.

'Over the years I've always relied on the dedication of the parishioners and their involvement in parish life,' the old man explained, 'but I must admit I've let things slip a little.' He peered over his glasses at his younger colleague and grinned. 'No doubt, a younger priest will be able to revive everything again.'

Marcel nodded in agreement and laughed at the old man's sincerity. 'That's the general idea,' he said. 'I have a few plans.'

By the time dinner was served in the formal dining room across the hall, the conversation had turned to more personal matters concerning certain families and the misfortunes that had affected them over the years.

The blustery housekeeper had prepared a special welcoming meal and as the pair sat down at the table, Father Lemieux expanded on some of his concerns. 'Not everything has been easy in this parish over the years,' he said, weighing his words as if he were afraid of saying too much. 'The village has had its share of tragedy as well as happy times. They are a tight-knit lot, you know, and the problems of one family can affect the whole community.' He smiled as he helped himself to food from the elaborate dishes. 'But let's not get into it now,' he went on. 'I'll show you around a little bit tomorrow and we can talk about any questions and concerns you might have then.'

Marcel got the distinct impression that the older priest had some intriguing information that he wanted to share but had some hesitation and reticence in doing so.

The evening passed quickly and Marcel, feeling quite exhausted now after his tiring journey, was quite happy to retire to his own room for the night. The priest's private quarters occupied the entire second floor of the old house, and Father Lemieux had kindly moved to the guest room for his last few days, allowing his successor to properly move in and unpack his belongings.

Marcel fell asleep with many thoughts on his mind. It had been quite enlightening to listen to Father Lemieux's musings and to hear his thoughts about the people of Maplewood Creek. But there was more to this village than the old man was letting on. Marcel had a few questions of his own, and he hoped to find some answers before his predecessor left for good on Monday morning.

Three

Over the weekend, the older priest introduced his young successor to the routines of parish life and community activity in the village. Everything was carefully explained from the expected services like baptisms, weddings and funerals, to the way that funds were collected and deposited in a Saint Stephen's bank account. Of course there was never enough money, he explained, and church property was always in need of repair and maintenance.

Father Lemieux pointed out improvements that had been made to the church and brought Marcel's attention to some of the more attractive features of the old building. 'It's a fine old church,' he said reverently. 'These wooden carvings, marble steps, fine old solid doors—you'll never find things like that in the modern buildings you see up in Fredericton.'

Marcel showed polite interest but cringed at the outdated mentality that seemed to shroud the whole place. The sight of an old-fashioned confessional box in the back corner provided an opportunity to ask some questions that weighed heavily on his mind. 'Tell me about the confessional, Father. What's the story behind that?'

'Ah! Isn't that a fine specimen?' The elderly priest beamed with pride as he led Marcel to the back of the church. 'This polished-oak confessional box is the original that was installed when the church was built more than a hundred years ago,' he said with the expertise of a true connoisseur. 'It's identical to the confessionals found in the great French cathedrals with a place for two penitents, one at each side.' He chuckled as he went on. 'It's not very comfortable, I must admit, but it's served its purpose for over a century so it's certainly earned its keep.'

'You do use it for its original purpose then?'

Father Lemieux turned, somewhat confused with the question. 'Of course. That's why it's here. What else would I use it for?'

'Well it's just that some priests I know prefer a face-to-face format rather than being cooped up in an old-fashioned confessional box. You know, they treat confession more like a confidential chat, person to person.'

The old man looked shocked and Marcel wondered if perhaps he'd said too much. 'It's just an observation, Father,' he added gently. 'I know it's not everyone's cup of tea.'

'I don't think I'd like that, but I suppose I'm of the old school,' Father Lemieux said, shaking his head. 'I don't think the people in this village would like that either. They like to tell their secrets and confessions anonymously in the dark safety of a confessional box.'

Marcel shuddered at the thought. 'I suppose I'll have to take things slowly for a while,' he said. 'I'll have to get to know people before I try out any new ideas.'

'Do you have a problem with hearing confessions, young man?'

Marcel was glad the old priest had asked that question. It saved him from broaching the topic himself and it allowed him to ask about the habits of the villagers when it came to these matters. 'As a matter of fact, it's something I'm quite apprehensive about,' he said with some hesitation. 'I loved doing baptisms and weddings while I was a deacon, and even funerals allowed me to work closely with people as they went through their grieving process but, quite frankly, the thought of hearing confessions in a claustrophobic box gives me the creeps. I've never done it of course—as you know, it's only about a month since I was ordained.'

The old man made no attempt to hide his shock and concern. 'But it will be part of your priestly duties' he said. 'People have to be given a chance to go to confession if they want to. You must have been fully trained for that part of your ministry while you were in the seminary program.'

'Yes, of course, but what I'm saying is that I'd much prefer to have a confidential chat or counselling session with parishioners who have worries or concerns on their minds. I don't really feel comfortable talking to faceless voices in the dark. It seems a bit spooky to me.'

The old priest shook his head slowly and looked at Marcel with tight lips as he took this in. 'That's a strange way of thinking,' he said gravely. 'But I think you'll have to keep in mind that the people in this village expect to be able to use the confessional box if they want to—that's the way it's always been around here.'

There seemed to be no point in pursuing that discussion any further and Marcel decided to stick to the basic facts. 'What's the routine for confessions then?' he asked. 'I mean have you been following a particular schedule or arrangement? I noticed there is no mention of it on the board at the main gates.'

'It used to be posted but that's not really a matter of any importance. Everyone knows that confessions are on Saturdays between 4pm and 5pm.'

Father Lemieux paused a moment and scratched his head before continuing. 'You know, to be honest young man, hardly anyone goes to confession these days. It's not like it used to be. I got into the habit of sitting in the confessional box week after week, but it was a rare occasion when anyone came in to confess. I mostly used the time to catch up on my reading, and I must admit, I've dozed off in there more than once.'

That says it all, Marcel thought to himself. What's the point of making these arrangements if they are no use to anyone? He realized that old routines would have to continue for a while until he was accepted by the community, but he made a mental note that sooner or later that old confessional box would have to go.

Father Lemieux shuffled towards the main doors. 'Let me show you the churchyard,' he mumbled. 'It's in a pretty bad state right now, but I've had a young man from the village tidying things up for me. There have been no new graves on church property for about seven years and all the old headstones are looking worse for wear. You'll probably want to continue the spring clean-up project I've started.'

The heavy front doors groaned as the two men pushed their way out into the churchyard. It was a bright March morning and as Marcel savoured the welcome fresh air he noticed a portly figure standing at the end of the stone pathway with his hands thrust deeply into his pockets. The man was looking around aimlessly as if were expecting to meet someone there, but as the screech of the unoiled hinges caught his attention he turned and stared at the two priests before walking towards them.

There was something familiar about this fellow, Marcel thought, and as the hulking figure approached it dawned on him that this was the same man who had sat next to him on the train from Fredericton the previous day. He was no longer wearing greasy, oil-stained jeans and he looked relatively presentable in his jacket and corduroy pants. Giving a cursory glance at Marcel the man focussed his attention on the obvious object of his visit. 'Father Lemieux,' he boomed with no hint of a smile, 'I thought I'd find you around here somewhere.'

The old priest shaded his eyes against the midday sun and squinted at the speaker who was obviously not someone he wanted to see. 'Denis,' he said coolly, 'what are you doing here?'

'I'm looking for that shit-arse son of mine. Is he around?'

Father Lemieux sighed. 'He's around here somewhere, Denis, but I hope you're not here to cause him any more grief. God knows Guy has had enough to put up with lately.'

The man raised his eyes to the sky and snorted derisively. 'Give me a break, Father. He is my son. I know he's got problems—that's why he should be listening to me.' He looked at Marcel as if expecting an introduction. 'Who's this then? Do I know you?'

Father Lemieux was about to speak up but his younger colleague beat him to it. 'Father Marcel Dion,' he said, extending a friendly hand. 'I think we travelled on the same train from Fredericton yesterday afternoon.'

'Oh yeah? I'm Denis LaPlante—I used to live in this god-damn village and my fool of a son still does. I'm trying to get him to move out. You'll die of boredom in this place, Reverend.'

The old priest shook his head in disapproval. 'No need for that, Denis. Father Dion is replacing me as pastor of St. Jude's, and I'm finally retiring. I'll be out of here Monday morning.'

'So I hear. I understand Dr. Martin is finally being replaced too. About time that old fool retired—he should have been struck off years ago. But what I'm really mad about is who's replacing him.' Denis spat on the ground as if to make his point more forcefully. 'Apparently, that idiot Bouchard has come down from Fredericton to take over—saw him on the train yesterday—and he'll be the new village doctor? Give me a break. The guy's nothing but bad news.'

Marcel smiled at the unwarranted outburst. 'I met Dr. Bouchard on the train yesterday,' he said shrugging his shoulders. 'He seemed fine to me. We were sitting across from each other and we had a good chat about one thing or another on our way into the village. I thought he seemed to be a nice friendly sort of man.'

Denis LaPlante snorted again. 'You don't know the half of it, Father.' He looked at Marcel with narrowed eyes then turned to the older man. 'So where's Guy then? I don't have all day.'

'As far as I know he's still cleaning up in the back cemetery.' The old priest waved his hand dismissively as if to hurry the unpleasant fellow on his way. 'You'll find him back there somewhere.'

With a scornful sniff, Denis turned on his heel and strode off towards the back of the building, muttering and complaining to himself, until he finally turned the corner and disappeared from view.

'Quite the character, isn't he?' Marcel chuckled at the unusual encounter, but seeing the grim expression on Father Lemieux's face he took a more sombre approach. 'What's he all about then?'

The old priest shook his head and sighed in frustration. 'He's caused plenty of trouble around the village over the past few years,' he said. 'Mind you, he's had some tough times in his life too. I suppose that accounts for some of the bitterness and bad attitude.'

'Is he from one of the problem families you mentioned.'

'The main one, I'd say.' Father Lemieux looked at his colleague as if he had plenty to say but was struggling to respect confidential information. 'Denis broke up with his wife, Jeanette, about ten years ago and went looking for work up in Fredericton. His son, Guy, is the young fellow who's been doing odd jobs for me around the churchyard.'

'And what about Guy? Is he anything like his dad?'

'Not at all—they're as different as chalk and cheese. Guy's had his problems though. He was just a teenager when Denis and Jeanette were going through their troubles, and he became a bit of a handful after the separation. Then to make matters worse, when Guy was about sixteen, Jeanette had a heart attack and died.'

'That must have been very difficult for him,' Marcel said, shaking his head sympathetically as he took this in.

Father Lemieux turned and pointed to a row of tidy gravestones along the gravel pathway. 'As a matter of fact,' he said, 'Jeanette was the last one to be buried in the churchyard here. I think that's what motivates Guy to come in and clean up the grave sites. He's very particular about keeping his mother's grave neat and tidy.'

Marcel tried to steer the conversation to another matter. 'What's this about Dr. Bouchard?' he asked. 'Denis LaPlante, seems to have it in for him for some reason.'

'I haven't a clue. I don't know anything about Dr. Bouchard, but if they were both up in Fredericton I suppose they've crossed each other's paths one way or another.' Father Lemieux sighed again before going on. 'Denis has been living in Fredericton for a few years but apparently he moved down to Saint Stephen recently. He's only ten miles away now—much too close for comfort I'd say. I think we were all better off when he was up north.'

'Why do you say that? Is he still causing problems?'

'Not really—it's just that I wish he'd give his son some space. Guy spent a year in Fredericton with his father and it didn't work out. He's only been back in the village for six months and he needs a chance to get his life back together. He needs some stress-free time for a while.'

'He sounds like a very needy young man.'

The old priest hesitated for a moment before answering. 'I suppose I should tell you this,' he said cautiously. 'You'll hear all about it anyway. I was away on holiday at the time, but when Guy arrived back in Maplewood Creek last September it seems he brought a woman with him—someone he'd met and married in Fredericton.'

'He does have a wife then?'

'Not any more. There was some kind of terrible accident and the poor woman drowned in the St. Croix river within a couple of days of arriving in the village. I heard all kinds of conflicting tales from parishioners when I got back, and even the papers had differing reports, so I don't know exactly what happened.'

Marcel listened to this tragic story, and he was anxious to hear more details. 'That must have been traumatic for the whole community,' he said. 'How did the family cope with that?'

'All I know is Guy was totally devastated. I've been working with him the best I can over the past few months, but he's a young man who doesn't say much. I've tried to give him a bit of counselling.'

'Has he had some proper professional help?'

'Not as such. Dr. Martin left the village practice just after Guy came back so there's been no medical facility around here for a while. I've been giving him jobs to do around church property to keep him occupied and to help get him back on an even keel. I think it would be good for him if you could continue with that arrangement. He's happy with a small fee and he's a good worker.'

'I'll certainly keep that in mind. I take it his father is no help then?

'None whatsoever. In fact, the less Guy sees of his father the better.' The old priest waved his palms to the ground, indicating that he'd said his last word on the subject, but Marcel was left with the feeling that he had a lot more to say.

By the time Father Lemieux's taxi arrived on Monday morning, Marcel felt he had received all information he needed to take over the parish of St. Jude's and he was eager to start his new job as a leader in the community. He knew what services would be required, and he was well informed about the procedures and traditions that the community expected. There was no problem with that. But his retiring predecessor had been strangely vague and cagey about past tragedies in the village. Marcel found himself wondering if his experience and skill in pastoral care would be sufficient for the needs of this unusual community.

Four

'A beautiful Monday morning, Father—and the first day of summer,' Louise Poirier announced as she bustled around the modest dining room, serving Marcel his breakfast as usual. The bright morning sunshine had put her into one of her talkative moods. 'Father Lemieux would never talk to anyone on a Monday,' she said, chuckling at the thought. 'That was his day off and, as he put it, if they need a priest on Monday they can damn well wait till Tuesday.'

Marcel smiled. His housekeeper had told him that several times before and it always amused him to think of the crotchety old priest expressing his views that way.

'Monday was his fishing day—during the spring and summer months, that is,' Mme Poirier continued. 'He'd spend all day down at the river on his day off and more often than not he'd come back with a nice salmon or two.' She put two slices of bread in the toaster and snapped down the lever. 'Mind you, salmon wasn't the only thing he brought back. He'd sometimes come home with the most awful rashes on his legs—the poison ivy down there is something fierce.'

Marcel nibbled on his bacon and eggs as he listened to his housekeeper's repetitive rambling. 'I've never had any desire to go fishing,' he said. 'It's never been my thing.'

'I never had the patience for fishing, neither,' Mme Poirier went on. 'But my brother used to take me down to the river quite a lot when we were kids. We were always intrigued about the St. Croix being the international border, and we used to amuse ourselves trying to throw rocks to the United States. It was far too wide of course but we thought it was amazing that it was almost possible to throw a rock to another country.' She laughed heartily at the memory. 'What will you be doing today then, Father? Is it golf as usual?'

'It is indeed. I'll be playing golf with Dr. Bouchard this morning, and it looks like we have a great day for it.' Marcel furrowed his brow as he went on. 'I don't know how we put up with it though. Maplewood Creek Golf Club is the absolute worst course I've ever played on.' He grinned at that observation and added, 'We don't have much choice I'm afraid.'

The bustling housekeeper removed burnt toast from the toaster, beaming happily at the mention of Pierre Bouchard's name. 'Ah, Dr. Bouchard,' she said. 'Now there's someone who's made a good impression in the village. Everyone says he's a breath of fresh air after old Dr. Martin. He's more up to date; uses modern methods—you know, proper prescriptions and all that.'

'He's a good man,' Marcel agreed, 'and by all accounts he's a good doctor too. Pierre and I have become good friends since we arrived here in March. We seem to have a lot in common.'

Mme Poirier scraped the toast and placed it in front of the priest on a large platter. 'You're doing very well, both you and the doctor,' she said. 'I hear people talking all the time, you know, but I've not heard a word against either of you.' She looked intently at Marcel and placed a greasy hand on her hip. 'And believe me, Father, that's unusual around here. Most newcomers to Maplewood Creek get gossiped to death.'

Marcel laughed as she bustled off to the kitchen chuckling to herself.

Everything seemed to be falling into place and a new vibrant community began to emerge in Maplewood Creek. For the first time in years, St. Jude's had a functional parish council, and committees with decision-making authority took care of everything from music to flowers. There was new enthusiasm in the parish community, and apart from occasional disagreements, which were to be expected, things were moving along very well. Interesting though—in three months not one single penitent had approached the new priest for confession.

Although Marcel had expressed his reservations about the whole idea of confessions, Father Lemieux had actually said very little about it. They were obviously not on the same wave length when it came to that topic. The old priest couldn't think beyond the long-standing tradition of private confessions in the confessional box and he insisted that the opportunity should always be provided for anyone who wanted it, even if no one ever actually came to confess.

It seemed like a strange arrangement but Marcel decided to continue the tradition until he was able to implement something better. This might have continued indefinitely, but one Saturday afternoon his priestly skills were tested to the limit when he finally encountered his very first penitent.

It was a Saturday afternoon like any other. Marcel took his place in the confessional box as usual and settled down to read the day's sports results in the local paper. He sighed as he tried to make himself comfortable on the hard, unpadded seat.

Why do I persist with this antiquated box, he thought. It seems to be such a waste of time. I suppose I should put the word out that I'll be available in the rectory for anyone who needs me.

The priest's musings were interrupted by a sound outside the confessional. The door on the penitent's side squeaked loudly as someone entered and knelt on the other side of the grill, and a male voice, distorted into a forced whisper, echoed through the enclosed space.

'Father…

'Yes, my friend.'

'Father…I'm under great stress…

'Yes, it's all right—when was your last confession?

'It's been a long time, Father.' The voice was emotional and strained, and Marcel thought it seemed to be deliberately disguised.

'What's on your mind, my friend? What do you wish to confess?'

'I can't find the words. I'm in such turmoil. I don't know where to begin.'

Marcel recalled the precepts drilled into him during his seminary training. Hate the sin but love the sinner, he'd always been taught. If a penitent is here confessing his guilt, it's because he wants to repent and turn his life around.

The priest leaned closer to the grill. 'Don't be afraid,' he said, trying to sound as encouraging as possible. 'We all have our faults. But we can improve ourselves and turn our backs on past failings. You have already shown great courage by coming here to confess.'

'My sin is unusual.'

'Speak it with courage, my friend. Don't be afraid.'

After a lengthy pause, the penitent blurted his shocking words of confession. 'I've committed murder,' he said. The voice drew back breath with a frightful cackling of air. 'I've committed murder, and I don't know where to turn.'

Dead silence followed these awful words and Marcel felt the hairs rising on the back of his neck. A shudder of panic travelled through his stunned body. The priest swallowed hard and he tried to respond but the words stuck in his dry throat. He leaned his head against the grill. 'Murder?' he stammered finally. 'What are you saying? You're confessing to murder?'

The bizarre whispering vocals continued, snivelling now, but strangely more confident since the ice was broken. 'Yes, I am, Father. I killed my wife.'

'You killed your wife?' Nothing had prepared Marcel for this ordeal. He searched for words but nothing came.

The disembodied voice continued to emanate from the darkness. 'It was some time ago, and now it's preying on my mind. I need absolution. Please help me, Father.'

Beads of sweat now formed on Marcel's brow. What was the proper response to such a confession? Shouldn't this man be confessing to the police first?

'Who knows about this?' he asked fearfully. 'Are you a wanted man?'

'No one knows, Father. I killed her but the death was wrongly recorded. No one suspected a murder but that's what it was. I deliberately killed her—and I need absolution…'

The priest breathed heavily as he tried to remain calm. He'd feared this part of his ministry more than any other, and now with his first penitent he was faced with the worst possible scenario. He knew he had to remain as calm as possible. 'It's not so simple,' he told his penitent. 'If you've committed murder you must give yourself up. You must go to the police and face the consequences of your actions.'

'The police? I can't possibly do that.'

'You must promise me. I must be sure that you will turn yourself in to the police and face the consequences of your actions. I must be convinced of your repentance before I can absolve you.'

The priest could hear his penitent's laboured breathing. There was no response to this admonition. Muffled sobs now filled the stress-filled confessional.

'Promise me you'll go to the police,' Marcel said. His voice was firmer now. He knew his priestly obligation. 'You must deal with this matter properly and justly. I cannot give you absolution until you solemnly promise that you will give yourself up.'

The agonizing voice moaned in the darkness. 'But my life will be finished if I give myself up. I need absolution before I can think about that.'

'If what you tell me is true, your wife's life is already finished. 'You've admitted moral responsibility for that. But you must accept legal responsibility for her death as well. You must confess to civil authorities.

This will prove your sincere repentance which is needed before I can give you absolution.

Again a dreadful silence ensued. A minute that felt like an hour passed before the hoarse whisper came through the darkness once more. 'If it's the only way. If I must—all right. I promise.'

Marcel drew his breath with difficulty, then exhaled in a long sigh. 'This is very difficult for me too,' he told the voice, 'but I can feel your remorse. I can feel your repentance.'

'Give me absolution, Father.'

Marcel raised his hand in blessing. 'Say your act of contrition,' he said, and he went through the motions, fulfilling the form of the sacrament. 'Absolvo te...I absolve you of your sins...'

It was done in a flash, and Marcel leaned back on the narrow, wooden bench, his heart still mercilessly pounding. He heard his penitent leave the confessional and he listened as the man's footsteps clattered on the stone floor of the church aisle. Finally, the squeak of the ancient hinges on the main doors told him that his penitent was gone.

Overcome by nerves and overwhelming nausea, the priest threw his head into his hands. Five minutes later, he could stand it no longer. He hurried from the confessional box and headed back to his private quarters in the parish residence.

Five

The rest of the weekend was difficult for Marcel. His thoughts kept taking him back to his dreadful ordeal in the confessional, and his dreams were dominated by the voice of a tortured man confessing to murder. The worst of it all was the isolation.

Marcel wished he could talk to his friend, Pierre Bouchard, about his ordeal but of course the secrets of the confessional were sacred and they could never be divulged to anyone. Not that he couldn't speak generally about the experience to an appropriate person such as Bishop Giguère or even a fellow priest, but even to them, no hint of his penitent's identity could ever be revealed. That would have posed no problem, given the anonymous circumstances of the confession but, thanks to Marcel's ever-vigilant housekeeper, the voice in the dark confessional box soon acquired a body and a face.

Two days after the nightmarish event, on Marcel's day off, Mme Poirier bustled into the dining room in her usual manner, bursting with news about a well-known young parishioner. 'Well,' she said, almost dropping the hot breakfast on Marcel's lap, 'hasn't that troubled young man, Guy LaPlante, left the village in a hurry? Not a word to anyone—just packed his bags and disappeared.'

Marcel narrowed his eyes. 'Guy LaPlante?'

'You know—the young fellow you had cleaning up the pathways in the churchyard a few weeks back. You hired him to finish the spring clean-up that Father Lemieux started.'

'Yes I do know who Guy LaPlante is. I haven't seen him around here lately, but I'm just wondering what's the big deal about him going away?'

'Well as you know, Father, he's a nice enough young man but he is a bit of an odd character. I know that's not a problem in itself but it's the secrecy that gets people talking. Most of us in the village spread the word to our friends and neighbours if we're going to be away for any length of time but Guy has just upped sticks and taken off. He was spotted with two big suitcases this morning waiting for the village bus.'

Marcel smiled at this scanty piece of information that qualified as big news in a small village. 'My understanding is that he's still very depressed over the death of his wife?' he said pragmatically. 'Perhaps he's taken a vacation or gone to visit family. Why should that be a problem?'

'It's not a problem as such—just unusual around here.'

Marcel had been making a conscious effort to avoid linking Saturday's traumatic confession with the death of Guy's wife, but the news of his departure brought that accident vividly to mind. 'Remind me, Louise,' he said cautiously. 'When did Guy's wife die? Last September, wasn't it?'

Mme Poirier poured out a cup of coffee from the old-fashioned pot. 'It was a few months before you came to Maplewood Creek, Father—towards the end of last summer. Yes, I believe it was at the end of September.'

'I never really heard any details about that accident—only what Father Lemieux told me and that wasn't very much. Nobody ever really speaks about it, do they?'

'Well it was a terrible tragedy. The whole village was upset about it at the time and I know Father Lemieux spent some time trying to help Guy deal with it. He was inconsolable. He's never been quite the same since, you know.'

'Has Guy always lived in the village?'

'Oh, yes, apart from the year he spent in Fredericton with his father. He was born here like the rest of us—I've known him since he was a little boy. As I say, he's always been a bit odd but I think he took a turn for the worse after that poor woman died. I've heard it said that Guy blames himself for not taking proper care of her.'

'So what happened exactly? How did his wife die?'

The bustling woman raised her eyebrows sceptically. 'If she was his wife,' she said with a confidential tone. 'Personally I don't think they were married at all—but that's another matter altogether. Anyway, as far as the accident is concerned, no one really knows what happened. I heard they were out walking by the river just after the two of them arrived in the village and somehow she fell in and drowned.'

'And you say Guy blames himself for that?'

'That's what I've heard. I know he took it very badly but, as I say, we were all ready and willing to give him support and understanding. We still are—but now he's left the village without a word to anyone after all this time. I don't know, Father. We're supposed to be his friends. I thought he might have been able to confide in us.' The harried housekeeper strode off to the kitchen, leaving the priest alone with his thoughts.

Louise could be a bit dramatic, Marcel thought, but there did seem to be a logical connection here that might be more than just a coincidence. Leaving his untouched breakfast, he walked over to the French windows and stared out at the ancient, weather-worn gravestones in the churchyard. This unfolding scenario seemed to be making some kind of sense. The disturbing confession, Denis LaPlante's behaviour that first weekend after his arrival in the village, and now Guy's sudden departure could all be related. Guy LaPlante might well have been the remorseful penitent who'd confessed to murder on Saturday afternoon.

Marcel recalled the conversation he'd had with his predecessor and how the old priest had been so secretive about the tragic death of Guy's wife. What did Father Lemieux know about this? Perhaps Guy LaPlante had actually confessed to murder before and left Father Lemieux knowing about it but unable to report it because of the so-called Seal of Confession. That would be a heavy burden for the old man to bear, but it might explain his tense manner and his desire to leave the village so quickly.

And what about Guy's father, Denis LaPlante? He was obviously an angry man with an axe to grind. Most of his anger seemed to be directed at his son, though he obviously had little time for Father Lemieux and he had made his feelings about Pierre Bouchard very clear indeed. Was he aware that his son was a murderer? And what was this important advice he'd talked about—had he advised his son to give himself up?

Everything seemed to fall neatly into place and after a few minutes of pondering the known facts, Marcel had convinced himself that Guy LaPlante had murdered his wife. That unfortunate young man must have deliberately drowned her, he thought, and then convinced everyone it was just an accident. Now, tormented with guilt, he's confessed to his crime and left the village in a hurry. I can only hope he has followed my direction and gone to Saint Stephen to give himself up.

The priest felt strangely relieved at the logical scenario he'd constructed. It saved him from having to deal with a frustrating dilemma about what to do and it was satisfying to know that Guy LaPlante was apparently doing the right thing. If he'd left the village to surrender to the police in Saint Stephen, the matter would be dealt with properly. Both Father Lemieux and Marcel himself would be relieved of that gnawing pang of conscience that told them they had a moral duty and a legal obligation to report a serious crime.

Marcel gradually came to terms with his upsetting experience in the confessional but he made up his mind that he'd never enter that box again. That very afternoon he called the church custodian, Henri Marceau, and told him to take it away. 'There's some good oak lumber there, Henri,' he told him. 'It's exactly what you need to build that shed you want for your back yard. Just get the thing out of the church as soon as you can. We're going to start having confessions the modern way—face to face.'

Over the following two or three weeks Marcel's work with the parish council and the various committees kept him occupied and involved, and by the middle of July he felt everything was more or less back to normal. He felt quite confident that Guy LaPlante had surrendered to the police. The burden of guilt had obviously been too much for the young fellow, he told himself repeatedly, and after his emotional confession he must have seen surrender as the honourable thing to do. Now it was up to civil law to take its just course.

The troublesome confession was no longer dominant in Marcel's mind. In fact, the priest had gently lulled himself into a haven of self satisfaction and false security, and he felt rather pleased with himself, quite convinced that he had performed his priestly duties in an exemplary manner. He'd given the right advice and he'd absolved a young man who'd bravely faced his wrongdoing.

Six

The last Monday in July was bright and glorious and Marcel looked forward to an early start at the golf course. Mme Poirier had become quite used to the routine. She hurried to clear away the breakfast dishes from the priest's table and send him on his way before he was delayed by trivial telephone calls. 'You'll be meeting Dr. Bouchard again this morning, I suppose, Father? Would you like me to pack you a lunch?'

'Oh, no thanks, Louise. No need for that. They have a bit of a snack bar at the club house. The food's terrible, mind you, but I'll manage just fine.' Marcel picked up his golf clubs from the front porch where he'd parked them earlier and he was on his way.

The Monday morning golf games with Pierre Bouchard had become something of a routine now. Marcel always looked forward to his day off and today he was feeling the joy of summer as he whistled his way down the country lane to the local golf course. The twenty-minute walk was even more pleasant than usual. With the sun shining and a light breeze blowing it felt good to be alive.

Pierre was waiting as usual by the tacky club house. 'So, Marcel, are you finally going to beat me today?' he teased. 'With weather like this there'll be no excuse for those bad shots into the trees.' They both laughed. It was a rare occasion when the doctor failed to win by a sizable margin.

'This could be the day,' the priest smiled. 'You never can tell.'

Maplewood Creek golf course was quiet at any time, but particularly so on Monday mornings. As usual Marcel and Pierre had practically the whole course to themselves. Nine holes went quickly and smoothly and following their usual custom they ended up in the club diner drinking lukewarm coffee out of paper cups. 'This is the life,' Marcel said contentedly. 'It may be a bit basic but I'd take simple village life over the hustle and bustle of Fredericton or Montreal any day—especially on a Monday morning.'

'You lived in Montreal then? You never mentioned that.'

Marcel laughed bemusedly. 'My secret life before Maplewood Creek, eh? No, there are a lot of things I haven't mentioned. I haven't heard much about your previous life either. Tell me about that.'

'Never mind my life. Tell me about Montreal. What were you doing there?

The priest sipped on his coffee and chuckled as he gathered his thoughts. Perhaps it was time to open up a bit. 'I worked in Montreal before I was a priest,' he said. 'There's more to me than you might think, Pierre. Being a priest is actually my second career.'

'Your second career?'

'Yes, my first life was very different. After university I started out my working life as a high-flying corporate banker in Montreal. I lived there for nearly ten years altogether.'

'That is quite different.'

They were hectic years really. I was very much involved in my job, rushing from one meeting to another. The hustle and bustle of business seemed to consume me in those days and it was no good for my health. Even worse, the pressure of it all was a terrible strain on my family.'

Pierre was intrigued with this bombardment of unexpected information. 'What family are you talking about,' he asked, leaning forward on the rickety table. 'Were you still living with your parents?'

'No, no. I was married at the time.'

'Married?'

'That's right. My wife, Clara, and I were both caught up in the rat race, always trying to buy bigger and better cars, a bigger home, better holidays—you know the pattern.' Marcel paused as he recalled the sad details. 'We realized too late that Clara was very sick.'

'What happened?'

'She was dying of cancer as it turned out. It was only after her death that I realized how foolish we'd been. We never made enough time for each other, you see, and I'll regret that for the rest of my life.'

The gobsmacked doctor folded his arms pensively and raised his eyebrows as he listened to these surprising details about his new friend's previous life. 'That's a very unusual background for a priest, isn't it?' he said, astonished at the priest's candour. 'I've come across quite a few priests in my work as a doctor, but I can't say I've ever met any who'd been married. Don't get me wrong though—I think it's great. It's an interesting dimension to your character and personality and it probably gives you a different perspective on lots of things.'

'I'm sure it does.'

Pierre stared briefly at his friend. 'Whatever made you become a priest though?' he asked. 'Where did that idea come from?'

'It wasn't a new idea, by any means,' Marcel told him. 'I'd toyed with the idea in my youth and it was only when I met Clara that any thoughts of the priesthood went out the window.' He smiled to himself as he reminisced. 'She was really something in those days,' he murmured, shaking his head. 'But when Clara died I missed her terribly and I wanted to do something totally different with my life. After a lot of soul searching, I decided to follow the old dream and study for the priesthood.'

'That's amazing. And are you happy with that decision now?'

'I've never looked back. They put me on the fast track in the seminary because of my age and background, and I felt quite honoured at being given my own parish right off the bat. I'm thirty-five years old and I have strong administrative experience, so apparently they thought I could handle it. Anyway, for the first time in years I feel like I'm really doing something worthwhile.' The priest raised his eyebrows and looked at his friend. 'How about you?'

Pierre seemed to be a bit hesitant about sharing his own past, but with a little prodding from Marcel he did confess to some similarities. 'I do know what it is to lose a wife,' he admitted ruefully. 'I suppose you could say my wife left me to look after someone else. It was all my own fault. I blame myself entirely.'

Marcel was sympathetic and understanding. 'Most marriages have their problems, Pierre. Sometimes no one is really to blame. People change and sometimes they need to move on.'

'Well it was a tumultuous stage in my life. I was angry and upset about it all of course, quite enraged in fact, but like you, I was totally engrossed in my work.'

'I suppose your wife was working as well.'

'My wife was even more involved in her work than I was in mine. I always felt that was a big part of the problem. Like you, we didn't leave enough time for each other and we foolishly thought our jobs were more important than family life. I must say, I do miss having her around.'

'You lived in Fredericton for a long time, didn't you? Did you run a medical practice up there?' Marcel asked. 'I imagine it would be more stressful in a big city. It must have been a very different kind of job.'

The priest detected reluctance in Pierre's voice as he struggled with his answer. 'I was involved in some investigative studies at the Fredericton Research Hospital,' he explained, 'but when this opportunity for a small country practice in Maplewood Creek came up I jumped at it. I'm really settling into this place now. The peace and quiet suit me just fine and the villagers seem to have accepted me well. I think I've put my old life behind me for good.'

Marcel laughed. 'I'm glad to hear it. I'm sure everyone values your work, Pierre. Of course I'm only here for as long as Bishop Giguère wants me here but I don't think he has plans to move me any time soon.'

'I hope not. You've helped me settle more than you realize. And as for these weekly golf games—we're the only two out here on a Monday morning. I'll have no one to play with if you leave.'

It was mid-afternoon by the time Marcel arrived back at the parish residence. To his surprise he was met at the front door by his flustered housekeeper. 'You've got a visitor, Father,' she informed him as he lugged his clubs up the walkway. 'You'll never guess who's here.'

'Not the bishop, surely?'

'No. It's Guy LaPlante. He's back.' Mme Poirier followed the priest into the hallway, fussing and fretting as if she'd seriously failed in her duties. 'I told him today's your day off, Father, but he insisted on waiting for you. He's in the parlour now.'

'Guy LaPlante? I thought you said he'd gone for good.' Marcel's heart sank as troublesome questions bombarded his mind. Shouldn't this man be in police custody? Does this mean he hasn't turned himself in to the police after all? Knowing what I know, how am I going to deal with this?

The confused young man was sitting in one of the large leather armchairs as Marcel entered the room. He stood politely and greeted the priest with a nervous handshake. 'I'm so sorry to intrude, Father. Please forgive me, but I needed to talk to you right away.'

'Not at all. I'm here for you any time, day or night.' Guy sat down again and Marcel drew up a chair to sit close by. 'What brings you here, Guy? They told me you'd left the village for good.'

'Oh no, Father. I never intended to leave permanently. I've been staying in Saint Stephen with my father and my sister over the past month or so. I've just arrived back this afternoon.'

'Well welcome back. I trust you had a pleasant break?'

'Everything was fine.' It was obvious that Guy had come with a burdened mind though he seemed hesitant to disclose the real purpose of his visit. After some useless small talk he scratched his chin nervously and forged bravely ahead. 'I should have talked to you sooner, Father,' he stammered nervously, 'but I've been at such a loss since Fran died and I've had great difficulty coming to terms with it. I blame myself, you see…'

Marcel felt his heart jump slightly as the woman's death was mentioned. Was this young man about to confess all over again? He leaned forward and said encouragingly. 'Tell me what happened, Guy. How did she die?

Guy's eyes welled up as he tried to speak. 'You may have heard, Father. She drowned in the river last September. We were walking along the river bank where the water flows fast through the rapids. I spent a lot of time down there when I was a boy and I wanted to show Fran where I used to play. There are some big rocks jutting from the river bank and into the water and I foolishly jumped onto them. I was fooling about and showing off the way I used to do when I was a kid.' The tortured man paused for a moment, unable to speak.

'It's all right,' Marcel told him gently. 'Just take your time.'

'Well anyway, I lost my footing and fell into the river. I'm not sure what happened next exactly, but suddenly Fran was in the river with me. The strong current started to carry her away, and I nearly drowned myself trying to save her, but the water was flowing so fast she just got swept away. They found her body two miles down stream.' Guy sobbed quietly at the memory of it.

The priest looked at him with sympathy and compassion. 'Have you thought about talking with Dr. Bouchard about this?' he asked encouragingly. 'I'm sure he would be able to help you deal with some of these issues. He's a very understanding man and very easy to talk to.'

'I know that, Father. I've been having a weekly counselling session with Dr. Bouchard, ever since he came to the village. He understands what I went through and he's been trying to help me.'

Marcel was pleased, though a little surprised, to hear this. The young man was obviously traumatized and he seemed to be blaming himself for no reason at all. There was no question of murder in this story. 'This seems to have been just a terrible accident, Guy,' he said gently. 'You did everything you could to save Fran and there's no reason to blame yourself for her death. A tragic accident doesn't make you a murderer.'

'Murderer?' Guy looked shocked at the suggestion. 'Oh no, Father, I didn't think anything like that. I just felt I'd been terribly negligent.'

Some time later, Guy LaPlante left the priest's residence, a comforted man. 'I think I'll be fine now, Father,' he said as he left the house. 'Thanks for listening. I know I have to get on with my life.'

Marcel watched him walk down the pathway alongside the churchyard and off towards his home. That poor young man, he thought, shaking his head. He's been torturing himself for no reason at all—not to mention what he's put me through. But at least now he's given a face-to-face account of the accident and that will actually do him some good. Not like that previous debacle in the confessional box…

The priest began to feel some special obligation towards Guy LaPlante after hearing the circumstances of the accident explained. The troubled man was obviously struggling with a number of past traumas and difficulties associated with his tumultuous childhood, and it was good that Dr. Bouchard was helping him to deal with that. Marcel made up his mind that he too would make himself available for the young man in order to help in any way he could.

Father Lemieux had been wise, he thought, to involve Guy in repair and maintenance projects on church property. It was a very practical way to keep him involved and it made it easier to engage him in casual conversations about how his life was going. Marcel felt pleased now that he'd continued this arrangement. The churchyard had to be kept in good condition anyway and as long as Guy was willing and able to do the work, the priest decided he'd be more than happy to pay him a small allowance to do so.

Over the following weeks, life in the village fell into a peaceful pattern again and once more all thoughts of that dreadful confession to murder gradually faded away. Marcel felt a great sense of contentment. His work with the people of Maplewood Creek, the leisurely golf games he enjoyed on his day off, and his friendship with Pierre Bouchard, all gave him a great deal of satisfaction. As the pleasant days of summer rolled on into autumn, life seemed to be very agreeable indeed.

All that was about to change.

Seven

'There's a message for you, Father. It looks like old Maurice Hubert is ill again. His wife called to say she'd like you to visit some time today if you can.' Mme Poirier left a note on Marcel's desk as he worked on Sunday's homily.

'That should be fine,' he said, picking up the note and staring at it absent-mindedly. 'He's not dying is he?'

'I shouldn't think so. He's getting old, but I still see him walking out most days. I know he's not been well since last weekend so I imagine he's just getting a bit bored and he'd like a visitor.'

Marcel felt in no rush. It was a pleasant September afternoon and a walk in the fresh air sounded quite appealing, especially as he'd been sitting at his desk for over an hour now and he was feeling somewhat cramped and restless. He was in fine spirits as he walked the short distance to the Huberts' house in the early afternoon sunshine.

Celine Hubert greeted her pastor at the door. 'So glad you could make it, Father,' she gushed as she ushered him through. 'Maurice is not so bad really. Dr. Bouchard was here this morning and he said the old boy has a few good years in him yet.' She laughed at the irreverent way she talked about her husband. 'Anyway,' she said, 'he'll be delighted to see you. Why don't you go up and have a chat? I'll get some fresh coffee rolling.'

The priest climbed the narrow staircase to Maurice's room where he found the old man sitting up in bed, reading a golf magazine and sipping on a bottle of ginger ale. 'Well, Maurice,' Marcel said jovially, 'you don't look ready for the last rites yet.'

Maurice laughed heartily. 'That's what Dr. Bouchard told me. No, I just wanted a visitor and a chat. Thanks for dropping by, Father.'

The two men chatted for a while about one thing or another. Maurice had been a keen golfer in his younger days and he was quite intrigued that his doctor and his parish priest were regular golf partners. 'Dr. Bouchard tells me you play on a regular basis. I'd love to join you,' he said regretfully, 'but I'm afraid my golfing days are over.'

It was a productive fifteen minutes. Marcel felt the visit was worthwhile and he felt content as he returned to the modest living room where Celine had a fresh pot of coffee ready. 'He's doing just fine,' the priest told her as he settled into one of the comfortable chairs by the fireside. 'We've had a good old chat about his golfing days. From what he tells me he was quite the player.'

'Oh he loved his golf all right.' Celine poured out two cups of coffee and handed one to Marcel. 'You've done a lot of good around here, Father,' she said, 'you and the doctor—in such a short time too. How long is it now since you both arrived in the village?'

'Just about six months now. We arrived on the same train you know, and we've been good friends ever since.'

'Well it's amazing what can be done in six months. I hardly recognize the parish now with all the activity and involvement.' Celine settled herself comfortably into her chair. 'And the changes you've made. I can tell you, Father, some people don't seem to like change but it's hard to find fault with anything you've done so far. That confessional, for example—getting rid of that old box was the best thing you ever did.'

Marcel laughed. 'You're probably right,' he said. 'I suppose it's a bit irreverent considering its eminent history, but I think it serves a much better purpose as a shed in Henri Marceau's garden. I used to spend an hour in that claustrophobic box every Saturday afternoon during my first three months in the village, biding my time and waiting for customers. You know, in all that time I only had one penitent—my very first penitent actually.'

Celine sipped on her coffee. 'It was a stuffy old thing,' she agreed. 'In the old days, Fr. Lemieux encouraged us to confess once a month and I'm sure someone designed that kneeler specially to make us do a bit of penance. It was absolute agony.' She chuckled as she rubbed her knees to emphasize her point. 'I still blame that hard kneeler for my bad knees.'

'Well a bit of penance never did anyone any harm, Celine,' the priest teased. He smiled at her dramatic portrayal. 'Was it really that bad, though?'

'It certainly was, and Dr. Bouchard agrees,' she went on. 'I was telling him the very same thing this morning. He joked about it, of course, but he told me he'd only ever been in that confessional box once, and it gave him sore knees for a week.'

Marcel furrowed his brow and looked quizzically at his talkative parishioner. 'Dr. Bouchard told you that?'

'He agreed with everything I said. He thought that kneeler was as hard as a rock and he complimented me for having put up with it for so long—joking of course.'

'No, no—I mean are you sure he said he was in the confessional box here at St. Jude's? Surely he must have been talking about somewhere else. He lived up in Fredericton for years, you know. He was probably talking about a church up there.'

'No, we were talking about St. Jude's church here in the village. He said he was in the confessional a couple of days before you got rid of it in June. He laughed when I told him Henri Marceau had made it into a garden shed. He thought that was a great idea.'

Marcel stroked his chin pensively as he tried to take in what was being said. 'But that means…,' he began. 'That means…'

'Oh, I see what you mean, Father. If you only heard one confession in that box, Dr. Bouchard must have been the one—your very first penitent.' Celine laughed loudly, oblivious to the deep implications of her words. 'Well I'm sure he feels very privileged, being a friend of yours and all.'

Marcel suddenly felt quite sick to his stomach. He placed his half full cup on the table beside him and stood up. 'I have to go, Celine,' he said hoarsely. 'I have a few things to finish up. You'll have to excuse me.'

'Oh, of course. I understand. Are you all right, Father? You seem to have gone quite pale all of a sudden.'

'I'll be fine. Too much coffee perhaps.'

But Marcel wasn't fine. That one piece of information innocently passed on by Celine Hubert had thrown an enormous wrench into the priest's otherwise peaceful life. The implications were enormous. If what Celine had said was true, then Pierre Bouchard must be the one who had confessed to murder—he must be the one who had murdered his wife. It was nothing to do with Guy LaPlante at all.

Marcel mulled this over as he walked back to his residence. Did the logic really lead to that conclusion? Surely he must be missing something? He was absolutely certain that he'd only ever received one penitent in the old confessional box, and until now he'd assumed that the person on the other side of the grill was a confused and upset Guy LaPlante, blaming himself for his wife's accidental drowning. But Celine Hubert was quite adamant that she and Pierre had discussed the uncomfortable conditions in the confessional. Could she be mistaken? If not, there was no escape from the logic—the doctor must have been the last one to use it. Indeed the only one to use it since Marcel had arrived in Maplewood Creek.

There seemed to be no escape from the cold logic. The bewildered priest could reach one conclusion only—a conclusion he desperately wanted to avoid. The disguised voice in the confessional box that Saturday afternoon belonged to Pierre Bouchard, not Guy LaPlante. But how could he believe such a thing? He'd been playing golf with his doctor friend virtually every week since that fateful June afternoon. Surely if Pierre had made that dreadful confession to murder, some hint of it would have come out one way or another in the conversations they'd had over the past few weeks.

Mme Poirier had just entered the residence with two bags of groceries when Marcel reached the house, still feeling dazed and confused. 'I'll not bother with dinner tonight, Louise,' he told her. 'I'm not feeling quite well and I need some quiet time by myself.' He hurriedly mounted the stairs two at a time and disappeared into his private quarters on the second floor.

Mme Poirier had been unable to utter a single word in the rush. She stood there holding the two bags, quite puzzled at the priest's unusual behaviour then, shrugging her shoulders, she left the bags on the kitchen counter and bustled off to her own apartment at the south side of the house.

Marcel checked his luminous watch as he sat there in the darkness. It was two-twenty-five. He'd been sitting in his leather armchair for several hours now, pondering his dilemma and wondering how he could ever find a satisfactory solution to the unexpected problem he now faced.

As far as he could make out, if it was really the doctor who had confessed to murdering his wife, Marcel had only three options—do nothing, refer the whole matter to the police, or directly confront Pierre Bouchard with the situation and ask him for an explanation. The perplexed priest had spent half the night wrestling with these possibilities, but each one presented such overwhelming difficulties that in the end they seemed to provide no real solution at all.

It was quite tempting to pretend that the conversation with Celine Hubert had never taken place. After all, if Maurice Hubert hadn't requested a visit from his pastor, Marcel would be none the wiser and the pleasant life he'd become used to in this quiet village would have continued uninterrupted. His friendship with the doctor would have been unaffected too. Marcel sighed heavily. If only the identity of his murderous penitent had not been revealed in this way there would be no reason to suspect Pierre Bouchard of anything.

But that was another puzzling piece of information. Why would someone who'd confessed to murder casually talk about his confession as if the whole thing were a big joke. He obviously didn't tell Celine anything about what he'd confessed but, even so, one would think that in the circumstances most people would simply keep their mouth shut.

Marcel recalled the emotional, heart-wrenching exchange between penitent and priest that Saturday afternoon. He had been quite convinced that the penitent was suffering from an emotional breakdown, filled with remorse over a dreadful murder and desperately seeking forgiveness and absolution. It was easy to imagine Guy LaPlante in such a state. He was a nervous kind of fellow, unsure of himself and easily rattled. But Dr. Bouchard, on the other hand, was a highly educated, self-assured professional and it was hard to picture him breaking down like that. Still, the dreadful remorse that a murderer must feel could lead anyone to the brink of despair, and apart from that, the known facts spoke for themselves. Guy LaPlante had fully explained himself—his wife had died in an accident—and it was Pierre, not Guy, who claimed to have entered the confessional box on that awful afternoon.

Doing nothing at all was out of the question, Marcel thought. He knew that he could never live with that. He saw Pierre Bouchard on a regular basis and they both looked forward to their weekly game of golf, lunch at the clubhouse, and a friendly chat. How could he possibly continue that routine knowing that his friend could be a murderer. And it was pointless trying to convince himself that, because it was knowledge obtained in the secrecy of confession, he didn't really know about it. The reality was that he did know, and his deepest convictions and sense of justice told him that he had a duty to do something about it.

So this is really a police matter, the priest told himself. I'll have to report it. I have to tell the police I have reason to suspect someone of murder. And what will they say? They'll ask me who I suspect and what evidence I have to support my suspicion. And that's where it will fall flat on its face. What could I possibly say? This man came to confession and confessed to murdering his wife? And did you see him face to face, they'll ask. Well no, he was in a dark cubicle behind a grill disguising his voice, I'd say. What a fiasco that would be. The whole thing would be quite impossible. And in any case, when all's said and done, priests don't report what penitents have told them in the secrecy of confession. Most people would consider that to be totally unethical.

Marcel leaned forward with his head in his hands. He desperately needed sleep now but he still had to decide on a course of action. It seemed his only option was to confront Dr. Bouchard directly and demand an explanation. If he could get Pierre to admit openly what he'd done, then at least it would be possible to counsel him and help him to face his responsibilities. There was one obvious difficulty with that, of course. A priest can't just say, by the way, you confessed to a murder in the confessional—what are you going to do about it? Confession is anonymous and the penitent doesn't expect it to be ever mentioned again. Officially, the priest knows nothing about it. And if I bring up the matter for discussion, Marcel thought, Pierre Bouchard could simply say he doesn't know what I'm talking about and that would be the end of that.

Marcel realized that his options were very limited. I have to give Pierre an opportunity to talk about this murder of his own free will, he decided. If I can get him to tell me exactly what happened I might be able to deal with it properly. Maybe his wife's death was accidental or at least due more to negligence than malice. After all, Guy LaPlante had blamed himself for his wife's death, but despite his crushing feelings of guilt, there was no question of murder. Maybe Pierre's wife had suffered a similar fate. Perhaps she'd suffered a terrible accident and Pierre was feeling guilty about it. Perhaps there's a plausible explanation. Perhaps…

Marcel desperately wanted to find a rational explanation, a justification, an excuse even. Pierre Bouchard was a good, responsible citizen, and come to think of it, he'd always talked about his wife as if she were still alive. Pierre had said very little about his wife but at least he'd been quite clear about one thing—she'd left him for someone else. That sounds like she's still alive, he thought, and if she's still alive he can't have murdered her. Perhaps there was a ray of hope. He sighed deeply. Maybe I'm jumping to irrational conclusions after all.

The tormented priest was totally exhausted and he could think about it no more. His closing eyelids were getting beyond his control as these troubling thoughts dominated his tired mind. He finally gave in. Closing his eyes and lying back in his comfortable chair, he fell into a fitful sleep.

It was six o'clock when Marcel opened his eyes again. The morning light was streaming in through the south window, an event that usually filled him with the joy of a new day. This morning, however, was a little different. He felt stiff and achy after being in the chair all night and the first thing that came to mind was the situation concerning Pierre Bouchard.

Marcel felt a little more hopeful with the new day however. Sleeping on the troublesome issue seemed to have helped considerably and he felt that a confidential chat with the doctor might resolve it, just as it had done with Guy LaPlante. It was still necessary for Pierre to initiate such a discussion, of course, but Marcel was confident that, under the right circumstances, he could guardedly start the ball rolling.

Saturday morning Mass was scheduled for 7 o'clock, but unlike the Sunday liturgy that filled the church to capacity, this service usually attracted very few participants. Only a dozen or so devoted souls tended make it to the church on a Saturday morning. They were almost always the same dedicated individuals, older parishioners who were determined to be there rain or shine. Marcel had a habit of chatting to these hardy folk for a while in the vestibule after Mass and he hated to disappoint them on this particular morning. He was tired and hungry, but he made the effort to shower and prepare himself for the service, and he doggedly went through the motions for these simple villagers who had become so dear to him.

By the time breakfast was served at 8.30 the bleary-eyed priest was ravenously hungry and he eagerly entered the dining room on the main floor. Mme Poirier was ready for him. She took her responsibilities seriously and became genuinely concerned when things didn't seem right. 'Are you feeling better this morning,

Father?' she greeted him, placing an extra large breakfast on the table. 'I was getting worried about you not eating since yesterday lunch.'

'Nothing to worry about,' Marcel told her with a smile. 'I had a few things to sort out but everything is falling into place now.'

'Well that's all right then, isn't it? Enjoy your breakfast, Father. If there's anything else you want I'll be right here in the kitchen.'

The fussy housekeeper turned and headed for the kitchen but Marcel stopped her. He needed information and Mme Poirier was the best source he had. 'You've lived in Maplewood Creek for a long time, Louise, haven't you?'

She stopped in her tracks and turned to face him, surprised at the sudden question. 'I was born in this village,' she said proudly. 'I grew up here, got married and got widowed here, and no doubt I'll be buried here when my time comes.'

The priest smiled at her honest approach to the inevitable events of life. 'I hope that won't be for a long time yet, Louise. But I was just wondering if I could pick your brains on something. Tell me, what was Dr. Martin like?'

'Dr. Martin? Well I suppose he was a good doctor in his time. He wasn't much good to us over the last few years, though. His own health became worse and worse as he got older. People had to go into Saint Stephen if they were really ill because Dr. Martin couldn't cope any more.'

'But why did he leave the village after living here for so long?'

'Well I suppose he was getting a bit old for the job and he wanted to retire to a warmer place. It was about a year ago. He left rather suddenly as it happened. No goodbyes or anything. In fact we went six months with no doctor at all after he left Maplewood Creek and it was only when Dr. Bouchard arrived that we got decent service again.'

Marcel pondered this response before continuing with his next question. 'What about Father Lemieux?' he asked thoughtfully. 'Did he get along all right with Dr. Martin?'

Mme Poirier wandered back to the table and leaned heavily on the chair facing the priest. 'They weren't friends if that's what you mean. Not like you and Dr. Bouchard. As you know, Father Lemieux wasn't exactly the picture of health, either. He had a doctor in Saint Stephen that he'd visit every two or three months for his medication so he didn't really have to deal with Dr. Martin at all. Now that you mention it though, I think the two of them had a falling out over something a few years ago. I've no idea what it was about. Father Lemieux never talked about it.'

Marcel buttered a piece of toast as he listened to his chatty housekeeper and then continued his casual investigation. 'And what about this business concerning Guy LaPlante's wife,' he said calmly. 'I know the police had to do an inquest because of the tragic accident, but was it Dr. Martin who signed her death certificate?'

Mme Poirier placed her hand on her chin and thought for a moment. 'I wouldn't think so,' she said. 'I couldn't really say because it was nothing to do with me, but I would imagine that Dr. Bouchard would have done that.'

Marcel looked up sharply and smiled. 'Dr. Bouchard? No, it couldn't have been him, Louise. That was long before he arrived in the village. He and I arrived here on the same day at the end of March—remember?'

'Well I know that of course but this was before Dr. Bouchard took over the practice. He was down here last September for about a week, helping Dr. Martin. I suppose that's when they were negotiating the take over. I know for a fact that Guy LaPlante's wife drowned while Dr. Bouchard was here. He was the first one on the scene when the alarm was called. It was too late, of course—she'd been swept away and he couldn't do anything to help her. Apparently, she was already dead when they pulled her out of the river.'

Eight

Marcel sat with his coffee and pondered the unexpected information that his housekeeper had just given him. So Pierre Bouchard had lied about his arrival in the village. The priest recalled the last leg of their train journey into Maplewood Creek a few months earlier when he and the doctor were the only two remaining passengers in the compartment. They'd laughed and joked about being newcomers to the village and it was Pierre who said first that he'd never been to Maplewood Creek before. Why would he lie about something like that?

It was a stupid sort of lie too, the priest thought. If Mme Poirier knew he'd been to Maplewood Creek before, dozens of other villagers must know as well. They wouldn't think anything of it, of course, and they'd casually blurt it out any old time. Pierre Bouchard must have known that the new parish priest would find out sooner or later so what was the point of trying to hide it?

Marcel was puzzled about another thing too. Why would his doctor friend be so secretive about the accidental drowning of Guy LaPlante's wife? He and Pierre had known each other for more than six months now, played golf virtually every week, and chatted frequently about life in the village. Yet Pierre Bouchard had never mentioned the tragic drowning and his involvement in the gruesome aftermath. They didn't tend to talk about their respective professional concerns, that was true of course, but surely it would be almost impossible to avoid a casual mention of such a tragedy.

Marcel was disillusioned and disappointed at the way things were relentlessly unfolding before his eyes. He hated the idea that Pierre Bouchard appeared to be less than honest, and it felt very uncomfortable to have a friend who obviously had a lot to hide. The nightmarish confession of murder kept creeping back into his mind despite his best efforts to avoid thinking about it, and he was alarmed at this frightening scenario of murder and intrigue that seemed to be developing. The worst thing of all was that his friend Pierre now seemed to be at the centre of it all.

Meanwhile, life had to go on. Saturday was a day for visiting the sick, and this morning Marcel had promised to go into Saint Stephen to visit a parishioner who was in the hospital there. He was still feeling the effects of sleep deprivation from the night before and he didn't relish the thought of travelling on the rickety old bus that took the villagers into town for their weekend shopping. Besides, he knew there was no escape from his parishioners once he boarded the bus and this morning he didn't feel like chatting. Everyone knew him and they had an endless supply of questions and anecdotes to fill the time on the half-hour trip. It was usually a good opportunity to relax and get to know people but on this particular morning alternate transportation seemed like a better idea.

Father Lemieux had left his old car behind when he retired and moved to Bangor, Maine. The old jalopy was nearly twelve years old now and it was in very poor shape so Marcel rarely made use of it. He had driven the ten-mile trip into Saint Stephen on occasion and that was about as far as he would trust it to go. But today he wasn't going to quibble about details—the old car would have to do. He quickly changed into more casual attire, burying his clerical collar deep beneath his blue turtle-neck sweater, and hurried down to dig out the car from its comfortable place in the cluttered garage.

Surprisingly, the car started without protesting too much, but the gas tank was near empty and Marcel had no choice but to putter over to the only gas bar in the village to fill up. Gaston Leduc was on duty. He'd worked there for years and he greeted the priest with a friendly smile as he pulled into the limited space in front of the shop. 'Driving yourself today, Father?' he teased. 'I used to tell Fr. Lemieux that this old banger had passed its sell-by date long ago. I can't believe you're still driving it.' He grinned, knowing the priest enjoyed a joke.

'Some of us have no choice, Gaston. Maybe I should ask for bigger contributions on the collection plate, then I could buy something better.'

'Oh well, if you put it like that—I guess maybe it will last a bit longer.' The two men laughed at the way a mere mention of money can change a person's point of view.

As Gaston proceeded to fill up the tank, Marcel wandered a few steps away and noticed a gleaming silver BMW parked on the opposite side of the road. It must be nice to drive a car like that, he thought, recalling ruefully how he had always driven a brand new Cadillac when he was a high-flying corporate banker in Montreal. Those days seemed so long ago. Strange, he thought, how cars don't seem to be very important any more.

As he stood waiting, the priest looked thoughtfully at the buildings facing him. There was a small commercial block housing a tiny general store and a pharmacy, and next to that was a venerable old house that was now serving as a doctor's surgery and residence. Marcel could clearly read the prominent sign displayed in front of it: Dr. Pierre Bouchard, M.D. General Practitioner.

Should I go over and have a word with him, Marcel thought. He'll be in there now for morning surgery. I could confront him with his lie and ask him for an explanation. Why did he tell me he'd never been to Maplewood Creek before? Mme Poirier and God knows how many others could confirm that he'd not only been here but he'd spent at least a few days with Dr. Martin and got involved in the tragedy of a woman's drowning. It didn't seem to make much sense.

On reflection, going over to complain seemed rather petty and counterproductive. People do things for a reason, Marcel thought, and in any case, my personal feelings about being deceived by a friend are not the issue. There is a much wider question to be considered here. Has a murder been committed and if it has, am I being involved in a criminal cover-up? And what about the Seal of Confession? Can that really excuse me from going to the police? He shuddered at the thought and he knew he'd have to get some kind of explanation from Pierre Bouchard before he could put it to rest.

Marcel was about to turn and check on Gaston's progress at the pump when he noticed an athletic-looking woman in jeans and leather jacket leaving the surgery. She was all business as she bounced out of the front doors, and the long blond hair and turned-up collar did not disguise the fact that she was some kind of hard-nosed professional on a mission. She strode towards the BMW, gave the priest a cursory glance, and then opened the driver's door and jumped in. In an instant, the engine roared to life and she was off down the road in a cloud of dust. One of Pierre's patients, Marcel thought, but maybe not. She's obviously not from the village so why would she drive into Maplewood Creek in a BMW when there are better health facilities in Saint Stephen? Who knows and what does it matter? He hurriedly paid for his gas and was soon on his way.

The drive to Saint Stephen was inevitably frustrating and wearisome due to the poor road conditions. It was an unpaved road most of the way, but even the occasional paved sections were full of potholes and crevices. Any attempt to drive at a reasonable speed tended to throw grit and gravel everywhere, and driving to town was really no faster than going by bus. But at least it gave the priest a chance to mull over some pressing questions in privacy.

Marcel tried to take advantage of the quiet half-hour by himself, but it was difficult to concentrate on anything as all his energy seemed to be spent on driving safely. As he reached his destination he put his mind to the job at hand. He'd come to Saint Stephen for a reason and now he had to give it his full attention. Everything else could wait.

The hospital in town was not large by any standards but it was relatively new and conveniently divided into sections according to the specific needs of the patients. Marcel had been there several times before. He had no difficulty finding the post-surgery section in the south wing, and as he made his way down the pristine corridors he pulled up his white collar to make it more visible, identifying himself as visiting clergy. At the end of the hall he found Marianne Boudreau in room thirty-two.

Marianne had suffered from a painful knee for a long time and now, as she recovered from invasive surgery, she was suffering from boredom as well. But she was delighted to see her pastor as he appeared at the door of her semi-private room, and she greeted him enthusiastically.

'Father Marcel,' she exclaimed. 'Thanks so much for coming. You've no idea how bored I'm getting in here by myself.'

Marcel grinned at the sight of her lying there with her leg propped up on cushions. 'You don't have a roommate then?'

'I do, but she's out for a walk, lucky thing. I can't put any weight on my knee for at least twenty-four hours so it looks like I'll be stuck in here for a while longer. With any luck I'll be going home tomorrow.'

The welcome visitor sat on the chair by the bed and helped himself to a few grapes from the bedside table. Marianne was on his church music committee and he valued her contribution to the thriving life of the parish. 'I hope it won't be too long,' he told her with a disingenuous straight face. 'St. Jude's is falling apart without you.'

'Oh sure, Father, as if... I think the parish will do just fine without me.'

The two of them chatted for several minutes about the mundane events of daily life. To Marcel, this was the essence of his priesthood—giving comfort and reassurance to those who needed it, taking an interest in the pains and problems of others, and being a true friend in a practical kind of way. He looked around the clean but modest room. 'Is there anything you need, Marianne? I'll be in Saint Stephen for most of the day so I can bring you anything you want from town.'

'I don't think so, Father. I've had one or two friends drop by and my nephew, Guy, was here last night with a few items I'd asked for. He's the one who brought me the grapes too.'

'Guy? I don't think I've met him, have I?'

'Of course you have. Guy LaPlante, my late sister's son.'

Marcel looked at her in surprise. 'Guy LaPlante?' he said. 'Is he your nephew? I had no idea.'

'Oh yes, he's my nephew all right. I know he's had his problems lately but things seem to be improving now. We've only just got back on proper speaking terms again and he's promised to visit me once in a while.'

The priest nodded, surprised that this piece of important information had escaped him for so long. 'I know things have been difficult for him. I've chatted with him on a number of occasions when he's been helping with jobs around the church, and he's told me a bit about the tragedy concerning his wife's death last year.'

Marianne raised her eyes to the ceiling. 'That fiasco,' she said. 'I still can't make any sense of it. I still don't really understand what happened.'

'What do you mean? I thought it was common knowledge that she drowned in a terrible accident.'

'Well, yes she did. But I mean the whole thing about him coming back from Fredericton out of the blue with that woman on his arm. There was something very odd about it right from the start—I only met Fran once but she didn't seem to suit my nephew at all. She was at least ten years older than Guy for one thing and I thought she acted more like his mother than his wife. It was because of her that Guy and I fell out, you know. I was confused and disappointed with the way he'd behaved and I really didn't believe that woman was his wife at all. I told my nephew that in no uncertain terms.'

'It must have been a traumatic experience for him. I understand they hadn't been together very long when she died?'

'Hardly any time at all. They'd just returned from Fredericton. I spent nearly a week getting Guy's house cleaned up and ready for them but she died the day after she arrived in the village. I was sorry about the accident of course, especially when I saw how devastated Guy was. He stayed with me for two or three weeks after her death but I found it difficult to do anything with him. He just clammed up and wouldn't tell me anything about her—how they'd met, where and when they'd got married, if they ever did—nothing at all. To this very day I don't really know who she was.'

Marcel was intrigued with this conversation. He recalled the conversation he'd had with Guy LaPlante after he'd been mysteriously missing for a month, supposedly staying with his father and sister in Saint Stephen. Guy was obviously a troubled young man and the priest felt compelled to check out his story with Marianne. 'I believe Guy has a sister living here in Saint Stephen with his father,' he said. 'Your niece—has she been in to visit?'

'A niece? Where ever did you hear that? No, Guy's mother, Jeanette, was my only sibling, and Guy was her only child. Since my husband died he's all the family I have.'

The priest frowned and shook his head. How does one get the real truth around here, he thought. He looked at Marianne, puzzled and disappointed. 'You know, Marianne,' he said, 'I've been trying to help your nephew with some of his problems. As you probably know, I kept him on to do repair and maintenance around the church when he was looking for work in the spring. Some time ago, I had a chat with him about some personal matters and I speak to him casually whenever I get the chance. But maybe if you could tell me a little bit about his background it will help me to understand him better.'

Marianne adjusted her bandaged leg on the pillows and tried to make herself comfortable. 'I can tell you a bit about his childhood,' she said. 'That's where his problems started, I've always said.'

The priest looked at her pleadingly. 'Anything at all that might help me to understand him.'

'Well, first of all, Guy's father, Denis LaPlante, left the family when his son was fourteen years old. He wasn't from Maplewood Creek originally you see, and he found village life boring and lifeless. When he split up with Jeanette he left Maplewood Creek altogether and found himself a job in Fredericton. My nephew had great difficulty accepting the break up at the time and Jeanette couldn't cope with his increasing anger and frustration. He was more or less out of his mother's control for a while.'

'I understand your sister passed away some time after the break up. What happened to her exactly?'

'She died two years later when Guy was about sixteen; she was only forty-seven. It was a heart attack apparently, but I've always said it was more like a broken heart. I know she was quite depressed and she was worried about her son and what she was going to do with him. Guy came to live with me after she died. I'd been a widow for a few years and I was quite happy to have him live with me.'

'That is so sad, Marianne, but how fortunate he was to have a kind aunt to take care of him. Did Guy live with you until he left home then?'

'That's right. He seemed to calm down after Jeanette died. But he missed her terribly and blamed himself for her death. He thought if he'd behaved better when he was younger she would never have developed a bad heart and she wouldn't have died.'

Marcel nodded. 'I can understand that. Young people so often blame themselves when in reality they are the innocent victims of their circumstances.'

'But Guy did seem to come to terms with it over time,' Marianne went on, 'though for a short time he did develop some worrying psychological problems. He'd imagine things sometimes—he'd think his friends were talking about him or trying to harm him in some way. Other times he'd feel guilty about things for no reason at all—things he hadn't even done. And, come to think of it, it's funny you should think I had a niece because when Guy was younger he went through a period where he imagined he had a sister. He'd pretend to phone her, and I know he wrote her a few letters because I found them in his room. It was a very troubling time for all of us'

'Did he get any professional help for these problems at the time?'

'Not from a specialist. Dr. Martin tried to help him and he did put him on some medication, but I've no idea what it was. It seemed to help though. By the time Guy was eighteen or nineteen he seemed to be a fine young man and much more stable. He even had a girl friends for a while, and he had a steady job at the gas bar in the village. He worked with Gaston Leduc who was his best friend in those days. As you probably know, Gaston works at the gas bar to this day, but he doesn't seem to be interested in Guy any more.'

The priest pondered over these revelations about Guy LaPlante's life. This young man was more complicated than he had thought and he wondered if the traumatic experiences of the past were still influencing his behaviour. More than likely, the tragic loss of a wife stirred up past memories of his mother's death and this would be a very difficult cross to bear. Having lost his own wife to a serious illness, Marcel knew how that felt.

Marianne looked at her perplexed pastor. 'I hope that puts a few things in proper perspective, Father. What are you thinking—are things any clearer?'

'Yes, indeed. Guy does seem to be a little mixed up doesn't he? But what did you mean about him coming back from Fredericton with that woman on his arm? Is that where he met her?'

'Yes it is. Guy lived with me until he was nearly twenty-two years old. Then he decided he'd had enough of Maplewood Creek and he wanted to go and live with his father.'

'So his father was still on the scene after the break up then?'

'In a way. Denis has kept in touch sporadically over the years. We knew he was living in Fredericton but he used to return to the village every few months before

Jeanette died. We didn't see him for a long time after that but he turned up again a couple of years ago trying to get Guy to go and live with him. I think he caught the lad at a bad time really.'

'What do you mean?'

'Well my nephew was desperate for a change and he was looking for an opportunity to leave the village, so when Denis showed up out of the blue and offered him a new life in Fredericton he couldn't resist. Denis had never been a good influence on his son though, and I was opposed to any permanent reunion. But Guy was adamant. Anyway, he was old enough to make up his own mind so off he went to Fredericton to live with his dad. I knew it wouldn't work out—and it didn't.'

'Why? What happened?'

'Guy wrote me a letter about three months after leaving the village. He'd found a job in a small engines repair shop and he was living in a cheap basement apartment. He said things didn't work out with his father. He was too controlling, he said, and wouldn't let him make his own decisions.' Marianne paused and stared at the wall as if she were afraid of saying too much. 'Denis was always a bit of a bully,' she said, turning to the priest. 'He always felt he knew best so it didn't surprise me at all that Guy wanted a place of his own.'

'But what about Guy's wife—girlfriend or whoever she was? How did that come about?'

'That was much later—the following summer in fact. Guy didn't communicate with me very often but I received a birthday card from him at the end of August last year which was most unusual. He wrote a short note with it saying he'd met a wonderful woman called Fran and he was going to bring her back with him to Maplewood Creek.'

Marcel stood up and walked over to the large window overlooking a well- manicured garden. He peered out as he mulled over the woman's words. 'That must have been a big surprise,' he said. 'Did he say why he wanted to return to the village?'

'He said his father was giving him some problems. Apparently Denis hated Fran and according to Guy he was trying to break them up. By that time, all my nephew wanted to do was to get away from Denis and return home with his new wife. He has legal ownership of his mother's old house, you know. I'd rented it out for him for several years but he knew there were no current tenants, and he wanted to move back in. As I told you, I got it cleaned up for him and three weeks later he showed up on my doorstep with Fran.'

Marcel turned from the window. 'That's quite a story, Marianne,' he said. 'I'm sorry to be asking so many questions but may I ask you one more thing?'

'Of course. Go ahead.'

'This wife of his, Fran—what was she like?'

'Well, as I said, I didn't care for her. Not that there was anything wrong with her as such. She was in her mid thirties and seemed to be an educated or professional type—totally unsuitable for Guy who's always been a blue collar worker. And there was something distinctly odd about the relationship. She wasn't like a wife at all. She seemed to be looking after him like a mother would do for a sick child. It was really quite weird and I was very upset with the whole situation.'

'Did you ever discuss any of this with her?

'Not really. We'd just been introduced. The first thing she told me was that she needed to talk to me about Guy, but that never actually happened.'

'Why was that?'

Marianne paused a moment before responding and pursed her lips as if to hold back the words. 'Well,' she said in lowered tone of voice, 'the woman drowned in the river before we had a chance to talk.'

Nine

The Sunday routines were more or less as normal. It was the busiest day of the week for Marcel as parishioners gathered at the church in a flurry of activity, first for Sunday Mass and then for socializing over coffee in the parish hall. Any special activities such as baptisms, anniversary celebrations, and children's special events took place in the afternoon, and the pastor was expected to be available for any of these on short notice. Marcel went through the motions, but he was preoccupied with a new dilemma now that seemed to have no simple solution—should he honour his Monday morning golf appointment with Pierre Bouchard, or should he find an excuse to cancel it?

Pierre rarely attended Sunday Mass so at least there were no worries about meeting him in the parish over the weekend. But Marcel thought maybe this Sunday would be one of those odd occasions when he would turn up. He shuddered at the prospect of a chance meeting. How could he act normally in the presence of a man he now suspected of murder? He hoped desperately to see no sign of Pierre among the throng of bubbly parishioners and as luck would have it, he wasn't disappointed. Marcel relaxed a little over the afternoon and busied himself with his normal duties. But Monday morning remained in the back of his mind—and it came all too soon.

It was a glorious morning in late September and Marcel would normally have felt on top of the world as he ate a leisurely breakfast and anticipated some quality time with a good friend. But today a cloud seemed to hang over everything. He worked hard and felt he deserved his day off though he made it clear that, unlike Father Lemieux, he was always available in an emergency, even on Mondays. This particular Monday might be shaping up as one of those emergencies, he thought, as he mentally planned what he would be saying to Pierre Bouchard.

'You seem to be in another world this morning, Father.' Mme Poirier fussed around the breakfast table as usual, adjusting the coffee pot and straightening up the toast. 'Is everything all right?'

Marcel looked up at his housekeeper. 'I have a few things on my mind,' he said, not betraying any of his inner feelings, 'but that's quite normal for a priest.' He laughed as he poured himself another cup of coffee, projecting an image of perfect normalcy. 'Anyway, this is my day off, isn't it?'

'You'll be playing golf, I suppose?'

'That's the general idea. I'm supposed to meet Dr. Bouchard at nine o'clock.'

'You'd better get moving then. I'll make sure no one delays you with a silly phone call. Some people around here don't seem to realize that a priest needs time out too.' She hurried off to the kitchen with a pile of dirty dishes.

Marcel had made no conscious decision about whether to meet Pierre Bouchard or not, but since he'd done nothing about cancelling their regular appointment, he found himself going through the usual routine, dressing for golf and picking up his golf clubs from the back of his untidy garage.

It was always a last-minute decision on whether to use the old car or not. Marcel usually left himself plenty of time and walked the short distance to the golf course, especially when the weather was fine. Occasionally, when he was running a little late, he would start up the old banger and drive himself down the lane and out of the village, but he always felt a bit lazy for doing so. Not only that, but Pierre had bought himself a new car from a dealer in Saint Stephen and the stark contrast between the two vehicles parked side by side was a bit of an embarrassment for the former bank professional.

There was no doubt about transportation this particular morning. Marcel was soon walking down the back lane towards Maplewood Creek Golf Club, a good half mile south of the village. He had a few pointed questions for his golf mate and he wanted to get them clear in his mind. A brisk walk on a beautiful, bright morning seemed to be an ideal way to clear his head and get things into some kind of perspective and logical order. It seemed to work. By the time he reached the club house steps twenty minutes later, the perturbed priest knew he had to somehow find answers to at least three pressing questions.

Pierre Bouchard was sitting alone at a small table in the club house café when Marcel walked in. He looked up as the door opened and grinned in his usual friendly manner. 'Over here, Marcel,' he called. 'I've ordered a coffee for you.'

It seemed like any other Monday morning and Marcel wondered again if he had somehow got things wrong. How could this professional man, his close friend, be guilty of something as serious as murder. There must be some logical explanation for the troubling bits of information that seemed to be coming from all directions. Surely Pierre will make it all clear today and things will be back to normal.

'Hi Pierre. Looks like we have the perfect day for it.' Marcel went through the motions and occupied the empty chair at the flimsy table. 'Thanks,' he said, taking a sip of the freshly poured coffee, 'I've already had too much of this stuff for breakfast but I guess another one won't do me any harm.'

Pierre laughed as he picked up his own paper cup. 'I don't know why we drink clubhouse coffee anyway. It's absolutely dreadful stuff like most other things in this place.' The two men relaxed and settled into their chairs. They'd become used to their Monday routine and they felt comfortable with it.

'We should get moving fairly soon,' Pierre said, looking at his watch. 'I can't hang around for lunch today. I have someone coming to see me before afternoon surgery but I should manage nine holes with no problem.'

'Oh—I was just about to say the opposite.' Marcel's voice cracked slightly, betraying a hint of nervous tension. 'I've a couple of things on my mind that I'd like to ask you about, Pierre. Do you mind if we sit awhile before we hit the course?'

The doctor raised his eyebrows and sank back into his chair. 'Sure, Marcel. What's bothering you? Am I going to be the father confessor today?' He grinned at his own joke but quickly adopted a more sober demeanour when he saw the priest's serious face.

Marcel cleared his throat and breathed in deeply. 'It's a couple of things I've been hearing around the parish, Pierre, and I'm a bit puzzled. Maybe you can clarify this for me. Most people in the village know that you and I arrived here on the same day last March. We seem to have become the two most prominent figures in the village and between us I thing we're doing a pretty good job. I want to keep it that way.'

'I can't disagree with that—so what's the problem?'

'Well I think we have to be more honest with each other. As you've said yourself, we both care about these people, and though our roles are quite different, at the end of the day we're both here to ensure the welfare of the community. We should be sharing information, not hiding it from each other.'

Pierre frowned deeply. 'What are you saying? I'm not honest with you?'

'It's just something my housekeeper was saying. It was always my understanding that you were new to Maplewood Creek the same as me—that we arrived here on the same day—but Mme Poirier says you were here about six months before that, working with Doctor Martin.'

Pierre Bouchard smiled broadly and leaned forward, resting his elbows on the table. 'Are you getting a bit paranoid, Marcel?' he said. 'That day last March when we arrived, I didn't know you at all. We met on the train for the first time, remember, and I didn't know anything about you. I was just arriving with my belongings to settle in the village on a permanent basis the same as you, and in that sense I was new to Maplewood Creek. That's what I meant and that's what I told you. Yes, I'd been down here a few months earlier to work some things out with Doctor Martin but I didn't want to bore you with any of that. I stayed with him for a day or two and then I had to return to my work in Fredericton. I had a lot of things to wind up.'

Marcel suddenly felt quite foolish. What a simple and logical explanation that was. How could he have let such a trivial matter bother him so much, he thought. He smiled and casually folded his arms. 'I suppose I might have read too much into it,' he said. 'I'm just surprised you've never mentioned it, that's all.'

'But why would I? It's never come up in conversation, has it? Is it important?'

'I guess not. But there's more to that story, isn't there? I understand a woman drowned in the river while you were here and you were called on to give some medical assistance. That's pretty dramatic. I can't understand why you haven't talked to me about that.'

Pierre's face took on a more serious expression and he took on a more sombre tone. 'Marcel,' he said, betraying a hint of irritation, 'I can't tell you everything, can I? People in this village don't like to talk about that tragic drowning—and if it comes to that neither do I. Besides, I have professional obligations the same as you. I can't really discuss that incident without betraying information about a patient of mine.'

Marcel sat back and folded his arms. 'You mean Guy LaPlante, don't you? You do know him? He's told me about the regular counselling sessions he's been having with you.'

Pierre was obviously uncomfortable with the question and his voice reflected some impatience now. 'Guy is one of my patients. Of course I know him. I've been working with him but I'm sure you understand that any details about his condition are highly confidential.'

'I do understand that of course, but it was his wife who drowned wasn't it?'

The question seemed to hit Pierre like a ton of bricks. 'What of it?' he said tersely.

Marcel bit his lip and hesitated before going on. 'As you know only too well, Pierre, Guy LaPlante has some serious problems. I've also been working with him on a couple of issues, including his wife's drowning. Has he ever said anything to you that might suggest some guilt on his part?'

Pierre Bouchard swallowed hard and his face flushed with annoyance. 'I don't believe this, Marcel. You think I can answer a question like that? How can you ask me such a thing? What if I asked you what one of your penitents had confessed in the secrecy of confession? You'd be appalled wouldn't you?' He stared angrily at the startled priest. 'And if I did ask you that you wouldn't tell me would you?'

Momentarily stunned by the direct and forceful question, Marcel hesitated and stared back. 'Well,' he began, 'I…'

'Well would you?"

'No, I don't suppose I would.'

'You're damn right you wouldn't. It would be total betrayal. And I'm not going to answer your question for the same reason.'

Marcel desperately wanted to end this conversation. Pierre was right of course. How could he possibly answer a question like that. The priest could see his friendship with the village doctor unravelling by the minute and he was anxious to contain the damage as much as he possibly could. Yet he needed to know the truth, for without it this thing could never be put to rest. 'Pierre,' he said, 'I'm sorry to press you on this, but at least tell me one thing. Were you ever in that old confessional box we used to have in the church?'

'What?'

'It's just that Celine Hubert said you had discussed it with her. Did you really make use of that confessional before it was taken away or did she misunderstand what you were saying?'

That was the last straw. Pierre slammed the table hard with his fist, spilling what was left of his coffee, and he stood up noisily, throwing his chair behind him. 'This is too much, Marcel,' he said. 'What is this—an interrogation? Are you discussing me with your parishioners now? I thought we were friends. Talk about being honest with each other. I don't think you have a clue.'

Marcel stood up from the table as his friend edged towards the door. 'I'm sorry to upset you like this, Pierre. I do understand your professional obligations to secrecy and I respect you for honouring them. As you say, I'm bound by the same obligations myself—actually, that's the root of the problem I'm having at the moment. Believe me, if I could tell you more I would. But please bear with me. I have to ask you one more thing.'

'And what might that be?' Pierre spat out.

'About your wife—would you ever go back to her?'

If Doctor Bouchard was angry before, now he was close to uncontrollable rage. He stared at the priest, red-faced and incredulous, then turned and headed for the door. 'I don't know what's going on, Father, but I've had enough of this,' he growled as he flung the door open. He turned before stepping outside and faced the priest once more. 'To answer your impertinent questions, yes I did enter that damned confessional box of yours once, and no I won't be going back to my wife. If you must know, my wife is dead. She died in an accident last September.'

Marcel stood on the wooden steps of the club house and watched Pierre Bouchard drive away in a cloud of dust. What have I done, he thought. That man is infuriated at the way I questioned him in such a clumsy and insensitive manner. I'm not sure he'll ever forgive me for it.

It was a depressing thought. Marcel valued his friendship with the village doctor and he had always felt that the two of them together had the potential to do a great deal of good in the community. He had hoped to resolve the nagging suspicions that haunted him but now things looked worse than ever. Pierre is angry for good reason though, he thought. I've obviously touched a sore spot and he seems to have plenty to hide. Not only that, but he's made it clear that he doesn't want to be questioned about these things. He's already acting like a guilty man and far from clearing himself of suspicion, he's just blurted out a few things that make it impossible for me to doubt any more his involvement in a woman's death.

But things were becoming very confusing. Marcel walked slowly down the steps with his hands pushed deeply into his pockets, staring at the gravelled driveway that led from the parking lot. He leaned heavily on the decorative rail at the front of the building, peering at the exit as if his friend were about to reappear any minute. What exactly have I discovered, he asked himself. Are there any more excuses or alibis for Pierre Bouchard, or is it certain now that he's the one who confessed to murder in the confessional that day? Judging by his parting comments it surely seemed that way.

Several things were quite puzzling, however. For one thing the irate doctor didn't seem to think his admission to using the confessional box was a problem. If he really was the penitent that Saturday afternoon, one would think he'd be careful to hide that fact from the priest. But not necessarily. He knew full well that any priest would guard the secrets of confession with his life, and if he was angry enough he might well resort to some revengeful taunting. I did it but you can't do anything about it, sort of thing. Marcel shook his head. He had to admit that Pierre Bouchard was not the sort of man who would stoop so low.

There was another slant on this whole thing of course. Pierre knew that the priest had made a habit of being in the church for confessions every Saturday afternoon and if he was the penitent who'd confessed to murder, he may have assumed that his confession was only one of many that day. There'd be no way for a priest to know who confessed what. But that's where he was wrong. Only one confession had been heard in that confessional box since Marcel had taken over the administration at St. Jude's, and he was the only person who knew that. It seemed that Pierre had just inadvertently admitted that the confession in question was made by him.

Marcel found the information about Pierre's wife to be the most troubling disclosure of all. He'd desperately clung to the hope that she was still alive and well somewhere, in which case his friend would no longer be suspect—but in that case it would have been difficult to explain the confession. He felt guilty about tricking his friend into revealing that bit of information though he knew it was an essential piece of the puzzle. He'd guessed, correctly as it happened, that by bringing up the question of whether or not Pierre would consider returning to his wife he would betray some information concerning her whereabouts. The doctor had obviously wanted to keep that fact to himself, but in his angry outburst he'd admitted that she was dead. That seemed odd too, Marcel thought. Pierre had never mentioned his wife's death before. He'd rarely mentioned her at all but he'd always given the impression that she was still alive, living with someone else.

Several Muskoka chairs were arranged in front of the club house and Marcel sank into one of them with a loud sigh. He just wanted to get on with his peaceful life in the parish, doing what priests are supposed to do, but the thought of walking back to the house now with his heavy golf bag seemed like such a burden. Pierre would normally have given him a lift back to the village but there was no chance of that today.

Technically, it was the priest's day off, though there was always plenty of work to do. At least two sick parishioners were due for a visit and he'd promised to meet with the liturgy committee as soon as possible to make some decisions for the season ahead. Guy LaPlante was a constant worry on Marcel's mind too. The young man seemed to have no work at the moment and the priest hated to see him wandering around the village on his own. He was harmless enough of course, but perhaps some more maintenance jobs could be found for him around the church.

The whole business about Guy's wife seemed to take on a new perspective now. Marcel had wanted to believe that Guy was the murder suspect in spite of his clumsy explanation about his wife's death. At least there'd be some way of explaining that. Guy was a disturbed young man with a whole range of problems that were not being properly dealt with, and he might well be more responsible for his wife's death than he was letting on. The troubled man had explained the details of his wife's drowning to Marcel in their confidential chat and it sounded like a very plausible explanation at the time. But who could verify that they were the accurate facts? As Guy's family doctor, Pierre Bouchard must know something, but he had been very careful not to disclose any information he might have about that.

Marcel rose from his chair and set out on his twenty-minute walk back to the village. He continued to mull the whole thing over in his mind as he gradually fell into a brisk pace, still unsure of his obligations and legal responsibilities. There seemed to be two possible scenarios. Either Pierre Bouchard had killed his wife and then confessed to it, or Guy LaPlante had somehow caused his wife's death and confessed to that. But on reflection there were other possibilities too. Suppose Pierre had killed Guy's wife. Or perhaps Guy had killed Pierre's wife. But then who confessed to what? One thing seemed to be very clear—Pierre Bouchard and Guy LaPlante had an awful lot in common.

The most annoying and frustrating thing, Marcel thought, is that there'd be no case at all if he hadn't heard his first penitent confess to murder. It would simply be a matter of two parishioners, each losing his wife to a tragic accident around the same time. A bit of a coincidence perhaps, but that's as far as it would go. Life would go on and everyone would be happy.

The house was in view now and Marcel relaxed his pace a little as he came up the back laneway. He allowed himself to consider briefly the possibility that the murderous penitent who was causing him so much grief was neither Pierre nor Guy. Perhaps it was someone from out of the village; perhaps it was a hoax; or perhaps he had imagined the whole thing. But it was no use. Too much independent evidence—evidence that had nothing to do with sacramental confession—was surfacing all around him. Two women were dead—that was known fact. Guy LaPlante was suffering from a variety of mental problems—his aunt had made that very clear. Pierre Bouchard had uncharacteristically lost his temper over a few personal questions posed by a good friend. And there seemed to be some strange connection between the two men involved. Something was definitely going on and Marcel knew it was time to get some professional advice about his legal and moral obligations.

Ten

Mme Poirier was vacuuming the front hall as Marcel came in. She jumped back in astonishment as he dragged his golf bag in and threw it into a corner with a loud clatter. 'Oh—Father Marcel,' she exclaimed, quickly turning off the noisy machine, 'I wasn't expecting you back for hours. What happened to the golf game?'

'Change of plan, I'm afraid.' Marcel headed for the stairs leading up to his private quarters but turned back to face his housekeeper as he mounted the first step. 'I have to take a short trip to Fredericton, Louise. I'll be gone for a couple of days so I'll need you to take care of a few things for me.'

'Certainly, Father. Nothing serious has happened has it? I mean you're not going for a funeral or anything?'

'Nothing like that. I have to arrange a meeting with Bishop Giguère but I'll be staying with a friend of mine, Father Gérard Rousseau. He's in St. Francis parish in Fredericton. I'll get you the phone number.'

'No need for that, Father. It'll be in the directory if I need it. What do you want me to do at the moment.'

Marcel thought for a minute. 'Well you could start by arranging a taxi for me. I'll need to catch the two o'clock train from Saint Stephen this afternoon so maybe you could call one of the cab companies up there. Meanwhile I have two or three phone calls to make.' He climbed the stairs two at a time and disappeared into his apartment.

Some time later the priest reappeared in the front hall with a small, black travel bag packed and ready to go. He dropped the bag at the front door and then made his way into the parlour where he sank into a comfortable arm chair. His busy housekeeper was dusting the coffee tables but stopped immediately when the priest entered the room. 'All set then, Father?' she asked. 'Is your accommodation worked out?'

'It's all arranged now. I'll be meeting with the bishop some time tomorrow morning. They have to fit me in so I'm not sure what time it will be, but you can contact me at Father Rousseau's place in case of an emergency. Things should be all right around here too. I've just talked to André on the liturgy committee. His team will conduct a short service in the church tomorrow morning. Now what about that taxi? What time are they coming for me?'

Mme Poirier moved her cleaning equipment to one side and sat down in the other armchair. 'I called a couple of cab companies in Saint Stephen, Father, but they are all ridiculously expensive. I don't know if you're aware of it or not, but Gaston Leduc in the village here operates a taxi service of sorts. It's nothing fancy, but he'll drive you into Saint Stephen for less than half the price—and he's right here on your doorstep. I've already called him and he says he can be here at 1.15 this afternoon if you wish.'

'Gaston? Oh, of course. That makes more sense doesn't it? Yes, if you want to confirm that with him you can tell him I'll be ready and waiting.'

Gaston Leduc was true to his word and his humble taxi pulled up in front of Marcel's door exactly on time. The priest hurried down the pathway and threw his travel bag into the back seat. Then he occupied the front passenger seat next to his youthful driver and prepared himself for the bumpy ride into Saint Stephen.

'So you're not driving your old jalopy today, Father?' Gaston grinned as he slipped the stick shift noisily into gear and pulled away from the curb with an almost imperceptible squeal of tires. 'Good for you, I say. I know this rig of mine has seen better days but I must say it's better than yours.'

Marcel laughed at his driver's unabashed honesty. He valued the easy, casual relationship he enjoyed with most of the villagers and did everything he could to encourage it. 'I can't disagree with that, Gaston. I suppose I should be looking for something better, but to tell you the truth, I don't really do much driving these days.'

'Well, if you need any help or advice about a new vehicle just let me know.' Gaston wound up his window, wincing at the annoying squeak created by the dry glass. 'You're headed for the station then, are you, Father?'

'That's right. I'm catching the two o'clock train to Fredericton. I'm surprised you were able to pick me up at such short notice. It's much appreciated.'

'My pleasure, Father. Anything to oblige.' He laughed heartily. 'Are you taking a bit of a holiday then?'

'A bit of business, more like. I'll be back tomorrow afternoon though. I should arrive into Saint Stephen about 4 o'clock. Perhaps you can pick me up and drive me back to the village?'

'No problem at all, Father. I'll be there on the dot.'

Marcel looked quizzically at his cheerful chauffeur. 'But what about your business, Gaston? Who's taking care of the gas bar and shop while you're out driving me?'

'Oh, I've locked up for a bit. They won't miss me for an hour or so. Things are usually pretty quiet on a weekday afternoon.'

Marcel shuffled in his seat in an attempt to get comfortable. 'You need to get yourself a good reliable assistant, Gaston. Someone to look after things when you're not there.' He hesitated a moment, not entirely sure whether to mention a controversial name. 'You know Guy LaPlante, don't you? I believe he's looking for work at the moment; he might be a good choice. Hasn't he worked with you before?'

Gaston pointedly ignored the question, and he turned onto the main road to Saint Stephen, dodging an extra large pot hole as he squealed around the corner. 'I don't know why we can't have better roads around here,' he complained. 'Just because we're a small village they think we don't need any proper services.'

'It does seem that way sometimes, doesn't it? But about Guy LaPlante—isn't he a friend of yours?'

Gaston paused before answering, slowly shaking his head. 'I wouldn't say that, Father—not any more. When we were teenagers we used to hang around together and we both worked at the gas bar for a while, but that's a long time ago. Guy has had a lot of problems. I see him around the village sometimes and we pass the time of day, but I couldn't trust him to hold down a proper job, not at the moment anyway. He can be a bit unreliable, you know. I'm manager of the gas bar and shop now and I have to be responsible for it.'

Marcel stretched his feet forward. This really was an uncomfortable taxi and he began to wonder if it might have been better after all to call one of the big companies in town. On the other hand, he thought, Gaston might be a wealth of information on some issues and unanswered questions, and for the next twenty minutes he has no escape. He looked at his driver, wondering where to begin. 'I thought you might be able to help him out, that's all,' he said, 'but I do see your point.'

'It's not that I don't want to help him out.' Gaston seemed somewhat uncomfortable with the issue of Guy's problems and he hesitated as he tried to explain. 'You see Guy's had a tough year and sometimes he has trouble distinguishing between what's real and what isn't, if you see what I mean, Father. He has an overworked imagination and he tends to get carried away with things.'

'I know he's had some difficult problems to deal with and I've been trying to help him. But you've known him for a long time—you would be in a good position to offer him some support. Has he always had these problems?'

'He was always a strange sort of kid but he seemed to do all right most of the time.' Gaston coughed, betraying a touch of caution. 'I don't want to talk out of turn, Father, but I think the real problem has always been Guy's dad.'

'Denis LaPlante?'

'You know him then?'

'I can't say I know him. I met him once when I first arrived in the village last March and I've seen him driving through on that motorcycle of his once or twice on a Saturday morning and that's about it. But I do know Guy's aunt, Marianne Boudreau, and she's mentioned her brother-in-law. She seems to think he had a big influence on Guy while he was growing up—not always positive, unfortunately.'

'Mme Boudreau, yes. Without her, Guy would have stood no chance at all. He moved in with his aunt when his mother died, and she was very helpful and understanding, more like a real mother actually.'

Marcel had heard all this before from Mme Boudreau but there were several questions on his mind about the part played by Denis LaPlante in this whole saga. 'So I've heard,' he said nodding in agreement, 'but my understanding was that Guy's dad left the family when his son was still quite young. I've also heard that he kept in touch with them on a regular basis? I mean after he moved to Fredericton?'

'He was supposed to be living in Fredericton. He hated the village but he was always coming back making a nuisance of himself when Guy and I were teenagers. As you know, he's a big heavily built fellow, a truck mechanic, and he liked to throw his weight around. He'd come back every few months and scare the hell out of Guy and his mother.' Gaston shook his head in disgust. 'A real bully he was. I never liked the guy.'

'What was the point of it all? I mean what was Denis LaPlante trying to gain by behaving that way?'

Gaston swerved heavily to avoid a large pot hole, causing the two men to sway to one side. 'Sorry about that, Father,' he grinned. 'What was he trying to gain?

Well it was the house, you see. It belonged to Guy's mother. Her parents had left it to her and it's worth quite a lot of money. When they split up, Denis LaPlante expected her to sell it and give him half the proceeds, but she refused. So he kept on giving her a hard time. Three years later she died of a heart attack, probably due to the stress I'd say.' He coughed again then added as an after thought, 'Of course I only know what Guy told me at the time.'

This quarrel over ownership was news to Marcel. He wondered if there could be any connection between the conflict over the house and Guy's current state of mind. 'After Mme LaPlante died, her husband still didn't get ownership of the house did he? I mean, my understanding was that the property was left to Guy?'

'That's right. Apparently his mother made it clear in her will that the ownership would be passed on to her son and not to his father. It was iron clad; Denis didn't have a leg to stand on.'

'That must have infuriated him.'

'Probably did—I don't know. He left the village for good after that. No one saw him around here for years, and for the first time in his life, Guy was able to settle down and live a more normal life with his aunt. Come to think about it, he was at his best during those late-teen years. He was more like a regular, normal young guy then with a job and a girl friend. I can't believe the way he's gone downhill since last September.'

There was plenty to think about and the two men travelled in silence for a while. Marcel noticed that the road was much improved now and the smooth paving told him they were within the township of Saint Stephen. They'd be at the station within a few minutes, yet there was still so much to ask. 'You mentioned last

September,' he said, trying to get in as many questions as possible. 'Why do you say that?'

'That's when Guy returned from Fredericton—about this time last year. He was working up there with his dad for about a year, you know.'

'Yes, I did know that, but that puzzles me. If Guy was so afraid of his father why did he want to go to live with him in Fredericton?'

Gaston geared down as he approached the large parking area in front of Saint Stephen railway station. 'That's always puzzled me too,' he said as he parked adeptly close to the curb. 'Guy was no longer a kid by then, of course. He was twenty-three when he left the village. Apparently his dad had visited out of the blue one day and then wrote several letters, more or less invited him up there. I suppose Guy was ready for a change—big town and all that. I think they lived together for a short time but it wasn't long before Guy found a place of his own. That's what Mme Boudreau told me anyway, and it didn't surprise me at all.'

Marcel made no attempt to leave the taxi. 'And when Guy returned to the village last year he brought a new wife along with him, didn't he?

Gaston raised his eyebrows and sneered. 'Along with the rest of the entourage.'

'What do you mean?'

'Well it wasn't just the new wife—and I've got my own thoughts about that. I hadn't seen Guy for over a year at that point and I was all for welcoming him back home with a bit of a party or celebration of some kind. His aunt had cleaned up the old house for him and this new woman he'd acquired. Everything should have been fine. But it obviously wasn't.'

'Why do you say that? What was the problem?'

'Well Guy had changed so much and he was on pins and needles all the time. I was supposed to be his best friend but he more or less ignored me and he wasn't himself at all. But the worst of it was this woman, Fran. She kept fussing around him all the time and I just felt like I was in the way. Mme Boudreau and I kept trying to help out on that first day when they arrived in the village, but they didn't seem to want any help. In fact they more or less asked us to leave.'

'Yes, but what's this entourage you mentioned?'

'Well the next morning Dr. Bouchard showed up. That was the first time I'd ever met him, but he obviously knew Guy and Fran. Mme Boudreau and I had gone round to visit again and Dr. Bouchard opened the door to us. He seemed to be all riled up and he said he couldn't invite us in because he was discussing some personal matters with Guy and Fran. He seemed anxious for us to leave so he could talk to them in private. I didn't know what the hell was going on.'

Marcel looked out of the passenger window as his thought process absorbed the new information. 'Who else was part of this entourage?'

'Guy's dad, Denis LaPlante. He arrived while we were literally still standing at Guy's front door and he quickly made his presence felt. It was chaos and confusion all around. He bellowed and yelled at Dr. Bouchard, obviously furious about something, though I never did figure out what he was so mad about. Something must have happened when they were all in Fredericton. Anyway, Mme Boudreau and I were quite disgusted with the whole thing so we just left them to it. The next morning we heard about that dreadful accident. Fran had drowned in the river later in the afternoon of the previous day.'

The puzzled priest bit his lower lip as he tried to gauge the significance of it all. 'So Dr. Bouchard, Denis LaPlante, Guy and his new wife were all at Guy's house when you left them?'

'That's right.'

'Did you see any of them again that day?'

'The only one I saw again that day was Guy's dad. He came into the gas bar mid afternoon to see if I could drive him into town. He was in a foul mood though; he sat down on the chair by my cash register frantically scratching his legs and using language that would shock a sailor. He said he must have walked through poison ivy somewhere and judging by the horrible rash all over his legs I'd say he was probably right. Anyway, I told him I wasn't available to drive him so he used my phone to call a taxi from Saint Stephen. They told him he'd have to wait for a couple of hours because they were so busy so he just sat there with a scowl on his face and waited for his ride. He had very little to say and I more or less ignored him. When his taxi finally arrived he just got up and left without a word.'

Marcel gave his driver a large bill, refusing any change, and then retrieved his travel bag from the back seat. He slowly climbed out of the taxi and stood there on the sidewalk with the passenger door wide open. 'It's a sad story, Gaston. I want to help Guy any way I can but there are so many complicated issues there. I mean, to lose a wife like that amid so much anger and confusion…'

Gaston leaned over to the open car door. 'I'll be here for you tomorrow, Father, but there's one last thing I'd say to you before I go. Sorry to be so blunt, but that woman, Fran, who Guy brought back from Fredericton—I don't know who the hell she was, but I don't believe for one moment she was his wife.' He pulled the door shut, gave the priest a quick thumbs up and quickly drove away.

Marcel stood and watched as the taxi turned the corner at the far end of the station and headed for the road back to Maplewood Creek. Then, with a head full of confused and conflicting thoughts, he walked into the busy station to begin his trip to Fredericton, quite unsure about why he was going and what he would discover when he got there.

Eleven

Guy LaPlante struggled with his well-worn can opener and with some difficulty he opened a large can of baked beans. As he scooped out a generous helping into a glass dish, two pieces of toast popped up from the toaster and he retrieved them gingerly, wincing slightly as it burnt his fingers. He quickly lathered the hot toast with a blob of butter from the plastic container on the kitchen counter and emptied the beans on top. Beans on toast was his favourite lunch, and he sat down at the kitchen table to enjoy them.

The view from the kitchen was impressive. Guy looked out at the green meadows behind his back fence and the thick forest beyond. He felt secure in the knowledge that he owned his own home and though his income was small, he could manage; he knew he'd always have a place to live. His grandparents had been wise to buy a half acre of land on which to build their dream home some fifty years earlier, and now Guy owned the whole property as his rightful inheritance.

It was a slow lunch. The troubled young man stared dreamily into space as he relaxed on a captain's chair that seemed to be far too fancy for the kitchen. For some reason he was feeling much better today, and for the first time in months, life seemed to have some positive aspects to it. Maybe the future wouldn't be so bad after all, he thought. There were some good people in his life now, and most of them seemed to have been doing everything possible to help him pick up the pieces after the traumatic events of the previous year.

But Guy felt mean and unappreciative. He'd been so absorbed in his own problems lately that he'd had no time for anyone else, and he'd shown very little gratitude to either friends or family. Not that he'd ever had much family to speak of, he thought, sniffing sarcastically at the memory of frequent domestic conflict during his stressful childhood.

Guy poured himself a glass of orange juice and wandered over to the French windows in the adjoining lounge. The garden was a mess, as always. He remembered his mother's dissatisfaction with it and her constant frustration with her husband and unruly son who refused to help her with any of the heavy work. He felt guilty about that now. I was such a brat, he thought to himself. I could have made things so much easier for her. How lucky she was though to have a caring sister who was willing to take me in. Aunt Marianne—how would he have managed without her?

Those times were different, Guy thought, especially after he'd got over his mother's death. He was at peace then and his life seemed to have some purpose to it. Work and play seemed to balance each other the way they should. He remembered how he and Gaston Leduc had worked so hard at the gas bar, late into the evening sometimes. And life wasn't all work in those days; they always had enough money to have a good time too. The two of them would drive into Saint Stephen almost every weekend and paint the town red, usually drinking too much and moving from one rowdy bar to another. More often than not, they didn't arrive back in the village till dawn. He laughed at the memory of it, and then took on a more sombre expression. It was one of those weekends in Saint Stephen when he'd met the girl of his dreams at the Dance-Etienne. Julie, he said out loud—whatever happened to you?

Julie had been a stabilizing factor in Guy LaPlante's life for a short period of time. She was an ordinary, down-to-earth sort of girl with an engaging manner that appealed to his sense of humour. She worked as a secretary at the main police station in Saint Stephen, and she frequently entertained her phobic boyfriend by mimicking the mannerisms of senior staff there. Her irreverent antics always caused Guy to break into fits of uncontrolled laughter, attracting the attention of all who happened to be around. The romance continued for almost a year before Julie moved away for a new job in Moncton. She had to get on with her life, she told him, and Guy never heard from her again.

It was after Julie moved away that Guy began to feel restless in Maplewood Creek. The village had become too small and restrictive for a young man and Guy yearned for something better. He thought about moving the few miles to Saint Stephen, but apart from the expense of renting accommodation there, the town seemed empty and sad without Julie, and every street corner seemed to remind him of the good times they'd had together. Even the weekend trips into town with

Gaston became boring. Guy found himself making excuses not to go, and before long the regular excursions to the bright lights of Saint Stephen were just a distant memory. Then one Saturday afternoon an unlikely opportunity appeared out of the blue. Guy's tetchy father, Denis LaPlante, arrived on his aunt's doorstep with a pasted-on smile and a bottle of wine.

Denis wasn't very welcome at the Boudreau residence, but he didn't come very often and he never stayed very long. Marianne was far too polite to turn him away and besides, she grudgingly accepted that, like any other father, he had a right to contact his son once in a while. Denis had blustered in with his usual clumsiness on that occasion. He'd plonked the bottle of wine on the kitchen counter and looked around for the main object of his visit asking, 'Where's that son of mine?' as if it were a regular weekly occurrence.

Guy was out, as it happened, but conveniently for Marianne, he made an appearance before Denis had quite finished drinking his own wine. The young man was surprised and not entirely pleased to see his absentee father sitting in his aunt's tidy living room, talking loudly and now feeling the effects of the cheap brew. 'Dad!' he mumbled. 'What the hell are you doing here?'

Denis plonked his glass on the coffee table and stood up. 'Well you may ask, son,' he said ambling towards his wary offspring. 'I'm here to offer you a chance to add some excitement to that dreary life of yours.' He inflicted an unwelcome bear hug on Guy's gangly frame and then returned unsteadily to his seat by the fireplace.

Over the next two or three hours, Denis talked about his life in Fredericton and the advantages of living in a bustling city. He wanted his son to join him there and start living a little. 'This village is no place for a young man,' he proclaimed. 'Sell that house of yours and use the money to set yourself up in business. I've got the perfect plan. We can open up a used car lot and offer service and repairs. There'll be no shortage of business up there. We'll make a fortune working together.'

Mention of selling the house had immediately raised a red flag for Marianne. She knew that Denis was still bitter about the settlement after Jeanette died. His wife had always maintained sole ownership of the property, thanks to a pre-nuptial agreement, and Denis had reluctantly accepted that even after the divorce, but when she died he had expected to inherit it from her. He was incensed to find that Jeanette had registered a will with a lawyer in town, stipulating that ownership was to be transferred to Guy and Guy alone. She kindly left everything else, which wasn't much, to her ex-husband.

By the time Denis left that afternoon, the Boudreau household was in an uproar. Guy was enthused about a new life in Fredericton and he would have foolishly put the house up for sale with no hesitation. It was left to Marianne to convince him not to do so. 'That house is under lease,' she explained. 'You have a professional couple living there and they are paying you a substantial rent for it. Don't give that up, whatever you do. It's your main source of income, and not only that, it's your future security.' She stopped short of telling her capricious nephew that as far as she was concerned, if he did sell the house, once the proceeds fell into his father's hands, that was the end of it. He'd never see that money again.

Guy suddenly realized he was day dreaming again and he quickly turned away from the window. This seemed to be a regular occurrence now as he tried to piece together the events of the past two years and make some sense of them but that wasn't necessarily a bad thing. Dr. Bouchard had assured him that mulling over both positive and negative experiences could be therapeutic and productive. He seemed to be right because things were definitely falling into place.

Guy put his empty glass down on the coffee table and looked around his pleasant lounge with an appreciative sigh. It felt so good to be the outright owner of this luxurious home. How he wished now that he'd ignored his father's persuasive exhortations to live with him in Fredericton. It was a bad idea from the start. He knew that now.

Denis LaPlante's only real interest had been the money that he felt was rightfully his through the sale of Guy's property, and he was determined to get it one way or another. That was the long and short of it. When he didn't get it he turned nasty. Guy of course was the one who suffered from his father's frustrations at first hand, but even Marianne, who had witnessed her brother-in-law's sinister side on more than one occasion, could not have imagined the lengths to which he was prepared to go.

The afternoon sun was still shining across the back garden, casting longer shadows now, but creating a striking bucolic environment that Guy found hard to resist. He started to open the French windows that led on to his pink-stone patio but stopped short when he heard his unusual jangle of doorbells ringing. He looked at his watch instinctively. 'Who the hell's that,' he said out loud. 'I wasn't expecting anyone today.'

The anxious young man felt his heart rate increase slightly as he headed for the front door. It's probably aunt Marianne, crutches and all, he thought. Just home from the hospital but no doubt she's worrying about me again. He flung open the door and faced his visitor head on with affected confidence and well-practiced artificial self assurance. Then he stopped dead in his tracks. 'Gaston!' he gulped in surprise. 'It's you!'

Gaston stood there grinning. 'Yes! It's me all right,' he said cautiously, not sure whether his visit would be welcome or not. 'I thought it was about time we talked—seriously I mean.'

A tense moment of awkward silence followed as Guy tried to assess the purpose of his old friend's visit. He'd always felt quite comfortable talking to Gaston Leduc, and although he wouldn't have chosen this particular moment for a chat, it seemed churlish and rude to turn his old friend away now. He laughed shyly. 'It has been a while, hasn't it? Come on in. I have a couple of beers in the fridge.'

The two men wandered through the hallway to Guy's kitchen. Both were somewhat self conscious as they struggled to deal with a strained friendship that had been neglected for too long. As Guy rummaged in the fridge, his old friend tried to make conversation. 'This is like old times when you were living here with your mother,' he said. 'We did spend a lot of time in this house when we were kids, didn't we? I don't know when I was last here—apart from the brief visit last summer of course when you'd just arrived back from Fredericton.'

Guy smirked as he opened two beer bottles and handed one to Gaston. 'I would have asked you over before now, you know. I wanted to in fact, but I really haven't been myself for some time. I'm sure you know that.'

'Yes, indeed. You've had a tough time of it since you came back to the village—a lot to deal with.'

'And long before that too. The last two years have been absolute hell.' Guy pointed with his beer bottle to the French windows in the lounge. 'Let's go outside. You'll remember the great view from the back. You can still hear the rapids from the patio.'

It was a pleasant afternoon. The heat of summer had now given way to that unique feeling of wellbeing that September brings, and as they settled into comfortable Muskoka chairs, Guy felt suddenly pleased to have a visit from an old friend. 'So what made you drop by today?' he asked. 'Was this a spur of the moment thing?'

Gaston took a long drink from his bottle. 'It was, I suppose—yes. Father Marcel was saying you might be looking for a job, and I thought you might be interested in working at the gas bar again. It would only be part time, of course.'

Guy looked up sharply at the mention of Marcel's name. 'Father Marcel?' he said quizzically. 'You've been talking to him?'

'Don't be alarmed,' Gaston laughed. 'We weren't discussing you.' A slight blush betrayed the blatant lie. They'd done nothing but discuss Guy's sad life all the way to Saint Stephen. 'No,' he went on, trying to reassure his old friend. 'I just drove him to the station this afternoon and your name came up.'

The suggestion of a job at the gas bar was quickly forgotten as the popular pastor became the focus of attention. 'I didn't know he was going away,' Guy said with a hint of concern in his voice. 'Where's he off to?'

'Fredericton, apparently. He said he has some business to attend to up there, but he'll be back tomorrow afternoon. I'll be picking him up in Saint Stephen when he arrives.'

Guy was relieved to hear that. 'Father Marcel has helped me a lot since he arrived in Maplewood Creek. He's a great guy. I've done a few small jobs for him around the church and I've had a casual chat with him on occasion. I find him very easy to talk to—very understanding. Without him and Dr. Bouchard I'd be in a bigger mess than I'm in now.' He laughed gently at the sad portrayal of his present state of mind.

'You say the last two years have been tough for you. I thought it was Fran's tragic accident last year that turned your world upside down. God knows, the death of a loved one must be the ultimate cross to bear.' Gaston was careful not to refer to her as Guy's wife. He was still unsure about who she was but quite convinced that her place in his old friend's life was nothing but a murky confusion in the mind of a troubled man.

Guy didn't respond immediately. Instead he stared dreamily at the thick wooded area at the far end of his property. His momentary silence was full of anticipation, and the distant gurgling sound of the river as it rushed through the rock-strewn rapids half a mile away added some background drama. 'Yes,' he said finally, 'Fran's death was the ultimate blow, but if I hadn't gone off to Fredericton in the first place, none of this would have happened. I would never have met Fran and I would have avoided a whole bunch of other problems as well. That father of mine—he has a lot to answer for.'

Gaston thought it was interesting that Fran would be included as one of the problems. 'It's just about two years ago since you left the village, isn't it?' he asked casually, not wanting to appear too inquisitive. 'I remember the day you left, full of excitement at the prospect of a new life in the big city. At that time I didn't think you'd ever come back.'

Guy responded with a cynical laugh. 'Actually, it was the beginning of two years of misery. I was just thinking before you came, leaving Maplewood Creek was the biggest mistake of my life.'

'What was the problem, then? I thought you and your dad had some kind of plan set up for a new business?'

'That's what I thought but, as it turned out, it all rested on the sale of this house. My dad's idea was to use the proceeds to invest in a repair shop and used car venture, but by then my aunt had convinced me not to sell, and that led to some horrific arguments between my dad and me. You wouldn't believe how vindictive and abusive he can be.'

Gaston grimaced sympathetically. 'Maybe I would,' he said. 'I've seen Denis lose his temper more than once. Didn't he have any funds of his own then?'

'Not a penny! I moved in with him, and from day one he hounded me to come up with some money. He cursed my mother because she didn't leave him the house when she died, and he was threatening violence to my aunt Marianne on a daily basis for persuading me not to sell. A couple of bitch sisters he called them. But the more he ranted, the more I realized I had to maintain ownership of this house. It became clear to me that my dad couldn't be trusted.'

'Is that why you moved out on your own?'

'It was more serious than that.' Guy paused as if he were afraid of saying too much. 'I couldn't move out at first because I had no job and no money, and I had nowhere to live. I suppose I could have returned to Maplewood Creek at that point, but I didn't even have the train fare to get home. I was stuck, you see.'

'But you did move out, didn't you?'

'Eventually I did—with some help. I managed to find a crappy job in a mechanic's workshop and it came with an equally crappy room.' Guy finished off his beer in a long, drawn-out swig and wiped his mouth with the back of his hand. 'You know, Gaston, I'm only just beginning to rethink those first few weeks in Fredericton. I haven't even talked to Fr. Marcel about this, but I have to tell you, things really did get bad after a while, to the point that I had to get medical help. You'll be surprised to know that I was registered in the psychiatric division for several months at the Fredericton Research Hospital.'

This revelation did not surprise Gaston in the least; he had suspected as much. Guy had always been a bit unstable since adolescence and with a father like Denis LaPlante it was hardly surprising that sooner or later he would go off the rails. But now he found that his curiosity was replacing the sympathy he had first shown. Had the relentless bullying by Denis LaPlante pushed his son over the edge? Gaston remained cool and controlled. 'That's terrible, Guy,' he said gently. "Whatever did your dad do to cause that?'

Guy hesitated again as if he were afraid to divulge too much personal information and when he spoke it was with a hushed, confidential tone. 'Well,' he said, 'among other things he told me some very upsetting things about my mother. You'll remember she died when we were teenagers.'

'I remember that. I have good memories of her. She was a fine lady.'

'Well, I've always believed she died of a heart attack—that's what I was told at the time. But according to my dad, she died of poisoning and it was all my fault.'

'Your fault?' Gaston looked astounded to hear this and waited, open mouthed, to hear his old friend's explanation.

'That's what he said. Do you remember that summer—we were about seventeen and we did a lot of stupid things, but one of our crazier ideas was to make some home-made wine using wild cranberries that we'd found down by the river? I gave my mother a complimentary bottle of that stuff, and that was just before she died. My dad said it was that wine that poisoned her.'

Gaston raised his eyebrows and shook his head emphatically. 'There's no way that could have caused her death, Guy. That wine, if you could call it that, was dreadful stuff, and we only made enough for four bottles. I seem to remember my parents dumping their complimentary bottle down the toilet, but I know I drank a full bottle myself, and as I recall, so did you. It didn't do us any harm so why would it have harmed your mother?'

'That's what I've asked myself a thousand times, but my dad insisted that it was my fault, and at the time I started to believe it. He said we must have confused some poisonous berries with cranberries. He happened to be in Maplewood Creek on one of his unwelcome visits to the house when she passed away, and according to him, although he knew she'd been poisoned, he let it pass when old Dr. Martin said she'd had a heart attack—to protect me, he said.'

Gaston shook his head in disgust. 'That's terrible, Guy. But surely you don't believe that now. I know Dr. Martin had a reputation for being a bit incompetent in his old age, but if he said it was a heart attack that killed your mother, that's what it was.'

Guy stood up and walked slowly to the edge of the patio, his hands pushed deep in his pockets. 'It's taken me a long time, but I can see that now,' he said, his back still turned to his companion. 'But two years ago in Fredericton it was a different situation—quite scary really. I felt completely at my dad's mercy, but it was when he started talking about involving the police that things really came to a head. He said he could continue to keep the poisoning business a secret if only I would sell the house and share the proceeds with him. He was obsessed with this house, you see; he still is.'

'You mean he actually tried to blackmail you?'

The troubled young man bit his lip and struggled for words as emotion threatened to get the better of him. 'Yes, he did, but I must have had a stubborn streak in me, because it was at that point that I packed up my things and left, even though I had nowhere to go.' Guy pointed to the distant trees and turned towards his friend. 'Let's go for a stroll,' he said. 'We can follow the old trail down to the river. I haven't been down there since…well for a long time.' He forced a tentative smile. 'Remember all the fishing we used to do down there when we were kids?'

Gaston groaned as he eased himself out of his comfortable chair. He sensed that Guy LaPlante had said enough for the moment and would rather talk about more pleasant things. He grinned as the two of them set off across the fields to the old river trail. 'Yes, we did a lot of fishing in those days,' he laughed, 'but I seem to remember catching more poison ivy than fish!'

Twelve

Gaston felt much more at ease with his old friend as the two of them beat back the overgrown bushes to reveal the trail they had once known so well. He was beginning to feel guilty now, wishing that he'd made contact sooner instead of trying to avoid involvement in Guy LaPlante's troubles. After all, he told himself, Guy was a childhood friend. They'd grown up together in a small, tight-knit community and shared so many memorable experiences throughout their adolescence. How could he abandon him now when he was so badly in need of a friend?

Gaston had known all along of course that his old friend was dealing with some difficult personal problems, but the revelations about Denis LaPlante's role in his son's breakdown seemed to place the whole saga in a very different light. And this woman, Fran, the woman who had died so tragically—who was she really and how had Guy become so tied up with her? Gaston was determined to find out more about the awful drowning that had occurred in the very river that was now before them.

The deafening sound of the rushing waters greeted the two men as they pushed their way to the river bank. It was an exhilarating sight and Gaston felt quite euphoric as he reminisced about the old days. 'Look at that,' he said breathlessly, pointing to a formation of rocks towards the middle of the rapids. 'When we were kids we used to dare each other to get to those rocks by using these smaller ones as stepping stones. Remember that? We must have been mad.'

'I remember.' Guy stared passively at the raging torrent, his hands now pressed firmly on his hips. 'I'm always awed by this sight,' he said wistfully. 'It reminds me of the Niagara River in many ways. I remember my mother taking me to Niagara Falls when I was about eleven years old, but it wasn't the falls that impressed me so much, it was the Niagara river—the ultimate in white water, the incredible force of the current. I know this isn't quite the same but it brings back those same feelings of awe.'

Gaston began to stroll leisurely along the river bank, picking up small rocks along the way to throw into the water. 'I've never been to Niagara,' he said musingly, 'but I can imagine. If it's like this it must be almost a spiritual experience to stand on the banks of the Niagara river and be fully absorbed by such incredible forces of nature.'

Guy grunted, becoming more absorbed in his own thoughts now. 'I imagine Father Lemieux must have thought this was a spiritual experience', he reflected. 'He always spent his day off down here, fishing for salmon. I suppose he just needed some peace and quiet after a busy weekend.'

'I'm sure you're right.' Gaston glanced at his friend staring at the gurgling waters and wondered if he dared mention Fran's name again. It might be a bit indelicate, he thought, given that the poor woman must have drowned close to this very spot; however he forged awkwardly ahead. He felt his nails digging into his palms as he heard his own voice raised over the thunder of the fast-moving water. 'What did Fran think of the rapids?' he asked rather gauchely. 'She must have been quite impressed.'

Guy seemed a bit surprised at the question but there was no strong reaction against it. It was almost as if he welcomed a chance to talk about her, or perhaps even to set the record straight. He knew only too well that the tragedy had been discussed around the village for months on end. All the villagers really knew, of course, was what they had read in the papers and deep down, Guy knew that those reports were not entirely accurate. He looked sombrely at his friend. 'Actually, Gaston,' he said with some hesitation, 'she hated water, especially raging torrents like this; it scared the shit out of her.'

'Did she tell you that?'

'Yes, she did.' Guy seemed reluctant to expand on his answer but as he fixated on the fast-moving current he continued in a somewhat monotonic voice. 'I was only joking really,' he said, 'but I remember pressing my hand into her back as we stood here. I started pushing her towards the edge, and I told her I was going to throw her into the river—you know, just fooling around.'

'My God, that sounds awful. How did she react to that?'

'Not very well I'm afraid. She became a bit hysterical. She told me she was afraid of fast-flowing rivers and any kind of deep water. She couldn't swim, you see, and she didn't appreciate the joke.'

'Well I can understand that. Let's face it—it can be a bit scary on this section of the river to anyone who's not used to it. It's different for us. We've played around here ever since we were kids and it's no big deal. But Fran—I can imagine she'd have been pretty scared.' Gaston noticed a look of embarrassment on his friend's strained face and thought perhaps this conversation might be leading to some unexpected confession of guilt. Could it be that this disturbed young man was somehow responsible for the woman's death? 'I'm sorry, Guy,' he said, hoping to lull him into saying more. 'This must be upsetting for you. I hope I haven't spoken out of turn.'

'Not at all. It's probably what I need—you know, to face the accident head on and deal with it properly. After all, it's over a year now.' Guy paused for a moment as if he were searching for words, then hastily added, 'She drowned at this very spot you know.'

'I thought it must have been around here.' Gaston stepped up onto a large rock on the river bank and then sat down heavily, dangling his feet over the edge. 'You must have discussed it with Dr. Martin at the time, though. I'm sure he would have been able to help you sort things out.'

'Actually, I found Dr. Martin to be totally useless.' Guy sat down beside his friend on the rock and continued languorously, 'but you'll remember Dr. Bouchard was down here that week. He helped me a lot, and when he moved into the village permanently last March he became my rock. It's only because of his expert counselling that I've been able to start thinking more coherently over the last little while.'

'Are you still seeing him then?

'Every week—I have a regular appointment. You know, it's strange how a tragic experience like that can become so murky. You'd think it would be forever clear in your mind, but it's not. Your mind can play such cruel tricks and you start getting confused about what's real and what isn't. As I say, it's only very recently that things are clearing in my mind, but even now I still get confused about what actually happened.'

'So what do you think happened? You said the accident happened right here. What do you remember exactly?'

Guy sighed deeply. 'Some things I remember clearly,' he said dolefully. 'I remember stepping onto those smaller rocks like we used to do when we were kids. Fran was going mad, telling me to get back, but I wanted to show her there was nothing to be afraid of. I was trying to show her how we used to get to the cluster of rocks in the middle of the river and I just kept going.'

'So did she step onto the rocks with you?'

'Heck, no! She was standing back by these trees behind us. She wouldn't come anywhere near the edge.'

Gaston wrinkled his brow with a look of confusion. 'How did she manage to fall in then?'

'That's one thing I'm still confused about. I remember slipping on the wet rocks and falling into the water myself. The next thing I knew, Fran was in the river with me and Dr. Bouchard was screaming like hell at me to try and save her.'

Gaston turned his head in astonishment. 'Dr. Bouchard? You mean he was down here with you?'

'As I say, it's still a bit confusing. But yes, he was there—he seemed to appear out of nowhere. He certainly hadn't walked down from the house with us.'

'Yes, I know that. I was still there when he went storming off to Dr. Martin's place.

'That was some time before Fran and I came down here. He told us he was going to see Dr. Martin. You'll probably remember Dr. Bouchard and my dad had a big yelling match that morning on my front door step. They both left the house soon after that, leaving me and Fran alone, and I didn't see them again until after the accident. Fran and I definitely walked down to the river alone.'

'But don't you think it seems strange—Dr. Bouchard being here right at the time when Fran drowned?'

'I haven't really thought about it as being strange but yes, I suppose it was a bit of a surprise at the time.'

'And did he never explain how he came to be there at that crucial moment?'

'Well we've discussed the accident countless times during my counselling sessions. Apparently he was still quite upset after his argument with my dad so he took a break from his discussion with Doctor Martin and he went out for a walk to mull things over. He came across me and Fran by the river purely by accident. He says he arrived at the rapids just in time to see Fran jumping in, apparently to save me from drowning.'

'That sounds a bit odd, doesn't it?' Gaston looked at his friend quizzically. 'I mean would she really have done that?'

'I've agonized endlessly over it. I've just told you she was terrified of water, and she couldn't swim, so why would she jump in? But even if she could swim, why would she have jumped in anyway? I certainly didn't need rescuing; I was clinging to the rocks and it was no problem to climb out.'

'What about Fran then? Did you try to save her?'

'Of course, but I didn't stand a chance. She got caught in the current and went under almost immediately. I tried desperately to find her and so did Dr. Bouchard. He was in the water up to his waist same as me, but he realized she was being washed away. He left me to it and clambered out over these rocks right about here where we're sitting. I remember seeing him running along the river bank desperately trying to catch sight of her. As you've probably heard, he was the one who found her two miles downstream a couple of hours later.'

'Yes, I did hear about that at the time.' Gaston was puzzled at this strange story and he wondered if his troubled friend had given an accurate account of the events surrounding the woman's death. By his own admission, Guy was still confused about what was real and what wasn't, and if he was still receiving counselling, he obviously had some unresolved issues. Yet, he seemed to be quite lucid and the passing of time had clearly allowed him to see things from a different perspective.

The two men sat there in silence for a minute, watching the surging white foam as it rushed around the rocks. Gaston knew that he might not get the opportunity to question his troubled friend again in such detail and he was determined to press on while he seemed willing to talk. 'What about your dad then?' he asked. 'Was he down here as well when the accident happened?'

'Guy shook his head emphatically. 'Oh no, there was no sign of him. I know Dr. Bouchard stayed in the village for the next few days after Fran died, but my dad took off and I didn't see him again for quite a long time.'

'Actually, I saw him that same afternoon. He called for a taxi from the gas bar and he had to wait more than an hour for it.' Gaston thought for a moment as another thought occurred to him. 'You say you didn't see your dad for a long time. He must have been at the funeral though?'

The question seemed to confuse Guy. He bit his lower lip and looked away as if the topic of Fran's funeral should be avoided, and when he spoke his voice was more subdued. 'You know Gaston,' he said, 'that's something else I can't fathom. I have no recollection at all about Fran's funeral. I don't even know if I was there. I was totally shattered by her death and I felt very guilty about how the accident happened. My aunt Marianne looked after me for the next few days and she told me that Dr. Bouchard had taken care of all the funeral arrangements. To this day I don't know exactly what happened and, as I say, my memory is still a blank when it comes to the actual funeral.'

Gaston saw an opportunity to clarify the relationship between his confused friend and the woman who'd drowned. 'Surely you would have been at your wife's funeral,' he said reassuringly. 'Surely, even if you were traumatized after that terrible accident, Dr. Bouchard would have made sure you were involved in some way. Have you never discussed that with him—as part of your counselling sessions I mean?'

'I've tried of course, but whenever that topic came up, Dr. Bouchard said we'd talk about it some other time. He seemed reluctant to discuss it.'

'Has he at least told you where your wife is buried?'

Guy looked closely at his inquisitive friend. He was about to speak but turned away as if he were unable to take the final step and admit that Fran was not his wife. He stared at the swirling waters resting his head in his hands and remained almost motionless until he finally spoke. 'I don't think I can talk about this any more,' he said. 'I really appreciate your friendship, Gaston, and I hope you will continue to support me. I still have some things to work out with Dr. Bouchard and I need to talk to Father Marcel again too. I'm afraid you'll have to bear with me a while longer.'

'I understand. Sorry if I've been asking too many questions.' Gaston looked at his watch and rose to his feet with some difficulty. 'I'll have to get back to the shop, anyway. I've left it unattended nearly all day and that's no way to run a business.'

'Are you still offering me a job then?' Guy looked at his old friend and smiled sheepishly. He'd got a few things off his chest and he was feeling a bit more self confident now. 'I know Father Marcel will be pleased to see me working. He's always encouraging me to get involved in something—good for the soul he tells me.'

'He's right, I'm sure. Let's give it some thought, Guy. Drop by one day and we'll talk about it.'

'I'll do that.' Guy stared into space for a minute as his thoughts roamed elsewhere. 'When did you say Father Marcel was returning?' he asked. 'I'd really like to have another chat with him sometime soon.'

'Tomorrow afternoon. I've promised to pick him up at the station when he gets back from Fredericton.'

Thirteen

'Father, I've killed my wife,' the disembodied voice whispered through the darkness.

'What?'

'Help me, Father. I've committed murder. I don't know where to turn.'

Marcel woke with a start as the train came to a grinding halt in Fredericton station, and he felt the sweat on his brow, cold and clammy now as it dripped onto his cheek. It had been a tiring two-hour journey from Maplewood Creek, and despite his best efforts, Marcel had dozed off as he prepared himself for this crucial meeting with the bishop. His ordeal in the confessional had become a recurring dream lately, and it took a moment for the priest to realize he had just relived it one more time.

Nothing seemed to have changed, Marcel thought, as he stepped down from the train, but it felt good to be back in Fredericton. He was dubious now about what he could really achieve from his meeting with the bishop. Would it be a waste of time, he wondered, or will some real, practical answers emerge from the discussion?

Marcel liked Bishop Giguère and he'd had many a thoughtful chat with him during his years of training in the seminary, but what could he do to help with the situation in Maplewood Creek? Two women dead, a murderer on the loose, a good friend under suspicion—and that dreadful confession. All the bishop could do really was to offer some good advice. Still, Marcel thought, it's advice that's needed right now—some words of wisdom to tell me what to do.

'Taxi, Father?' Marcel jumped as someone laid a heavy hand on his shoulder. He turned and found himself staring into the grinning face of Gérard Rousseau. 'And about time too,' his priest friend teased. 'You must have come up on the freight train.'

'Rousseau, you maniac. You nearly gave me a heart attack. How long have you been waiting?' The two shook hands, happy to be in the company of a priestly colleague, an event that happened all too rarely in Marcel's estimation.

'Not that long really. About twenty minutes I suppose.' Father Rousseau pulled the travel bag from his friend's hand and pointed to the taxi rank at the intersection. 'I came down by cab,' he grinned. 'There's no way I'd drive down here at this time of day.'

Gérard Rousseau was a good five years older than Marcel, and he'd already celebrated ten years in the priesthood. A casual observer might think of him as being a bit worldly for a priest—he was an avid ice hockey player and enjoyed a couple of beers with the guys after a vigorous game—but someone more realistic and perceptive would see him as a down-to-earth, well-adjusted individual who knew what he was about. He knew what was important and was not. He was there to serve the people in the community to the best of his ability, and he had no compunction about putting silly rules and regulations conveniently to one side.

'Well, Marcel, you've survived your first six months. How's life treating you down there in the sticks?' Gérard opened the back door of a yellow cab waiting in line and threw his friend's luggage onto the back seat. 'Hop in,' he said. 'You can tell me what brings you so urgently to the big city as we fight the traffic.'

Marcel settled into the cab's comfortable leather seat, yawning now as he began to feel the effects of his journey. The familiar surroundings were a welcome sight on this fine September afternoon..

'You have an appointment with the bishop, then? Is there a problem?' Gérard looked at his colleague with some anticipation. 'Not that it's any of my business of course.'

Marcel laughed. 'Just a couple of things that need some clarification,' he said. 'As a matter of fact, I'd like to pick your brains on something I'm struggling with. You might have some thoughts. But we can talk about it later—perhaps this evening over a glass of wine.

'Of course. That's what friends are for.' Gérard spent the rest of the taxi ride to the suburbs pointing out landmarks and some impressive new buildings that had appeared over the course of the summer, grumbling from time to time that they didn't necessarily improve the landscape.

Marcel was quite happy to conclude the short trip to St. Francis church, anxious to freshen up and relax a little. His friend led him into the comfortable private quarters of the priests' residence . 'Remember this place?' he laughed. 'You can have your old room back. Take your time—I usually eat late. I've asked Monique to have dinner ready for about seven. You'll probably be starving by then.

It was sheer joy to take a shower and change into something more comfortable, and by the time Marcel came down for dinner, he was indeed starving. The smell of good cooking from the kitchen spurred him on, and he entered the dining room to find Gérard already seated at the table. 'Make yourself at home, buddy,' he said. 'Monique has prepared a special dinner in your honour.'

Even as he spoke, Monique pushed a loaded trolley into the dining room from the adjoining kitchen. The young woman could only be described as beautiful. She was trim and healthy and her bubbly personality added to her uncommon attractiveness. She was about thirty years old, but her youthful, fresh complexion and shoulder-length auburn hair made her look much younger. Marcel couldn't help but compare her to his own housekeeper, Mme Poirier, and he wondered how Gérard managed to justify such a desirable candidate for the live-in position. Resident housekeepers were supposed to be "super adulta", that is mature adults, according to Canon Law and Monique hardly qualified. But this wasn't the time to mention it. Marcel smiled at Gérard's hospitable housekeeper as she approached the table. 'You must be Monique,' he said. 'It's a pleasure to meet you.'

'Father Dion,' she replied, with a gentle, contagious laugh. 'It's so nice to have you staying with us. Welcome to St. Francis residence.' She spoke with a delicate French accent and exuded the confidence and charm that one might normally expect of the lady of the house.

Gérard looked rather self satisfied as Monique placed several dishes of food on the table. He placed a gentle hand over hers. 'Actually, Father Dion spent the whole summer here last year,' he said. Their eyes met affectionately and the older priest coughed before adding, 'It was before your time.'

'Oh, I see,' she said, pouring wine into the crystal glasses. 'Well, welcome back, Father. I hope you will enjoy your short visit.'

Marcel nodded. 'Thanks--this looks like a meal for royalty.'

Monique smiled shyly, acknowledging the compliment, and then pushed the empty trolley towards the door. She turned before leaving the room. 'I'll leave you and Father Dion to it, Gérard. I'm going out for a while, but I'll be back later. I'll see you then.'

The priest glanced at his friend before replying. 'That's fine, dear. Marcel and I have a lot to talk about. Don't worry about us—we can take care of ourselves.' Monique pushed the trolley out of the room, and quietly closed the door behind her.

An awkward moment of silence followed as the implications of this short exchange were made clear. Marcel, anxious to avoid any embarrassment to his friend, spoke first. 'She's charming,' he said nonchalantly. 'but whatever happened to Mme Gaudette? She looked after me so well when I was here last summer.'

'Marie Gaudette? She retired at Christmas, poor soul. Marie was housekeeper in this parish for more than twenty years, but she wasn't well, you know. Her arthritis was a problem and I think she was quite happy to retire.' Gérard tried to sound casual and relaxed, but he was aware of the unasked questions that filled the air. He began to serve himself from one of the dishes before him, but stopped midstream to look Marcel in the eye. 'You'll be wondering how Monique fits in I suppose?'

Marcel shrugged his shoulders. 'Well, it is slightly obvious,' he said, 'but I've never been one to make judgments.' He served himself and steered the conversation to more mundane topics—local politics, hockey scores, and common acquaintances.

By the time dinner was over, the two men were well at ease with each other, and Gérard adopted a more serious tone as he poured each of them a second glass of wine. 'We've got things to talk about, Marcel,' he said. 'Let's move over to the lounge where we can be more comfortable.'

The lounge was a peaceful, relaxing room, but it looked more like a professor's study with its oak paneling and neatly stocked bookshelves. The two men made themselves comfortable, engaging in some irrelevant small talk as if to preface the more serious discussion that was to follow. But this didn't last long.

'So what's on your mind, my friend?' Gérard sat back in his leather armchair with his feet on the small coffee table in front of him. He sipped on red wine, facing the younger priest who occupied an identical leather armchair. 'You said you wanted to pick my brain on something.'

'Yes, indeed; but let me ask you a question first.' Marcel took a short drink from his glass and thought for a moment before speaking. 'What do you do about confessions in your parish?

'Confessions?'

'Yes—I mean, do you have a regular weekly schedule, or do your parishioners approach you on the matter? And more to the point, do you still use a confessional box or is it more of a face-to-face sort of thing?'

Gérard laughed, somewhat amused at the younger priest's serious demeanour. 'You know,' he said with a grin, 'there are two confessionals in the church here, but they haven't been used for their original purpose for years. I use them for storage. As far as confessions are concerned, I encourage people to come and talk to me if they have anything on their minds, and I welcome them with open arms when they do. As often as not, we'll sit here in this very room over a coffee. I don't judge them; I just help them to put things in proper perspective, face up to their responsibilities, and get on with their lives.'

'Yes, I thought you'd say something like that. I've been trying to do the same. But what about confidentiality? What about the so-called Seal of Confession? When you're face to face with someone, don't you find it's a problem when you know who your penitent is, especially where serious matters are concerned?'

'I can't say I do.' Gérard took on a more serious air. 'Obviously we respect the privacy of what is said. Like other professionals, we accept that personal discussions are confidential, and any revelations or confessions of guilt, if you like, are made in confidence. But when you get down to it, our obligations are not that much different from those of counselors, social workers, or lawyers. Our penitents, if you want to call them that, expect us to guard their secrets, and that's what we try to do.'

Marcel took a slow, deliberate drink from his glass as he absorbed this point of view. 'But isn't it more than that?' he asked finally. 'It seems to me that priests have always had more obligation to secrecy than other professionals such as the ones you mention. When you read the references in Canon Law, for example, it's downright scary to see what our responsibilities are, and the dire consequences for any priest who dares to betray confessional secrets.'

'Like we'll be deposed and made life-long ignominious wanderers?' Gérard chuckled at the ancient edict he was quoting. 'No, seriously,' he said, 'your point is well taken, Marcel, but you have to remember that these decrees and statutes go back centuries. That's a twelfth-century edict I'm quoting there. Of course we have to respect confidences, but we have to get away from this culture of magic and make-believe if we are going to serve our people in the twentieth century and beyond.'

Marcel raised his eyebrows and looked at his bluntly-speaking colleague. 'You mean there are circumstances where you might have to betray a confidence then?'

'I'd hope not, but we have to be realistic.' He sat back and stared at the wine glass in his hand. 'I'm thinking of abuse cases—physical, sexual, or emotional—whether it's abuse of a minor or of anyone else. There was a time when the Seal of Confession was accepted by civil authorities as well as by the Church, and no one expected priests to report anything to the police. But times have changed. That's why I say we have to be realistic. No one is above the law in today's world. Teachers, doctors, nurses—they all have a legal obligation to report abuse when they become aware of it, so why should we be exempt from that same obligation?'

Gérard paused for a moment as he pondered his own words, then added, 'And another thing comes to mind too. As you know, we've had offenders within the ranks of the priesthood as well as in every other sector of society. Most priests prefer to confess to their bishop rather than to their colleagues, and it's obvious that many of these abusive priests of the past did exactly that—they confessed to their bishop.'

'That's understandable, I suppose.

'Yes, but the problem with that, of course, is that in the past it tied the bishop's hands. He couldn't reveal what had been confessed and he couldn't report the abuse to civil authorities unless there was hard evidence of abuse from other sources. All he could do really was to counsel the perpetrators, give them a year or two in a monastery, and then move them to new locations, giving them a chance to start over.'

Marcel nodded in agreement. 'And now it's coming back to haunt us.

'Exactly. Those same bishops are now accused of a systemic cover-up, all because of the Seal of Confession. So I'm not sure the Seal of Confession can work the way it used to.'

'It's hard to disagree.' Marcel placed his empty glass on the table and sat back in his chair. 'So what would you do, Gérard, if someone confessed to you that he'd committed a serious crime? I mean really serious.'

'It depends what kind of crime, I suppose. As I say, if it was a case of abusing a minor I'd definitely report it—I don't think I'd have a choice in the current environment. But I'd feel no obligation to report other crimes like theft or fraud. Even lawyers are exempt from giving evidence against their own clients. '

'What about murder?' Marcel bit his lip as if to hold back the words.

'Murder? I think I'd die of shock if that happened.' Gérard laughed out loud at the thought of it. 'Remember that old movie, I Confess? The murderer confesses to Montgomery Clift that he's just murdered someone in his church, and even though the priest himself is accused of the murder, he can't say a thing about it. It makes good movie material but it's bull shit. I'm sure I'd drag the guy down to the police station and make him confess to the police.

'Really? Are you serious about that?'

'I'm being a bit facetious, I know, but think about it. As an upright citizen, a leader in the community, you know that someone's a murderer. You can't just do nothing about it, can you? In today's society, there's no justification and no excuse in covering up a serious crime. Mind you, it would be a tough call, and I hope and pray it never happens to me, because if it came right down to it I'm not sure how I'd handle that.'

Marcel paused for a moment before responding, then looking his friend directly in the eye, he said, 'The fact is Gérard, it has happened to me. Someone has confessed a murder to me. I think I know who it is, and I'm very confused about what, if anything, I should do. I was hoping you could enlighten me on the moral and legal implications.'

It was more of a bombshell than Marcel had anticipated. Gérard was speechless at this revelation, and he stared wide-eyed at his junior colleague as if he'd just received news of his mother's death. 'You're kidding,' he said finally in a strange voice. 'You mean someone actually confessed to you that he'd committed murder—and he told you that face-to-face?'

'Not face-to-face, no. When I first arrived in Maplewood Creek I decided to continue Father Lemieux's tradition of waiting in the confessional box for penitents every Saturday afternoon. For the first three months no one ever actually came to confess and then one day, out of the blue, someone shuffled in, all emotional, and said he'd murdered his wife.'

Gérard looked puzzled. 'So you didn't actually see the person?'

'No, it was just a voice in the darkness.'

'What are you saying then? You recognized his voice?'

Marcel felt a bit embarrassed at his clumsy attempt to explain. 'Not really,' he said, resting his chin in his hand. 'In fact, I should say not at all. The person was obviously trying to disguise his voice—you know, speaking in a forced whisper, as if he were afraid of being recognized.'

'I don't get it.' Gérard shuffled in his chair as he tried to make sense of what he was being told. 'If you didn't see your penitent and you didn't recognize his voice, how can you know who the guy was?'

'Only from information I discovered later. It was the only confession I ever heard in that confessional box, and from the idle chatter of one of my parishioners, I figured out who had made that confession. I put two and two together, so to speak.'

'And has there been talk of a murder in the village?' Gérard was more perplexed than ever. 'I mean are the police looking for a suspect in a murder case? Does a dead body figure in this mystery?'

Marcel paused before answering. He knew he had to weigh his words carefully. 'I'm aware of two men in the village who have lost their wives recently,' he said slowly, 'supposedly in accidents. I don't really know any details about either of these deaths, except that one of the women drowned in the St. Croix river. Apparently, an inquest ruled it as accidental. But in any case, I feel that the circumstances about that particular death may have been explained satisfactorily. It's the other one that concerns me.'

'How so?'

'Because I'm ninety percent certain it was that woman's husband who confessed to murder in the confessional box.

'And the only way you know that is through information you received outside of the priest-penitent relationship?'

'That's right.'

Gérard leaned forward and looked at his friend. 'If you're going to talk to the bishop about this, Marcel, you might get different advice, but I'd say you have a civil duty to do something about it. I'd go further—I'd say you have a legal obligation to make it known to the police. No matter what you think about the Seal of Confession, if you have evidence of a murder, especially if it's evidence that comes from outside the confessional, the law requires you to make it known to the proper authorities. That's my opinion anyway.'

'I came to that conclusion myself..." Marcel began to explain, but he was interrupted by the sound of someone entering the front door. 'What's that?' he said, momentarily startled.

'Don't panic—it's Monique. I guess she's back.' Gérard rose quickly from his chair and slipped out into the hallway, leaving the lounge door slightly ajar. The hushed conversation that followed was barely audible and the words were not clear.

Marcel wondered whether he should close the door to avoid the temptation to listen in on matters that might not concern him, but before he had a chance to do so, his friend was back in the room and settling once more into his chair. 'It's fine,' he said. 'I meant to clear the dining table before she got back. But no matter—she's doing it now.'

The intense discussion seemed to have lost its momentum after the sudden interruption, but Marcel tried to pick up his train of thought. 'You were saying I have an obligation to do something about it,' he said. 'I came to that conclusion after a lot of soul searching, and I finally gave the person concerned a chance to talk about it in the open. The idea was to counsel him about his obligations and offer him some help in dealing with the matter in a responsible way. I would have helped him to find a suitable lawyer, for example, and I would have willingly accompanied him to give details at the main police station in Saint Stephen.'

Gérard seemed relieved to hear this. 'That's good then. It's what I would have advised. And how did that work out?'

'It was a complete disaster. The man was incensed at my questions and I've probably lost any good will that might have helped me work things out with him.'

'Oh, no. And I suppose he knows you're on to his case now?'

Marcel shook his head. 'Actually I don't think he does. That's one thing that puzzles me. He seemed to have no clue what I was getting at and I began to think I was barking up the wrong tree. But, strangely enough, he confirmed that his wife had died recently, and he implied that it was he who'd made the one and only confession I heard in that wretched confessional box.'

'Did he say how she died?'

'Well, he said it was in an accident, but he didn't volunteer any details.'

The discussion could have gone on endlessly. The two priests examined every angle, moral and legal, and while they agreed that the situation could not be left as it was, it was difficult to identify a clear course of action. Gérard claimed that he would have no hesitation in notifying the police of a possible crime, but Marcel was not so sure he'd be able to do that. In the end though, he knew that the weight of responsibility rested on his shoulders. He would have to decide whether to face his friend, Pierre Bouchard, again on the matter or whether to let sleeping dogs lie. In any case, it would be interesting to hear what Bishop Giguère had to say. No doubt Marcel's superior would feel committed to the party line about the Seal of Confession, but perhaps his expertise on moral theology would find a satisfactory way through. He could only hope so.

Marcel was suddenly aware of being exhausted after his long, event-filled day. It seemed an age away since his heated discussion with Dr. Bouchard in Maplewood Creek that very morning, and now after the tiring journey to Fredericton and the long discussion with Gérard, his weariness was all too evident. 'I've got to get some sleep,' he said stifling a yawn. 'I'll need a clear head tomorrow morning for my meeting with Giguère.'

Gérard checked his watch. 'I'm pretty beat myself,' he said, blinking his eyes. 'Go ahead, Marcel. Get to bed. You need some sleep. I'm going into the church for fifteen minutes to finish up my breviary.' He rose from his chair and made for the door. 'See you in the morning,' he mumbled over his shoulder; then he hurriedly left the room.

Marcel remained in his chair for a few moments before following his colleague out of the door. It took some effort to climb the stairs, but once in his room, he was able to unwind a little. He too had his breviary to finish, and he relaxed in the comfortable chair by his bed, dozing slightly as he read the familiar words of prayer.

Some time later, a creaking of stairs told him that Gérard was retiring to his room down the hall. Marcel prepared himself for bed, allowing his host ample time to finish his ablutions in the bathroom opposite his room before heading there himself. He didn't have to wait long. He opened his door and peered into the dimly-lit hallway. A gentle patter of slippered footsteps caught his attention, and Marcel watched as Monique, even more beautiful in her silk, pale blue negligee, slipped quietly into Gérard's room.

Fourteen

'The bishop will see you now, Father.' Monsignor Duval took his role as bishop's assistant very seriously, and he led Marcel to the door of the Episcopal office with a comportment of importance and formality. He knocked sharply, opened the door, and announced the visitor to his superior. 'Father Dion is here for his appointment, Bishop.' He stood back, allowing Marcel to enter, and then gracefully withdrew from the scene.

Bishop Giguère was a man of some stature and dignity, but he was far less formal and bureaucratic than his right-hand man. 'Marcel, come on in,' he said, smiling as he rose from the ornate chair behind his desk. 'So good to see you. How are things down in the village?'

He led his guest to more comfortable furniture in front of the French windows. 'Let's sit here for a while where we can relax and chat in peace,' he said. 'What can I get for you? Coffee, perhaps, or would you prefer something stronger?'

'Coffee is fine, thank you, Bishop.' Marcel appreciated the warm welcome. He felt at ease with his mentor and settled into one of the red, felt-covered chairs while the bishop ordered coffee through the intercom on his desk.

'Thank you for seeing me at such short notice, Bishop,' Marcel said. 'I know you must have a busy schedule.' He was aware that he'd been fast-tracked into this meeting and it had crossed his mind that there might be a reason for that. Appointments with the bishop usually required a few days notice, but if it was a question of special privilege, any mention of it was being studiously avoided.

'No problem at all.' Bishop Giguère joined his protégé and occupied the matching chair on the other side of the solid wooden coffee table. 'Always available when needed,' he laughed. 'But tell me, Marcel, how are you enjoying Maplewood Creek? My assignments as parish priest were always in busy towns and cities and I always thought it must be wonderful to be pastor in a small, tight-knit community.'

Marcel smiled. 'I have to say, I love the unique atmosphere of the village, Bishop, and my parishioners are wonderful, genuine people. It's been a great joy to serve them over the past six months.' He coughed as if to emphasize his point and added, 'I look forward to being there for some years to come.'

The small talk was easy and comfortable, and the two men chatted until the coffee was brought in on a small, silver serving trolley. The middle-aged maid arranged the cups and saucers, obviously self assured and comfortable in her job. 'Would you like me to pour it now, Bishop,' she asked, 'or should I just leave it with you?'

'It's fine, Antoinette. You can leave it with us. Thanks so much.'

The woman quietly left the room, leaving the two clerics to deal with the business at hand. Bishop Giguère poured out two cups of coffee, handing one to Marcel and lifting the other to his chest as he leaned back in his chair. 'You said you had some matters of importance to discuss with me,' he said. 'Is there anything bothering you, Marcel?'

This was the moment of truth. Marcel felt his heart jump a little as he realized there was no going back now. He knew in the end he would have to decide his own course of action, but he still hoped his superior would provide a loop hole—anything that would help him solve the nagging dilemma that seemed to preoccupy his thoughts so much. His voice sounded somewhat strained as he spoke. 'You could say that, Bishop,' he said, 'but I wanted to call on your expertise with moral theology and perhaps Canon Law in relation to a troubling experience I've had in my parish.'

'Oh dear! That does sound ominous.' The words were spoken light-heartedly and Bishop Giguère smiled broadly as he settled back to listen. 'We all have questions and concerns, Father, and it's quite right and proper to ask for advice. There's no shame in that. Tell me what's on your mind.'

Marcel wondered if things had suddenly become more formal. The bishop never called him Father except on official occasions; perhaps he was adopting a more sober approach now, sensing that he was about to be faced with a serious problem. 'It's to do with a confession, Bishop,' Marcel went on. 'A man has confessed to murder and I'm quite confused about what action I should take.'

If there was a stunned silence following that bold statement, it lasted for only a split second. Bishop Giguère was an astute administrator as well as an outstanding scholar, and he was not easily fazed. He looked Marcel in the eye. 'I'm not sure what you mean,' he said attentively. 'What exactly is the problem?'

'Well, I find myself on the horns of a difficult dilemma. On the one hand, I have a moral obligation to respect the confidence of the confessional, and on the other hand, I feel I have a civil obligation to inform the authorities of a murder that's been brought to my attention. Where does one draw the line?'

'Draw the line? Father Dion, there is no line. Your sacred duty as a priest is to guard confessional secrets with your life. You can never betray your penitent, no matter what he has confessed. This is one of the most important principles of pastoral care. Surely that must have been drilled into you during your seminary training program.'

Deep down, Marcel had expected the bishop to take a hard line, but he hoped there might be room for a special case. 'Well, yes, of course, Bishop,' he replied, 'but this confession has caused me great distress, and I feel there are some unusual circumstances that might call for a different course of action.'

Bishop Giguère carefully placed his coffee cup on the table and sat back with his fingers interlocked on his chest. 'I can understand your distress, Marcel,' he said, 'but that's the nature of the priesthood. We've all had to deal with these difficult circumstances. I've had murderers confess to me, and I know that chill to the heart, that shiver down the spine as the penitent speaks his confession. But as priests, we can never allow ourselves to be the judge. We absolve the sinner and leave the judgement to God—and then put it out of our minds.'

There was empathy in the bishop's words, and for the first time, Marcel felt he was no longer alone. 'This has happened to you then, Bishop?' he whispered, somewhat taken aback. 'You've heard confessions to murder?'

'It was a long time ago. When I was a young priest I was assigned to the prison ministry at the penitentiary in Moncton for about eighteen months, and I worked with some hardened criminals there. Through care and counselling, I helped some of them to face up to the harm they had done and to accept responsibility for their crimes. Two inmates eventually repented and confessed to murder. It was a great joy for me to give them absolution. Both eventually died in prison but it was a comfort to know that they had made peace with their Creator.'

Marcel felt his heart sink as he detected the fundamental difference between the two cases. 'With respect, Bishop,' he said with some disappointment, 'that hardly compares to my predicament. Your penitents had been tried and convicted, and you had no duty or obligation to report anything. My penitent is a murderer on the loose, and by not reporting him I could be compromising the safety or even the lives of others.'

The bishop hesitated a moment, gently biting his lower lip. 'You say there are special circumstances. What do you mean by that?'

'Well, I was given information about this man, my penitent, that links him with a suspicious death—information obtained outside of the priest-penitent relationship I mean. Evidence that makes him a clear suspect.'

'You know the identity of your penitent then?'

'Yes, I'm afraid I do—and that's the problem.'

Bishop Giguère sighed and raised his eyes to the ceiling. 'That's why I'm an advocate of the private confessional box, Marcel. These face-to-face confessions are all well and good, but when a serious crime is involved it puts a priest in a very difficult position.'

'As a matter of fact, Bishop, the confession was made privately in the secrecy of the confessional box.' Marcel noted the raised eyebrows and felt the same air of confusion that surrounded his discussion with Gérard Rousseau on the previous evening. He thought it might be expedient to offer an explanation before the bishop had a chance to ask for one. 'As I have said, it was information given to me outside of the priest-penitent relationship that convinced me of the penitent's identity,' he explained. 'It was only then that I felt any civil duty to report a crime.'

The bishop looked dubious and folded his arms as if to take a strong position on one side of the argument. 'Don't you see a certain lack of logic in your position, Marcel? Let me put it this way. Without the confession, would you have any real evidence that a crime has been committed?'

'Well, no. I don't suppose I would. I'd be aware of a death—two in fact that seem to be related—but apparently both were ruled accidental.'

'And let me ask you this. Are you a hundred percent sure of your penitent's identity? Can you swear to it?'

'I'm almost certain—in fact, I'm tempted to say I'm certain. I know who this man is from what he told me outside of the confessional.

'But how do you know that the man you spoke to outside of the confessional is the same man who confessed to you in the confessional?' Bishop Giguère removed the pectoral cross from his chest and placed it firmly on the table. 'Put your hand on this cross, Marcel, and swear that you know the identity of your penitent with one hundred percent certainty.'

Marcel swallowed hard. 'I don't think I could do that, Bishop. I must admit there is some doubt, however small it may be.'

'And that's my point. I'm relieved to hear you say that, Marcel, because if you had no doubt at all about this man's identity you would be tempted to report him to the civil authorities. Yet the seal of confession obligates you to silence. All a priest can do in a situation like this is to counsel the penitent to give himself up to the police at the time of the confession. You could even make that a condition of absolution. If you did that, you have fulfilled your moral obligation.'

Marcel felt somewhat relieved to hear his superior's words as they seemed to indicate a clear course of action, yet nagging questions persisted. 'But isn't there a legal obligation as well?' he asked with some frustration in his voice. 'The Church has faced many charges of systemic cover-up in recent years regarding serious crimes, and I fear that civil authorities no longer respect our claim to immunity on religious grounds. If we have information, however obtained, don't they expect us to report it?'

The bishop was unyielding. 'Father Dion,' he said with some authority, 'many professionals claim exemption from the normal legal requirement to report crimes when their information was obtained under client confidentiality. Lawyers, doctors, newspaper reporters even, cannot be forced to break confidences, and when it comes to secrets of the confessional, everyone recognizes the priest-penitent relationship as a particularly strong, unwavering bond of confidential interaction.' He leaned forward, raising an episcopal finger to emphasize his point. 'You know, Father, throughout the history of the Church we have had good priests, bad priests, and lots of mediocre ones, but rarely have we had priests who broke the seal of the confessional. Don't ever think it can be done. Apart from any serious moral questions, the penalties under Canon Law are very severe for a priest who violates the seal. Such a miscreant priest incurs an automatic excommunication, and he would never again be allowed to practice his priesthood.'

The words were strong and instructive and Marcel shuddered a little at the deep implications for any decision he might make. He remained silent for a moment as he pondered the bishop's words. Maybe there was no murder after all, he thought. Perhaps he could simply forget the whole thing and get on with his life in the village, doing the work he loved with the generous and simple folk of Maplewood Creek. But that was wishful thinking, he told himself. He knew what he knew and his deep sense of duty would not let him forget it. Guy LaPlante's wife was dead and so was Pierre Bouchard's. There was some strange connection between those two deaths; he was convinced of that. And at least one of those women, perhaps both, had been murdered; he was convinced of that too. How could he not pursue this bedevilling mystery? How could he not do everything possible to make sure justice was done?

'What are you thinking, Marcel? Have I answered your concerns?' Bishop Giguère's tone was gentler now. He had made his case and he had every confidence that the inexperienced priest before him would faithfully follow his direction.

'Tell me, Bishop. What should I do?'

'I can only repeat what I've already said. If you have evidence of a crime, based on information you have obtained outside of the confessional, you have a moral and legal duty to report it to civil authorities. But any knowledge gained through confessional secrets must remain with you alone forever. You must examine carefully what you know and how you know it and make your decisions accordingly.'

Marcel nodded slowly, though he was not quite convinced. 'Well thank you, Bishop. I do appreciate your insight into this problem. As you say, I must consider my position carefully and do what is right and just. I do take my responsibility seriously, especially in terms of confidentiality. I'll pray over it and I'll make the right decisions.'

'I'm sure you will, Marcel. I have every confidence in you.'

The two men rose from their chairs and Marcel prepared to leave. As they moved towards the door Bishop Giguère continued the small talk they had begun earlier. 'I meant to ask you, Marcel,' he said quite casually, 'do you know Pierre Bouchard? I understand he took over a medical practice in Maplewood Creek about the same time you moved down there.'

The question was like a shot to the heart, and Marcel felt the blood drain from his face as he turned to face his superior. 'Pierre Bouchard?' he stammered. 'You mean Dr. Bouchard? I didn't realize you knew him.'

'I can't say I knew him well.' Bishop Giguère seemed oblivious to the priest's nervous reaction to his question. 'No, it's just that he and his wife used to run the psychiatric unit at the Research Hospital here in

Fredericton. He was the resident consultant for the diocese for a few years, and I had occasion to refer two or three priests to him—for depression and such like. He seemed to be a man of integrity and I respected his judgment. I just wondered if you'd met him down there.'

'I have met him, actually. In fact I know him quite well.'

'You do? Then please give him my regards. I was so sorry to hear about his wife's tragic accident last year. I believe she was highly regarded at the hospital.'

Marcel felt his heart pounding as they discussed his prime murder suspect but, anxious to find new information, he forced himself to remain calm and controlled. 'He's told me about his wife's death, Bishop, but he's never discussed any details with me. I presume the accident took place here. Was it something that happened in relation to her work at the hospital?'

'I really don't know where it was or what actually happened. I was at a convention in Vancouver at the time, but I do know the funeral was conducted by Monsignor Duval at the cathedral here in Fredericton. He tells me the place was packed.

'And I suppose Dr. Bouchard gave up his position at the hospital after her death?'

Bishop Giguère shrugged his shoulders. 'Apparently so. It's hard to understand why a high-profile psychiatrist like Dr. Bouchard would up sticks and move to a small country village like Maplewood Creek. But as you know only too well, Marcel, the death of a spouse can be traumatic, and it often leads the survivor to seek a completely new way of life.'

Marcel nodded in agreement. 'That is so true, Bishop. So true.'

Fifteen

Marcel left the bishop's residence in a bit of a daze. He knew Pierre Bouchard had done some research at the Fredericton Research Hospital but it was news indeed that he and his wife had worked together as psychiatrists. That had never been mentioned during the weekly golf games over the spring and summer, and he wondered about the implications of this new information.

The confused priest checked his watch pensively as he walked out onto the street. It was twelve noon. The train to Saint Stephen was scheduled to leave at 2:30 so he had plenty of time to have lunch, and then get on his way. He had planned to have lunch with Gérard in town before heading for the station, but now he wondered if he should cancel that comforting finale to his trip in order to pursue a more audacious plan. A visit to the hospital might contribute a vital piece to this perplexing puzzle, and if it did, perhaps a clear course of action might yet be revealed.

Marcel recalled Bishop Giguère's last piece of advice. Consider what you know and how you know it, he'd said. That was the key. There would be no question of breaking confessional secrets if all the information came from outside sources, and the more information he could get the better he'd understand what was going on.

The sight of a public telephone on the corner of Regent Street and Brunswick provided an irresistible opportunity to implement this new plan, and Marcel eagerly entered the box, fumbling with his change and mentally recalling the numbers needed to make his call. As luck would have it, Gérard was out but Monique listened to the breathless message and promised to pass on the crucial information. Marcel wouldn't be able to make it for lunch after all, and as he'd already picked up his travel bag before leaving, he wouldn't be returning to the St. Francis residence either, but he'd be in touch later.

The Research Hospital was only two or three blocks away and as there was no taxi in sight, Marcel headed out on foot. He maintained a brisk pace, churning an avalanche of questions over in his mind. Who should he speak to? What exactly did he need to ask? Would anyone really be willing to give him information?

Marcel knew that confidential information would never be passed on to a casual visitor, but he hoped at least to find out what happened to Pierre's wife. Something told him that if he could only find out how and where she died a big part of this mystery might be solved and he'd be able to eliminate his friend as a murder suspect once and for all. If someone at the hospital could only tell him that Mme Bouchard had fallen down the stairs, or had been electrocuted, or had been killed by some other explainable accident, Pierre would be off the hook. That would be so liberating, Marcel thought. If that turned out to be the case, then he and Pierre could perhaps work together to help that tormented soul, Guy LaPlante, to get his life into some kind of order. The death of Guy's wife, or partner if that is what she turned out to be, was obviously central to the young man's troubles, but with a skilled doctor and a dedicated pastor at his service, surely some satisfactory solutions could be found.

The priest realized he was out of breath now. He slowed his pace a little, but suddenly the grand entrance to the hospital was before him. He felt a little nervous as climbed the handful of marble steps to the main doors, anticipating an awkward introduction to complete strangers. He opened his coat a little and adjusted his scarf to expose the clerical collar. The priestly attire could be very useful on occasions like this, he thought. Hospitals might be cool to some visitors but the arrival of a priest or minister is seen as a regular occurrence in the day-to-day life of a busy hospital. His appearance at the main desk would be no surprise.

The reception area was large and impressive, and as Marcel approached the desk he was greeted with a welcoming smile from the young woman who sat behind it. She wore a large name tag on her lapel indicating that her name was Marie-Claire. 'Good afternoon, Father,' she said cheerfully. 'Who are you here to see today?'

This was an encouraging start and, Marcel heard himself reply with no hesitation. 'Hello. I'm Father Marcel Dion. I'm here to see the head of the psychiatric unit. Is he available?'

Marie-Claire ran her finger down the list on a paper before her. 'What time was your appointment, Father. I don't see your name here. Is Dr. LaFontaine expecting you?'

This was a bonus. Already he had a name to work with. 'Not as such. I'm a friend of Dr. Bouchard and I was hoping to have a quick word with Dr. LaFontaine if he's free. It's a matter of mutual interest.'

The mention of Dr. Bouchard's name obviously rang a bell with the young woman and she reacted immediately. 'Dr. Bouchard?' she asked raising her eyebrows in surprise. 'Of course—we have great memories of her. She is still very much missed around here. I'm sure Dr. LaFontaine will want to see you.'

This response caught Marcel by surprise. 'Actually,' he said sheepishly, 'It's Pierre Bouchard who I know. I didn't know his wife at all.'

'Oh, I'm so sorry—I just assumed…' Marie-Claire rose from her desk and peered over her glasses at the large double doors beyond the reception area. 'As a matter of fact,' she said, 'Dr. LaFontaine just entered the cafeteria about five minutes ago. If he's alone he might welcome a quick word. He replaced Dr. Bouchard as head of the psychiatric department, as I'm sure you know, and I think he'll be anxious to hear any news.' She led her visitor across the hallway and pointed to a distinguished-looking character in his late fifties, sitting alone at a table on the far side of the cafeteria. 'There,' she said, 'the man with the white fluffy beard all alone with his paper. That's him.'

Marcel felt his heart-rate increase somewhat as he crossed the room. Perhaps the pleasant young receptionist had been a little too accommodating and maybe the doctor would not appreciate the intrusion during his lunch break. But there was no turning back now. The unwavering priest helped himself to a ready-poured cup of coffee from the end of the counter, and then with a forced air of self confidence he resolutely approached the unsuspecting psychiatrist. 'Dr. LaFontaine,' he said with a smile. 'My name is Father Marcel Dion. I don't think we've met but I'm a friend of Pierre Bouchard. May I join you for a minute?'

The doctor looked up from his paper in surprise. 'Oh,' he said, taken aback at the sudden interruption, 'yes, by all means. A friend of Pierre you say?'

Marcel laughed, trying to break the ice. 'Pierre and I work in Maplewood Creek in related fields, you might say. I'm the village pastor and he's the village doctor. We also play golf together on a fairly regular basis.'

It was apparently the right thing to say. 'Oh well, if you're brave enough to play golf with that fellow, you certainly have my sympathies.' He stretched out a friendly hand. 'René LaFontaine—pleased to meet you, Father.'

Marcel sat down and tried to appear casual. 'I don't want to take up your lunch break, René,' he said, sipping on his coffee, 'but I thought as long as I'm here in Fredericton, I should touch base with you. Pierre would never forgive me if I didn't. I believe he's quite proud of the work he did here.'

'Is that what he told you? The scoundrel—it was his wife who did all the work around here. Pierre was always off on some project or other but it was Frances who got involved in the nitty-gritty of the day-to-day grind. She was totally dedicated to her work here.'

'Pierre never talks much about his late wife, but I understand she more or less ran things in the psychiatric unit.'

'That's right. She was very intense, you know. Once she got her hands on a particular case she couldn't put it down, especially if it was something related to her field of research.'

'Was she dealing with individual patients then? I mean, did her research involve specific cases here at the hospital?'

'Oh, yes of course. We generally referred unusual cases to her. She was very much into illusionary syndromes—guilt, fantasy beliefs and that kind of thing. She's written extensively on those kinds of problems and we recognized her as a bit of an expert.' René looked at the inquisitive priest, his brow wrinkled with uneasiness. 'I suppose you must have heard all about it?'

'Some of it, certainly. But I understood Pierre was involved in some of those cases as well.'

'Not really. At least not very often. In fact it was one of those extreme cases that led to all the trouble between Pierre and Frances. Their disagreements got to be a bit public around here—quite embarrassing really. And then we got that awful news about the accident. It was a bad time for the department and as with so many cases like that, it was our patients who ultimately suffered for it.'

Marcel needed information but didn't want to appear too nosey. He sipped again on his coffee and tried to give the impression of being quite familiar with all the particulars. 'Yes,' he said with an air of compassion, 'it was very sad. Did you ever hear any details about the accident?'

'Just the bare facts really. Pierre was devastated of course, and he said very little about it. It took him several weeks to wind up his affairs in the department here and he was clearly suffering from his loss during that time. I think he was more than ready to leave when the time came.' René paused reflectively for a moment and then added pointedly, 'One thing has always puzzled me though. I could never understand why he wanted to move to the exact place where she drowned.'

'She drowned?'

The sharp note of surprise in Marcel's voice caught his companion's attention. 'Yes, didn't you know that?'

'Well, no. Pierre never talked about it, and I've always hesitated to bring the topic up. I'm his pastor as well as his friend, you know, and I just assumed he'd talk about the accident if he wanted to.'

'Of course—I understand. But yes, apparently she drowned in a river down there while they were working on a case that Frances was involved with.' The doctor shook his head sadly. 'Poor Pierre. It must have been a terrible experience for him, and then he had to go through the trauma of transporting the body back to Fredericton for the funeral. It was a sad time.'

These revelations were disturbing and rather unexpected, but still more information was needed and Marcel wondered how much more the doctor was willing to say. As long as this compliant psychiatrist was willing to talk there would be no shortage of questions. 'You know,' the priest said, trying to sound casual, 'Pierre told me that his wife had left him for another man. He was a bit vague about it and I got the feeling that he wasn't quite telling the truth. Do you know—did she actually leave him or was that a bit of an exaggeration?'

René laughed and shook his head at this. 'That's Pierre dramatizing,' he said mockingly. 'I've heard him talk like that when Frances got too absorbed in a case and she'd spend days at a time with patients and their families. She's left me for another man again, he'd say sarcastically. Mind you, the time she put into her work was a bit ridiculous sometimes, I must admit, and this final case was definitely over the top. She would never have left Pierre though. She had a great admiration for him personally and for his knowledge and skills.'

'What was it then that Pierre was so annoyed about?'

'Annoyed? That doesn't begin to describe it. He was absolutely furious.' René smiled as he recalled the details. 'Frances had been working with a very disturbed young man who apparently revealed something to her that she thought would require police intervention. She wouldn't betray patient confidentiality of course, even to Pierre, but when this man wanted to return to his home village she decided to go with him to get to the bottom of the problem. She was afraid that his illusions would get him into trouble with the law, you see.'

'And his home village was Maplewood Creek?'

'That's right. Pierre was dead set against it though and he expressed his feelings very loud and clear. He thought that was way beyond the call of duty and he did everything he could to persuade Francis to change her mind but it was no use. She'd made up her mind and she accompanied the young fellow back to Maplewood Creek with the intention of talking to his family doctor. I don't know what happened. Pierre was livid about it and he followed her down to the village the next day— to bring her back, he said. The next thing we heard, Frances was dead and a big funeral was being planned for her here in Fredericton.'

Marcel coughed nervously, unsure of how far this discussion could go. 'I know you can't reveal names, doctor, but I think I know who this young man is. I believe he is one of my parishioners and I've been working with him on some very difficult personal issues over the past few months.' He put down his empty coffee cup and looked at René pleadingly. 'Do you mind if I ask you one more thing?'

The question seemed to shake the loquacious doctor into a more professional frame of mind. 'I think maybe I've said too much already, Father,' he said with a guilty look on his face. 'Are you sure this was just a casual visit, or are you here to extract confidential information from me?'

'I'm sorry, René. I don't want to put you in a compromising position. We all have patient or client confidences to keep, but I am genuinely concerned about this troubled young parishioner of mine. I'm afraid he may be blamed for something he hasn't done.'

'What was it you wanted to ask?'

'You mentioned his family. Did he have any family here in Fredericton?'

Dr. LaFontaine raised his eyebrows and sighed deeply. 'You do know then? We seem to be talking about the same young man, don't we? Yes, from what Frances told me, this patient's father was a big part of the problem. He strongly objected to the counselling and treatment that his son was receiving here and he instigated one or two loud, violent exchanges in Frances's office. He was quite unreasonable. Frances was always very professional, but this man persistently accused her of developing an unhealthy relationship with his son. Totally unfounded and ridiculous of course, but in the end it was that accusation that got Pierre so involved. He banned the obnoxious fellow from visiting the hospital and told him to stay out of his wife's way.'

Marcel pondered this for a moment. 'It does seem a bit over the top, doesn't it? But the young man, whose name we can't mention, had a very poor grasp of reality, didn't he? Perhaps he told his father things that weren't true—things that were just figments of his imagination, and maybe the father took them too seriously.'

'It's possible, of course. Frances was becoming a bit concerned because the young guy did seem to be developing a romantic crush on her. In fact, it got beyond that; she told me ...' René suddenly stopped dead in his tracks as if he realized he was out of line. 'You know, Father, I'd better stop right there,' he said, shaking his head. 'I've said far too much about this case. I think you'll have to talk to Pierre if you need any more information. After all, he's right there in the village, and if this patient is still as needy as you say, Pierre will know what to do.' He held out a hand with the clear message that it was time to go. 'Goodbye, Father. Thanks for dropping by.'

This short meeting had produced information far beyond Marcel's wildest expectations and his head was reeling from the profound implications of all that René LaFontaine had just told him. The puzzle was becoming ever more complicated. He boarded a waiting taxi outside the main entrance to the hospital and absent-mindedly gave his directions to the driver. Sitting deep into the comfortable soft leather of the back seat he pondered the flood of new information that had bombarded his mind over the past twenty-four hours. There seemed to be far more questions than answers now. What had really happened to Pierre Bouchard's wife? Why was she so obsessed with Guy LaPlante and his problems? And what about this woman, Fran, whom Guy claimed was his wife?

By the time Marcel reached the station, one thing seemed to be perfectly clear—Pierre's wife and Guy's wife were one and the same person.

Sixteen

Everything had changed now. Marcel settled into the corner of a quiet railway compartment for his trip home, and as the train moved slowly forward he tried to put things into proper perspective. He needed to clarify things in his mind and he needed to know exactly what he was trying to achieve, given that things were now not quite as they had originally appeared. The perplexed priest was determined to live up to his legal and moral obligations; he wanted to do the right thing but after his meeting with Dr. LaFontaine he had the distinct feeling that he'd been holding the wrong end of the stick.

The train fell into a gentle, soothing sway as it picked up speed and Marcel closed his eyes and sighed heavily. If only Clara were here with me now, he thought, she'd surely have some words of wisdom that would put me on the right track. He smiled as he remembered how she always clung so stubbornly to her decisions once she'd made up her mind. Clara was a firm pragmatist and she would have had no time for this useless vacillation—this back-and-forth nonsense that can be so disruptive and unsettling for one's life.

It would take a good two hours to reach Saint Stephen and Marcel was determined to have some kind of viable plan in place before he reached his destination. He mentally reviewed the events that had initiated this strange state of affairs. Where was it all leading, he wondered, and how had he got himself into such an exasperating position?

It was the confession of course that had started the unwanted ball rolling; without the confession there would be no case at all. To be sure, some unpleasant things had happened but why had they taken on such sinister implications? Pierre Bouchard's wife, who happened to be a prominent psychiatrist, had drowned in a terrible accident in the course of her work with a mentally ill patient. That's a tragic event, certainly, but why must it be viewed as a suspicious death? Only because a disembodied voice in the darkness of an old-fashioned confessional box had confessed to murder. But is that really relevant? For one thing, there was no way of knowing that the penitent who confessed that day was confessing to the murder of Fran Bouchard. Perhaps he was confessing to a crime that was totally unrelated to the events in Maplewood Creek. But that seemed very unlikely. The small, tight-knit community was very self contained and Marcel felt quite sure there was a definite connection between Fran's drowning and the confession to murder. He was even more convinced of this now after meeting with Dr. LaFontaine. The strange behaviour of Guy LaPlante and his troublesome father, the surreptitious activities of Pierre Bouchard, and the secrets that Fran Bouchard had apparently taken to her grave were all part of a mystery that needed to be solved.

In light of the new information, it seemed now that the identity of the penitent himself was still far from clear. Pierre Bouchard had admitted to being in the confessional box that Saturday afternoon and that was difficult to explain, but it seemed very unlikely that he was the mysterious penitent that day. He simply wasn't the type. Although he showed up for Mass once in a while, Pierre was not a devout member of the parish and it was hard to imagine him as an emotional, guilt-ridden penitent confessing to murder. Besides, Marcel told himself reassuringly, it was Guy LaPlante who was at the scene of Fran's death—not Pierre Bouchard. Guy had made that perfectly clear when he showed up at the rectory and described the events leading to Fran's death.

The details about the drowning of course were still a bit muddled. There was only Guy's word for what happened down at the river that day and with his history of mental illness there was every reason to wonder about the accuracy of his account. He was known to have difficulty distinguishing between reality and make-believe. According to Dr. LaFontaine, he was being treated for that very problem by Fran Bouchard, and the fact that she was willing to accompany her patient back to his home village a hundred miles away seemed to suggest that there were some very serious implications surrounding his case. René LaFontaine had also mentioned that police involvement was being considered. Fran had apparently discovered something about Guy that needed to be reported and if that was so, how would her troubled patient have reacted to that news? Given the romantic fascination he seemed to have towards his psychiatrist, the reaction might well have been one of rage and anger—and perhaps violence.

Marcel found himself leaning towards his original belief that the penitent in the confessional box that fateful day was Guy LaPlante. He recalled how the voice had been deliberately changed into a hoarse whisper in an apparent attempt to avoid recognition. Guy had been working around the church on a regular basis and he was becoming quite well known to his new pastor, so it would make sense for him to try to disguise his voice while making such a shocking confession.

But more to the point, this troubled man was emotionally unstable and, unlike Dr. Bouchard, he would be quite capable of issuing that gut-wrenching outburst in the confessional box. It was entirely possible that in his disturbed mind he'd felt betrayed by the woman he was so attached to, and in a fit of rage he'd pushed her to her death in the swirling waters of the St. Croix river. If that was the case, Guy would have been filled with remorse and that could easily have led him to make the emotional confession of guilt. Not only that, but Denis LaPlante might well be aware of his son's actions as well and that would account for his inexorable browbeating of his son at every possible opportunity. Was Denis pressing his son to give himself up? Father Lemieux had clearly resented the constant harrying and he'd made his feeling known to Denis in no uncertain terms. Given the edgy relationship between Denis and Father Lemieux, there was every reason to believe that the elderly priest knew all about Guy LaPlante's activities too.

Marcel opened his eyes and looked out at the peaceful fall scenery around him as the train made its way south. The leaves had turned now and the brilliant colours of autumn cast a radiant glow on the surrounding countryside, creating a beautiful world of cool tranquility. It was the time of year when feelings of serenity and wellbeing should be most prevalent and the perturbed priest resented the intrusion of this troublesome mystery that so occupied his thoughts. But he knew there could be no peace until the mystery reached a satisfactory conclusion, and so far that conclusion was being tiresomely elusive. Marcel shuffled into a more comfortable position and continued his thoughtful analysis as the train journeyed on.

It would have been easy to rest with the theory that Guy LaPlante was somehow responsible for Fran's death and leave it at that. After all, the unfortunate young man was suffering from a serious mental illness through no fault of his own, and Pierre Bouchard seemed to be dealing with that in a manner best known to him. He was a skilled and experienced psychiatrist. He'd know what to do and when all the facts were known no doubt he'd be in touch with the appropriate authorities and the whole matter would be properly resolved. Marcel liked that scenario. It relieved him of any responsibility to carry things further and it would allow him to resume his peaceful life as pastor of St. Jude's. But things were not so simple. Another more troubling scenario was distinctly possible too, and much as Marcel wanted to avoid it he knew he was compelled to face it head on.

Dr. LaFontaine had brought attention to a developing conflict between Pierre and Fran Bouchard and he had shown some concern about the noisy differences of opinion that were being expressed in their respective department offices. Pierre obviously resented his wife's intensive involvement with Guy LaPlante and his problems, and he must have been incensed at having to continually shield her from Denis LaPlante's abusive outbursts. No doubt he would have been more than happy to give the LaPlantes their marching orders and get them off their list of patients. But it seems Fran would have none of it. It was an exciting case in her field of research and she was determined to follow it through to the bitter end whether her husband liked it or not.

Marcel could only imagine Pierre's anger and frustration when his wife announced that she would be taking her patient back to Maplewood Creek. She must have had serious reasons for such unusual and drastic action but patient confidentiality would have prevented her from fully explaining them to her husband. According to René LaFontaine, Pierre was absolutely furious, but even this depiction must have been quite an understatement given that the mentally disturbed young man was introducing Fran as his own wife to all and sundry. That would be enough to push any reasonable man beyond his normal limits, and in such a state of anger and resentment anything would be possible.

Suppose Pierre, in a fit of uncharacteristic rage, had pushed Fran into the river. No doubt it would have instantly shocked him into reality and he would have tried to save her once he realized what he had done. But suppose he couldn't save her—suppose she drowned before he was able pull her out? He would have panicked and he'd probably have tried to convince himself that it was just a terrible accident. More importantly, he would have tried to convince everyone else it was an accident too, but it would be difficult to explain and the doctor's reputation and livelihood would be on the line. Better to blame it on Guy

LaPlante who might never be convicted of any crime because of his mental illness.

Guy was already suffering from delusions and it would be easy for someone with Pierre's knowledge and skill to convince him that Fran's death was all his fault. Pierre probably felt there was some truth to that anyway. He was already angry with his wife's troubled patient because of the turmoil and disruption he had caused. Perhaps he felt it was only right and just that responsibility for Fran's death should rest squarely on Guy LaPlante's shoulders.

This theory still left one nagging question unanswered of course. Guy had fully explained the circumstances of Fran's drowning and he had made no mention of Pierre being present when the accident occurred. His account gave the impression that Guy and Fran were alone when they went down to the river that afternoon. If Pierre Bouchard was with them, why wouldn't Guy have mentioned it?

There was another thing too. If the doctor was responsible for his wife's death that day, why would he move to Maplewood Creek permanently? He was adamantly averse to going there in the first place. Surely, after taking his wife's body back to Fredericton and dealing with the trauma of a rather public funeral, it would have made more sense for him to try and pick up the pieces and get on with his life in a familiar environment. But he didn't do that. He quit his lucrative psychiatric post at the hospital and moved lock, stock and barrel to Maplewood Creek. He obviously had some compelling reason to return to the village. Was it to find peace and tranquility after the traumatic death of his wife? Or was it to deal with some unfinished business?

Dr. LaFontaine seemed to say that Pierre was depressed and preoccupied with Fran's death as he wound up his affairs at the research hospital, and when the time came he was anxious to be on his way. But he had obviously worked out an appropriate time schedule for the take over with Dr. Martin in the days following the accident. He must have made his decision to move into the village at the time of Fran's death. But why would he have done that? Had Fran confided some new, dramatic information about her real reasons for bringing her vulnerable patient home? If that was the case, perhaps Pierre had decided to take over the work where she left off. That's one possibility but, on the other hand, perhaps he just wanted to be in a position where he could manipulate Guy LaPlante and make sure responsibility for his wife's death rested firmly on that young man's shoulders.

It was interesting, Marcel thought, that the confession to murder came so soon after Pierre Bouchard's return to Maplewood Creek. The doctor had been reluctant to admit that Guy was his regular patient but it was clear some ongoing treatment was underway, and it was quite possible that this treatment was in reality a sort of hypnosis designed to reinforce the young man's guilt complex. This would account for the heart-rending confession to murder that day, assuming that the beleaguered penitent was indeed Guy LaPlante, and it would also explain the young man's troubled state of mind when he met with his pastor that first time. Guy had described the details of the tragedy and how he felt so responsible for Fran's death, even though it was several months after the event. Something had obviously stirred things up in the young man's mind and it seemed reasonable to suspect that Dr. Bouchard's counselling sessions had something to do with it.

Marcel reluctantly had to admit that this scenario was a distinct possibility and indeed it seemed to provide answers to some very troubling questions.

An ear-piercing screech of brakes roused the priest from his reflective reverie as the train gradually slowed down for a brief stop at Maxwell Crossing, a tiny settlement several miles north of Saint Stephen. Not far to go now, the priest thought, shuffling again to find a more comfortable position on the hard seat, but still no clear solution to this maddening puzzle. No definite answers and no obvious course of action—yet one thing was emerging from these jumbled thoughts. It seemed now that the emphasis should be one of compassion and concern for a distressed and tormented young man who was obviously in urgent need of protection.

Guy LaPlante was struggling with an inner turmoil so severe that reality and fiction were frequently indistinguishable to him. No matter what he'd done he should not be held fully responsible. He was being treated for a serious mental illness and if he had somehow caused the death of his dedicated benefactor, the blame was not entirely his.

But Marcel was afraid that the situation could be much worse than that. If Guy had committed no crime at all and he was simply being used as a scapegoat for someone else's wrongdoing then something had to be done, and the beleaguered priest knew that his course of action was clear. He would have to use every means possible to make sure that justice prevailed. Protecting the innocent was surely one of the most fundamental obligations of his priesthood.

As the train moved forward to complete the last leg of its journey Marcel recalled what Dr. LaFontaine had told him about Fran Bouchard's reasons for undertaking the long journey to Maplewood Creek. She felt she had to accompany Guy to his home village, he explained, because she was afraid that her patient was in some kind of danger. She thought he might be victimized in some way or blamed for something he hadn't done. But what could that be and who was the perpetrator of these false allegations? It could hardly be Pierre Bouchard who hadn't really been involved with his wife's patient, but what about Guy's obstreperous father, Denis LaPlante? Denis was angry about the whole idea of his son's psychiatric treatment at the research hospital and according to René LaFontaine he had been belligerent and abusive on more than one occasion. Could it be that he was responsible for Fran's death? He certainly had a motive and, come to think about it, he had followed the pair back to the village and quite likely had ample opportunity to push the poor woman into the St. Croix river while he was there. Perhaps Fran died because she knew too much.

Yes, Marcel told himself emphatically, Denis LaPlante's involvement was something to consider. He was not a nice person and Guy's aunt, Marianne Boudreau, had described him as a bully, a loud, belligerent man who had made a habit of intimidating his family. Gaston had reinforced that image too and even Father Lemieux had expressed his concerns and disapproval of the man's boorish behaviour.

According to Gaston, Denis LaPlante was obsessed with obtaining ownership of his late wife's house and there seemed to be no limits to what he might do to achieve it. Perhaps he had resorted to some underhand dealings in an attempt to defraud his son of his rightful inheritance, some kind of threat perhaps, or an ongoing pattern of intimidation that had pushed Guy over the edge. If that was the case, no wonder he didn't want a professional psychiatrist like Fran Bouchard probing and questioning. Guy would soon break down under professional psychiatric care and it wouldn't be long before he'd be revealing details of his father's criminal behaviour. Denis would do almost anything to prevent that from happening—but would he go as far as murder?

If Fran had obtained incriminating information from her troubled patient, could Denis LaPlante have caused her death to prevent her from revealing it? Marcel wanted to believe he could. Denis would make a far better murderer than Pierre Bouchard, he thought, and it would seem so fitting for such an obnoxious individual to receive his just desserts. But Marcel had to keep his thoughts in check—wishful thinking was not very productive and there was no justification for rash judgement. It was essential to stick with the known facts.

Denis was a difficult man, that was certainly true, but there were plenty of reasons for thinking that the murderer could not be him. For one thing, confession was definitely not his style. The man had no time for religion and the parish community and it would be a gigantic stretch of the imagination to believe that he deliberately drowned a woman and then went hurrying off to confess his guilt to the new priest. That emotional, guilt-ridden outburst in the confessional box was definitely not something that could be pinned on to Denis LaPlante.

Another thing too—if Denis was responsible for Fran's death he would have scurried off into hiding somewhere but apparently that didn't happen. In fact it was just the opposite. According to Father Lemieux, Denis kept coming back to the village to give his son a hard time and although he still seemed to visit Fredericton on occasion, he'd moved down to Saint

Stephen permanently to be nearer to the village. That's hardly the approach that would be taken by a man trying to hide a serious crime.

In the end of course, the fact still remained that Guy had given a perfectly believable description of the way Fran Bouchard died. Marcel recalled that the troubled young man had appeared quite reasonable that day and although he was overcome with feelings of guilt, Guy himself clearly believed her drowning was an accident. He'd made no mention of his father being on the scene so there was no obvious way of tying Denis LaPlante to Fran's death. It was difficult to corroborate Guy's story of course because he was the only witness and given his precarious mental state, there had to be some doubt about its accuracy.

As the train approached the busy station in Saint Stephen, Marcel felt no further ahead in solving the mystery of Fran Bouchard's tragic drowning, but at least he knew where his primary duty lay. He was now quite convinced that Guy LaPlante was in need of support and protection. Fran had obviously discovered something so vital about the young man's life that she felt it necessary to accompany him back to his home village to deal with it head on, and there was every reason to suspect that her death might have resulted from that decision. But now it seemed that Guy himself might be held accountable for the tragic drowning. He may well have caused his psychiatrist's death either by accident or during a period of mental unbalance, or he may be a scapegoat victim being forced to bear the guilt of someone else's crime. Either way, he needed a strong advocate to stand in his defence and Marcel was ready to assume that role.

The question now was who to trust. Both Pierre Bouchard and Denis LaPlante seemed to have plenty to hide and it was difficult to know what was going on between them. Both had a considerable influence over Guy and yet they obviously hated each other. Were they pulling in opposite directions? Was one trying to harm the young man in some way while the other sought to protect him? Marcel had the feeling that the two adversaries were racing to an imminent finish line and Guy LaPlante's fate would ultimately depend on who won.

The careworn priest left the train and made his way to the exits with the pressing crowd. He was looking forward to seeing Gaston Leduc again. At least Gaston was a genuine young man who had his old friend's best interests at heart, and perhaps he could help. After all, he'd grown up with Guy LaPlante and they had shared many experiences throughout their childhood and adolescence. Maybe he could offer some insights that might help them find answers to some of these bothersome questions.

A gentle rain was beginning to fall as Marcel walked out onto the street. Several taxis were lined up and waiting for prospective customers and anxious drivers looked hopefully as passengers hurried from the station. But it was the beat-up vehicle at the end of the line that caught the priest's attention as Gaston's grinning face appeared from the open door. 'This way, Father,' the exuberant young man yelled, wildly waving his arms. 'Taxi at your service.'

Seventeen

Marcel threw his luggage into the back of the grungy taxi and then carefully squeezed himself into the front passenger seat. 'Gaston,' he said with a appreciative smile, 'so good of you to meet me off the train like this. I hope you haven't been waiting long.'

'Not at all, Father. I've told you it's a pleasure. Any time you need a ride just give me a call.' The young man grinned as he nodded towards his fellow taxi drivers all waiting in line. 'These guys will be a bit pissed off though. They'll be wondering why you picked the scruffiest cab—right from the back of the line too.' The tires squealed as Gaston made a rapid U-turn and made for the road back to the village. 'It's just as well though,' he added as an after thought. 'I don't suppose they'd want to be going to Maplewood Creek anyway, especially with this rain starting. The pot holes are bad enough in dry weather but once they start filling up with water it can be a bit of a challenge.'

Marcel tried to get comfortable in the cramped seat as he anticipated the rough ride home, but despite the discomfort he felt a deep sense of satisfaction at the thought of returning to the village and the work he loved so much. It would be so good to get back, he thought, even though he'd be faced with some mounting problems and a whole slew of uncertainties about where to go from here. 'Well, Gaston,' he said with a contented sigh, 'a lot's happened since I last saw you but now I just want to get home and get on with my life.'

Gaston glanced at his passenger and laughed out loud. 'Good grief, Father,' he said, grinning in amusement, 'you talk as if you've been away for weeks. It was only yesterday afternoon when I dropped you off. What's been going on? I take it you've had a successful trip.'

'You could say that I suppose. Was it really yesterday afternoon? I must be losing track of time. It feels like much longer—so much seems to have happened in the last twenty-four hours.'

'Well, you know what they say—time passes quickly when you're having fun. Or maybe you were just too busy.' Gaston took on a more serious tone as he adjusted the flapping windshield wipers. 'As a matter of fact, Father, I've been pretty busy myself over the last twenty-four hours. There's a couple of things I need to talk to you about.' He looked at the tired priest as if to beg approval. 'This might not be the time though—you might be a bit too tired at the moment.'

Marcel laughed. 'Well, I can't go anywhere can I? I'm a captive audience for the next half hour so you might as well go right ahead. Have things been a bit busy at the shop?'

Gaston sighed and shook his head. 'That's the least of my worries,' he said. 'No, I've been thinking a lot about our conversation yesterday. You seemed to be very concerned about Guy LaPlante and I think I should be doing something to help. He was always a good friend of mine, you know, and I feel I should have been there for him over the past few months. I feel quite bad about it now'

'You mean about offering him a part-time job or something.'

'More than that. I should tell you, Father, I went to visit him yesterday after I dropped you off and we had quite a long chat about the old days. He's not himself though. I get the feeling that he's still deeply troubled about something.'

Marcel perked up at this news. 'You've had a chat with him? Well I'm glad to hear that, Gaston. And I think you're right about something still troubling him—there's definitely something going on though I can't quite put my finger on it. Whatever it is, that young man needs a good friend right now and I'd say you're in the best position to help.'

'Actually, he thinks very highly of you, Father. I was hoping you'd be able to talk to him yourself and maybe find out what's bothering him.'

Marcel cleared his throat and hesitated slightly before speaking. 'I may be going out on a limb a bit here, Gaston, but I've been giving a great deal of thought to this over the past day or two. I'm sure you'll understand that I have to think of my professional obligation to protect confidentialities, but I want to ask you if you can help me with something.'

'Something concerning Guy LaPlante?'

'That's right. But I can't stress enough that what I'm going to tell you is in the strictest confidence. I'm breaking the rules a bit because I believe there's a serious need to do so. As I say, I think you are in a unique position to help and that's really why I need to confide in you. Can I count on your absolute discretion?'

Gaston swallowed hard and glanced quickly at his passenger, a little startled at the sombre tone in the priest's voice. 'So it's really serious then,' he said quietly. 'Yes, of course you can trust me.' He fiddled uncomfortably with the windshield wiper lever and added as if to explain, 'I'm happy to do anything that will help Guy get back on his feet.'

Marcel sank deeper into his seat and thought for a moment. 'This trip to Fredericton that I've just done,' he began, 'this trip—I needed to find some answers to a few troubling questions. As it turned out I found out much more than I wanted to and I've returned with more vexing questions than ever and some serious concerns about Guy.'

'So the purpose of your trip was to help Guy LaPlante then?

'It didn't start out that way but that's the way it seems to have ended. The fact is, Gaston, I believe Guy may be in some kind of danger.'

The rain was noticeably heavier now and a flash of lightning followed by a distant clap of thunder seemed to add emphasis to Marcel's words. Gaston slowed down to adjust to the worsening road conditions. 'What kind of danger do you mean, Father?' he asked, betraying a hint of apprehension in his voice. 'Are you saying you think someone's trying to harm him?'

'That's what we have to find out. I can't share all the information with you, Gaston, but I have reason to believe that someone may be using Guy as a scapegoat for a crime he didn't commit.'

The darkening sky appeared ever more menacing and a deafening torrent of rain began to crash heavily on the windshield. Gaston slowed down almost to a standstill and then pulled towards the side of the unpaved road. 'This is getting pretty bad,' he said. 'I think I'd better pull over for a while until the worst of this rain is over. I'm sure it's just passing through.' He parked his battered taxi precariously close to the ditch and then forcefully pulled on the squeaky parking brake. 'Did you discover something about Guy while you were in Fredericton?' he asked. 'I mean did something happen to Guy while he was working up there with his father last year—something that might explain his current frame of mind?'

Marcel pulled up his coat collar and folded his arms tightly. 'Actually, I think a lot must have happened. It seems he had some kind of breakdown during that year and he was receiving professional help for it.' The priest hesitated as he weighed his words. 'Do you remember the last thing you said when you dropped me off yesterday? We were talking about Fran, the woman who drowned in the St. Croix river last September, and you said you didn't believe for one moment that she was Guy's wife. What made you say that?'

'I never believed she was his wife from the moment I met her.'

'But where did the idea come from? Did Guy say she was his wife?'

Gaston thought for a moment. 'Come to think of it, I don't think I ever heard him say that. It was Guy's aunt, Marianne Boudreau, who first mentioned it to me. She came into the shop one day all in a fluster. She said Guy had written her a letter saying he was returning to

Maplewood Creek with his new wife, and he'd asked her to get the house ready for them. She was quite upset about it. I think that's why she asked me to be with her when Guy and Fran arrived back in the village.'

Marcel raised his eyebrows and smiled wryly. 'Actually, Fran was Dr. Bouchard's wife. She was a psychiatrist from the Fredericton Research Hospital and Guy was her patient.'

'Dr. Bouchard's wife? You're kidding.' Gaston whistled in surprise. 'Guy told me he was a patient at the hospital in Fredericton but why would he have told everyone Fran was his wife? It doesn't make a scrap of sense.'

'I must admit it's hard to explain,' the priest said gently. 'It might be related to his confused state of mind—you know, his confusion with reality and his run-away imagination. But I think it might be simpler than that. He may have told Marianne he was bringing a new wife home as a bit of an ego booster, or even as some kind of silly joke. Apparently it was Mme Boudreau who told people that Fran was Guy's wife the week before he arrived back in the village and the news must have spread around. Of course, once she met Fran in person, she knew that it couldn't possibly be true.'

Gaston stroked his chin pensively as he took this in. 'You know, Father,' he said, 'that is a bit of a surprise, but it does make one thing clear. It explains why Dr. Bouchard was in Maplewood Creek the day Fran drowned. He was pretty mad at her that morning and he was still yelling at her when he opened the door to me and Mme Boudreau. I couldn't figure out why at the time, but if she was the doctor's wife and everyone had been led to believe she was Guy's wife it's no wonder Dr. Bouchard was a bit irate. I do remember him saying he wanted Fran to accompany him back to Fredericton. That makes sense now.'

'Yes I was thinking about that too. I spoke to one of the doctors at the hospital today, someone who worked with Dr. Bouchard, and according to him Pierre's only reason for following his wife down to the village that day was to persuade her to give up the case and return home. But remind me again, Gaston. Did you tell me you didn't see Dr. Bouchard again that afternoon once you'd both left Guy's house?'

'I didn't see him but he was obviously still around. Guy told me he was there when Fran fell in the river. Dr. Bouchard was a witness to that, you know. Apparently he jumped into the water himself in an attempt to save her.'

Marcel looked up sharply. 'No, no, Gaston, I think you must have misunderstood that. Dr. Bouchard was called to deal with the emergency and I believe he pulled her body from the river some time later, but he wasn't there when she actually fell in.'

'That's what I thought too but Guy was adamant, Father. As I said, we had a long chat. We took a stroll down to the river yesterday afternoon and Guy pointed out the actual spot where the accident took place. I know he does tend to be a bit confused but he was very clear about that.'

'What did he say exactly?'

'Apparently Guy himself slipped from the rocks into the river and the next thing he knew, Fran was in the water with him. But then it seems Dr. Bouchard appeared from nowhere and he was standing on the river bank when Guy looked up.'

Marcel shook his head in disbelief. 'That's something I didn't know,' he said. 'If Pierre was actually present when his wife fell in it casts a different light on the whole thing. But it's strange that Guy didn't tell me about that.'

Gaston looked a little confused. 'Isn't Dr. Bouchard a friend of yours, Father? Surely you don't think he pushed Fran into the river.'

"I'm not saying that he did. Dr. Bouchard is a good man and yes, I do consider him a friend of mine but, you know, Gaston, sometimes good people make bad mistakes. We are all capable of making mistakes and when we do we have to take full responsibility for them. Fran's drowning may be a case of negligence or worse, but my main concern right now is that Guy may be being blamed for it or for something else that he didn't do—or at least for something that's not entirely his fault.'

Gaston stared out of the window and sighed. 'I should tell you, Father, Guy may not be entirely innocent. I know he can't be held fully responsible for his actions, and he does seem to be a little confused on certain details, but I think he may have been trying to tell me something yesterday afternoon in his own muddling way.'

'What do you mean? What has he said?'

'After I left him yesterday I was mulling over some of the things we were discussing and there was one thing he said that stuck in my mind—something I found quite disturbing. He was giving me an account of what happened at the river on the day that Fran drowned and he seemed to be on the point of admitting to some blame for her death. I got the distinct impression that he could have been the one who pushed Fran into the river.'

'Are you saying he admitted to that?'

'Not exactly, but he talked about pretending to push her in, joking around, and trying to scare her. You know what they say: many a true word is spoken in jest. I wondered if he was trying to tell me that it was he who pushed her in without saying it in so many words.'

Marcel thought for a moment. 'It's a possibility of course,' he said slowly, 'but as you say, we have to remember that Guy is mentally ill. Not only is he not fully responsible for his actions but we also have to take everything he says with a grain of salt. I don't think we can take him completely seriously.'

'That's true of course, but what do you mean when you say he might be blamed for something he didn't do?'

Marcel again struggled for words. 'It's something I discovered about Fran's work in Fredericton. The doctor I talked to earlier today told me that Fran had come across something that raised a red flag during her counselling sessions with Guy LaPlante. She thought police intervention might be called for and she was worried that her patient might be wrongly blamed for something. It seems she needed to check some records with Dr. Martin and that's why she found it necessary to bring Guy back to Maplewood Creek.'

The two men sat in quiet thought for a moment while the rain and relentless rhythm of the windshield wipers filled the silence. Pondering the priest's words, Gaston hesitated a little before speaking up. 'I think I know what Fran might have had in mind,' he said quietly. 'Something else that Guy told me yesterday—he told me his father blamed him for his mother's death.'

'What?' Marcel felt his heart leap angrily in his chest. 'Denis blamed Guy for his mother's death? That's outrageous! I don't think there is any doubt that she died of a heart attack about seven years ago, so what's that all about?'

Gaston shuffled uncomfortably in his seat at the priest's strong reaction to this news. 'Yes, it was about seven years ago when she died,' he said. 'I remember it well. We were teenagers at the time. Guy reminded me that we'd made some home brew that summer—a kind of cranberry juice that we called home-made wine. It tasted foul but it was completely harmless and in fact both Guy and I drank a bottleful with no ill effects. Apparently Denis LaPlante claims his wife drank some of it too and it poisoned her. I know for sure that is completely false, but the problem is Guy believed it. I think it could have been the trauma of being accused of such a thing that pushed him over the edge.'

Marcel did not respond immediately. This news could be the missing piece of the puzzle, he thought. Could it be that Guy's urgent need for counselling and treatment resulted from his belief that he was responsible for his mother's death. Fran, of course, wouldn't have known what to make of it. She wouldn't have known whether it was true or not, and as Denis LaPlante was so uncooperative she would have had no choice but to talk with the doctor who had signed the death certificate. That of course would be Dr. Martin in Maplewood Creek. Yes, this was beginning to make more sense now. Marcel looked quizzically at his youthful associate. 'Does Guy still feel responsible for his mother's death then?' he asked. 'Is he still fretting over it?'

'Oh no, he realizes that the wine story can't be true. At least that's what he told me. But I think he still resents his dad for suggesting such a thing.'

Marcel shook his head in annoyance. 'That's understandable,' he said, 'but why would Denis LaPlante say something like that? Why would he accuse his son of such a dreadful thing?'

'I don't know, but Guy seems to think it was because of the house. According to him, his dad was trying to blackmail him into selling the old family home. I think it may have had the opposite effect though. Apparently Guy dug his heels in after that and made up his mind that the house was not for sale.'

'Yes, but it was also after that that he needed psychiatric help. It's quite possible that Fran discovered this thing about his mother's death during the counselling sessions. Maybe that's what she was so concerned about; maybe that's why she brought Guy home to Maplewood Creek.'

The rain was noticeably lighter now and only the occasional rumble of distant thunder could be heard as the storm moved through. Gaston looked around and adjusted his twisted seat belt. 'We'd better get moving,' he said. 'I hate driving this road once it gets dark and it looks like there's precious little daylight left. The road's a mess. I'd better take it easy over these potholes but it shouldn't take us too long to reach the village.'

As the taxi moved slowly forward a single blinding light approached from the opposite direction and the unmistakable roar of a motorcycle engine filled the air. Marcel shielded his eyes from the glare and chuckled in amusement as the noisy machine passed. 'Someone's brave,' he said. 'I wouldn't fancy driving this road on two wheels tonight. He'll be shaken to bits by the time he reaches Saint Stephen.'

'Did you see who that was, Father?' Gaston turned his head and watched as the motorcycle bounced away over the water-logged potholes. 'That was Denis LaPlante. Who could mistake that bulky frame of his?' He shook his head and laughed. 'You'd wonder why the man keeps coming back when he hates the village so much.'

'He must have his reasons,' Marcel shrugged. 'I suppose he's visiting that poor son of his.'

It seemed like everything had been said for the moment and the two men travelled in silence for a while. Occasionally they were thrown gently from side to side as the well-used vehicle negotiated rough patches on the gravel road. As they approached the village, the church with its imposing spire and the tall trees that surrounded it first came into view. It was a welcoming sight, but the storm had left behind an unstable, drizzly air mass that cast a sombre dreariness on everything, and drops of heavy rain were still dripping from the sodden trees. Quite a fitting reception, Marcel thought as he finally reached home on this dreary, late-September day. There were so many unanswered questions and a multitude of problems to deal with. And so much work to be done—most of which threatened to be rather unpleasant.

Gaston picked up speed now as he hit the paved road at last, and he drove more confidently as he entered the village. He pulled up outside the main gates of the parish church and leaned back comfortably into the driver's seat. 'Well, that's it, Father,' he said with a grin. 'You're home.'

Marcel reached out and retrieved his travel bag from the back seat. 'I guess I am, Gaston. Thanks for everything,' he said, holding out an appreciative hand. 'I will be needing your help, you know. Let's keep in touch.'

'Any time, Father. Just let me know what you want me to do. I suppose you'll be meeting with Guy fairly soon then?'

'That's the plan.' Marcel paused tight-lipped for a moment as a thought occurred to him. 'Maybe we should both have a chat with him,' he said thoughtfully.

'We could go together. If he's comfortable with that we might be able to figure out what's going on.'

'Sure. If you think that would be useful just give me a call. I can always close shop for a while if you need me.' With his signature thumbs up signal Gaston was quickly on his way and Marcel watched as he drove the short distance downhill to his humble business on the other side of the whistle-stop station. He's a good man, the priest told himself. If anyone can help Guy LaPlante get back on his feet it's his old friend Gaston.

Glancing briefly at the cloud-darkened sky, Marcel pulled up his coat collar against the light drizzle and made his way up the walkway to the parish residence. He remembered his first walk up this very path some six months earlier and how the front door had been flung open before he even reached it on that occasion. To his astonishment, the memory was suddenly relived. Mme Poirier stood there on the doorstep; her face was an ashen grey and evidence of a stress-filled crying session lay heavily on her cheeks. 'Oh, Father Marcel,' she groaned. 'Thank God you're back. Something terrible has happened—something awful.'

Marcel hurried up the steps and threw his luggage on the porch. 'Louise,' he said anxiously. 'What's happened? Whatever's the matter?'

'Oh, Father,' the distressed woman wailed. 'I've lived in this village all my life and nothing like this has ever happened before. We've had some vandalism in the churchyard. I can't believe anyone could be so disrespectful.'

'But what is it, Louise? What have they done?'

'It's one of the graves, Father,' the distraught woman sobbed. 'Someone's been in there and desecrated one of the graves.'

Marcel felt a sense of outrage as the words sank in and he sighed in frustration. 'You mean someone's disfigured it with graffiti? Have they spray painted something on the headstone?'

'Disfigured it? No they've smashed it. They've ripped the headstone right off and broken it in two.'

Eighteen

Marcel woke from a deep sleep and tried to make sense of the morning weather forecast as it blared out of his bedside radio. Light breezes and clear blue skies were being promised by the cheerful announcer and the priest, even in his semi-conscious torpor, felt inner joy at the dawn of a new day. He rose quickly and through force of habit stumbled towards the picture window and retracted the blind. Through bleary eyes he could see there was no sign of yesterday's storm now. The first struggling rays of sunlight on the horizon were already casting a pleasant tinge on the village below and they seemed to be giving some promising hints of a beautiful day to follow.

Marcel loved this view. The original planners did well to build the church and residence on top of the hill, he thought, and how appropriate it was to have the pastor's room looking out over his parishioners' neatly laid out cottages. The pleasing spectacle always gave him an overwhelming sense of purpose and a reinforcement of his function as protector of the flock. What better way to start the day? After a minute or two of silent prayer, the priest wasted no time in starting his daybreak routine. His immediate task now was to get ready and prepare himself for the morning services.

The initial feelings of euphoria soon gave way to more mundane and troubling thoughts as Marcel recalled the mayhem of the previous evening. It had been a difficult and frustrating experience to arrive home to yet another problem and the priest had shown little patience for it. Louise Poirier was a fine, dedicated housekeeper but she seemed to be quite incapable of putting things into a proper perspective, and her habit of blaming herself for everything and anything that went wrong at the parish headquarters was especially disconcerting. This business about the vandalized grave was no exception. As far as she was concerned the violent intrusion was all her fault because she had not been vigilant about checking the comings and goings of visitors to the church premises. 'I feel so guilty,' she kept saying, and no amount of reassurance from her forgiving pastor seemed to make any difference.

In the end, through sheer exhaustion, Marcel had tried to downplay the vandalism as something that could happen anywhere. 'We'll talk about it tomorrow, Louise,' he'd told her with a hint of irritation in his voice. 'We can't do anything about it now. It's still raining and it's too dark to see anything anyway. These things happen and we'll have to try and deal with them the best we can.'

'But shouldn't we call the police?' she'd asked anxiously. 'Surely they'll need to know.'

'I'll take a look at the grave site tomorrow morning and we can decide then whether we need to call the police department in Saint Stephen.' This seemed to help and the hapless housekeeper finally retired for the night with a mug of comforting cocoa, leaving the priest to take care of his own evening meal.

Although Marcel had been in no mood for dealing with new problems the minute he'd arrived back from his tiring trip, he knew that the issue of the desecrated grave had to be addressed now in the cold light of day. He felt angry that such a thing could have happened and he particularly hated to think about it on this beautiful autumn morning, but he felt a pressing need to get the facts straight. The dragged-out drama of Mme Poirier's self retribution had made it difficult to focus on any details and Marcel realized that he still had no idea who's grave had been vandalized and to what extent the grave site had been damaged. He'd be able to ask Mme Poirier for more information over breakfast before checking things out for himself. Meanwhile, the harried priest made a concerted effort to put the whole thing out of his mind until after Mass.

There was no sign of Mme Poirier when Marcel sat down to breakfast in the formal dining room some time later, but she was obviously around somewhere. The morning paper had been placed in its usual position on the table and the aroma of fresh-brewing coffee was emanating from the kitchen. The priest picked up the neatly-folded newspaper and glanced quickly at the hockey scores on the back page but his scrutiny didn't last long. Within a minute or two the crestfallen housekeeper appeared carrying a hot plate between two hefty oven mitts. With a weaker smile than usual she placed the cooked breakfast on the table in front of her pastor. 'Good morning, Father,' she said quietly. 'I hope you slept well.'

Marcel looked up and smiled kindly, trying to make the upset woman feel a little more relaxed. 'Morning, Louise,' he said cheerfully. 'How about yourself. Did you finally manage to get some sleep?'

'Eventually,' she murmured dolefully. Mme Poirier removed her oven mitts and placed them carefully under her arm. 'But I was thinking about what you were saying, Father. I realize things can happen despite one's best efforts and all we can do is deal with problems as they arise. I'm sorry if I made too much of a fuss last night.'

'Not at all. You're quite right to be concerned and we will have to deal with the vandalism issue this morning. Why don't we go out and have a look at the damage after breakfast and we'll take it from there?'

Mme Poirier nodded in agreement. 'I guess I wasn't making much sense last night, was I? But I do feel much better now.' She headed once more for the kitchen but turned as she reached the door. 'I'll bring your coffee in, Father. Is there anything else you need?'

'Everything's fine, Louise. But bring the coffee in and pour yourself a cup. You can sit here and chat to me while I'm eating. Now that you're calmer you can start from the beginning and tell me exactly what happened while I was away.'

The bustling housekeeper was pleased with this invitation as it gave her a chance to vindicate herself and show that she'd handled things to the best of her ability. She quickly returned with the steaming pot and poured out two cups of coffee before pulling out a chair opposite Marcel and installing herself at the table. 'Everything was going just fine after you left on Monday afternoon,' she said firmly. 'Just the usual parishioners around. André dropped by to pick up the readings for Tuesday's liturgy and some of the choir people were in the church to sort out the music for next week.'

'No strangers then?'

Mme Poirier sipped on her coffee and thought for a moment. 'There was one,' she said thoughtfully, 'but I didn't think anything of it at the time. A woman I've never met rang the doorbell yesterday afternoon and asked to speak to you.'

'Not someone from the village then?'

'Definitely not. She was very officious, long blond hair, leather jacket, and a bit hard-faced, I say.'

Marcel frowned and sat back in his chair. 'What did she want?' he asked, a hint of displeasure in his voice. 'Did she know me by name?'

'Well she just said she needed to speak to Reverend Dion about an urgent matter. When I said you hadn't arrived back from your trip she said she'd be back, but she wouldn't leave a message.'

'And she didn't give a name?'

'No, the woman seemed to be in quite a hurry. She practically ran down the walkway and drove off in an expensive-looking silver car. Come to think of it, there was a man sitting in the car waiting for her.'

Marcel raised his eyebrows questioningly. 'A man, you say? What was he like?'

'I really don't know—I was standing at the front door and he was too far away. It could've been anyone.'

'Could it have been Dr. Bouchard?'

Mme Poirier reacted in surprise at the mention of the village doctor. 'Dr. Bouchard?' she said. 'I hardly think so but as I say, it could've been anyone.'

'It was just a thought.' Marcel reflected on that possibility for a moment, wondering what the implications of this visit might be. 'What about this silver car?' he asked. 'Could that have been a BMW by any chance?'

Mme Poirier laughed. 'It could've been I suppose. I don't know what a BMW looks like. It was definitely an expensive car though.'

Marcel carefully placed his knife and fork on his unfinished breakfast. This woman with the blond hair could be the same woman he'd seen leaving Pierre Bouchard's surgery on Saturday morning, he thought. What could she possibly want with the village pastor? And could this have anything to do with the damage in the cemetery? He looked pensively at his housekeeper. 'Tell me about this grave then, Louise? When did you find out about that?'

Mme Poirier topped up her cup and took a large sip. This is what she really wanted to talk about. 'That was later in the afternoon just before the storm moved in,' she said adamantly. 'Marianne Boudreau was over for the choir practice at four o'clock and apparently she came across the vandalized grave as she came through the churchyard. She's still on crutches after her knee surgery, you know, so I don't know why she felt it necessary to go for choir practice. Anyway, she came hobbling round to the residence and hammered on the door. It gave me quite a shock. She was beside herself, crying and weeping so I brought her in and made her a cup of tea before going out to see the damage for myself.'

Marcel hesitated for a moment before asking the next question, although in the back of his mind he already knew the answer. 'Which grave has been vandalized, Louise?' He bit his tongue as the question slipped out.

The harried housekeeper gaped incredulously. 'Which grave?' she said in astonishment. 'It's the grave of Mariannes's sister, Jeanette LaPlante. I'm sure I must have told you that last night, Father.'

The priest felt his heart jump as his fears were confirmed. I knew it, he thought, shaking his head in dismay. This is one more piece to the wretched puzzle? 'Actually you didn't tell me, Louise,' he said gently, 'but no matter. I didn't ask either, partly because I was afraid of what the answer might be. This is Denis LaPlante's wife we're talking about, right?'

'Yes, and Guy LaPlante's mother. That young man has been taking care of his mother's grave devotedly over the past few months—especially since that terrible drowning accident last summer. I feel so sorry for him; he doesn't deserve any of this at all.'

Marcel felt a surge of annoyance running through him as he pondered the distress that this senseless act had caused. Who's responsible for this, he wondered, and what's the purpose of it all? He pushed his breakfast plate aside with some irritation and looked at his troubled housekeeper who seemed ready to burst into tears again. 'So what did Marianne have to say about it? Did she have any ideas about who might have done such a thing?'

'Oh, she had some ideas all right. She was very distraught of course and it took her a while to calm down, but she made it very clear that she holds her brother in law responsible. She might be off the mark but I know for a fact that Denis LaPlante was in the village yesterday afternoon. I heard that noisy motorcycle of his and I saw him driving down the hill towards the station after Marianne had gone.'

Marcel nodded in agreement. 'I know he was here. Gaston and I saw him leaving the village as we arrived back last night. But did either of you see him on church property during the day?'

'I didn't, and I'm pretty sure Marianne didn't either. I think it was just the first thought that came to her head. Denis has been such a pain over the years and he was always at loggerheads with Jeanette after they separated. I suppose Marianne just assumed that he'd do something like this for spite.'

The priest stroked his chin and tried to look at the situation logically. 'It doesn't make much sense, though, does it? Why would he damage his wife's grave, no matter how bad their relationship was, and what would he have to gain by doing such a dreadful thing? It would do him no good at all.'

'That's true and he'd know how much it would upset Guy. I'd have to say that, rough as he is, Denis does care about his son.'

Marcel wasn't too sure about that and he didn't respond to his housekeeper's kind observation. Maybe upsetting Guy in one way or another was part of a pernicious plan to get control of him and perhaps persuade him to make some decisions that would benefit his father. By all accounts Denis was still intent on gaining possession of Guy's house and that seemed to be a project that occupied a great deal of his time. Still, he thought, vandalizing his wife's grave would be a bit over the top and it would hardly lead to any desirable results. The priest pushed back his chair and purposefully stood up. 'Anyway,' he said, 'it's time we went out and assessed the damage. Let's have a look at the grave site and then I think a call to the police in Saint Stephen might be in order.' Another thought suddenly occurred to him. 'By the way, Louise, has Guy been told anything about this fiasco?'

'I assume he has. Marianne was going over to see him yesterday after she left here.'

Marcel frowned. 'That would have been quite difficult for her,' he said grimly. 'There's no way of knowing how Guy would react to something like that. I hope she broke the news gently.'

The two of them made their way to the front door but they were suddenly stopped in their tracks when the vestibule telephone rang loudly, causing Marcel to jump in surprise as he passed by. 'Goodness me! You have the volume on that thing set way too high, Louise,' he laughed. 'I nearly jump out of my skin when it rings in my ear like that.'

'I'm sorry, Father—it's just that don't like to miss a call. People do expect someone to answer and I'm usually busy in some other part of the house.' Mme Poirier briskly wiped her hands on her apron and grabbed the phone. 'I'd better answer it,' she said. 'It might be Marianne and she'll want to know what's going on. I'll see you outside in a few minutes.'

Marcel wandered out onto the front porch and stood there with his arms folded tightly across his chest. This bit of vandalism really didn't make much sense, he thought, and it was difficult to see how it had anything to do with the problems at hand. Perhaps it was just coincidence that Jeanette LaPlante's grave had been damaged. That might be the most rational conclusion given that none of the characters in this puzzle seemed to be likely suspects. Denis was not overly bright but he wouldn't have been stupid enough to vandalize his own wife's grave. Guy wouldn't have done it either. He was quite conscientious about his work in the churchyard and he always paid particular attention to his mother's grave. And certainly, Pierre wouldn't do such a thing. He was a professional man far above such wonton destruction—unless of course, he wanted to make it look like someone else had done it. One other possibility remained—perhaps someone was trying to warn this meddling priest to butt out and mind his own business.

Marcel's musings were rudely interrupted as the front door was flung open and Mme Poirier reappeared on the porch, flustered and red faced. 'It's the police,' she said breathlessly. 'They want to talk to you urgently.'

'The police? What do they want?'

'I've no idea. But you'd better take the call, Father; I've left it on hold for you.'

The priest felt his heart pounding as he strode briskly to the phone, but he was not at all surprised to be receiving an urgent call from the police. It was something that had to happen sooner or later, he thought, and subconsciously he'd known that all along. With a sweaty palm he picked up the receiver and spoke directly into it. 'Marcel Dion speaking,' he said confidently. 'How can I help you?'

The officious male voice at the other end got right down to business. 'Reverend Dion, this is Detective Sergeant Jean Marchand calling from the Investigation Centre here in Saint Stephen. I hope I've caught you at an opportune moment.'

Marcel swallowed hard. 'Certainly,' he replied bravely. 'How can I help?'

'I'm calling on behalf of Chief Inspector Boivin and myself, sir. We tried to contact you on Tuesday but I understand you were away in Fredericton for a couple of days.'

'That's right. I returned last evening. What's this all about?'

'It's a delicate matter, sir. I don't want to alarm you unduly, and I do apologize for contacting you by telephone rather than in person. The fact is, we are on the point of concluding a murder investigation in the village and you seem to have inadvertently involved yourself in the case. We have some concern for your safety but, as I say, I don't think you need to be overly worried—just take sensible precautions.'

The words seemed to confirm Marcel's worst fears in an instant. This was obviously about Pierre Bouchard's wife. So Fran had definitely been murdered then. There seemed to be no doubt about it now. It was dreadful news in its own right of course, but at least it took away that awful uncertainty that had plagued him for so long. 'Why do you say that, Sergeant,' he asked courteously. 'In what way am I involved?'

'I'm sure you'll understand, sir, that I can't talk about the case. We are about to make an arrest and it's important that none of us do anything that would jeopardize that. But we are aware that you've been making inquiries at the Research Hospital in Fredericton about a death that occurred in Maplewood Creek last year. Apparently you were given some confidential information about certain parties who are relevant to the case and that poses a problem for us. I must ask you to keep that information to yourself until after an arrest has been made. Can I count on your cooperation, sir?'

'Well, yes, of course. But how did you know about my visit to the hospital? Has someone reported that to you?'

'I can't tell you that, sir. I know you have responsibilities to your parishioners but if you could just lie low for the next few hours—we expect to make an arrest later today.'

Marcel's mind was working overtime and a torrent of questions flooded his mind. What were the implications of this new twist and what did it all mean for Guy? Was that unfortunate young man about to be arrested? Or was it Pierre? And could this have anything to do with the latest problem in the churchyard? 'There is one thing that I should tell you, Sergeant,' he said cautiously. 'I was about to call the police on a matter that may or may not be related to your murder case. We've had some vandalism in the cemetery here at the church. One of the headstones has been removed and smashed. You may need to check it out.'

'Yes, sir, we're fully aware of that. We know about the headstone and it's all under control. Please don't touch anything at the grave site for now. We'll explain later.'

Marcel was astonished to hear this. 'You mean it's already been reported?'

'Let's just say we know about it, sir. Chief Inspector Boivin and I will meet with you as soon as possible and this will all become clear. I'll have to leave it at that for now, but thank you again for your help and cooperation. We'll talk again very soon.' Sergeant Marchand hung up abruptly, leaving the bewildered priest standing there and wondering where this strange case would lead him next. He had a weird sinking feeling in the pit of his stomach as he made his way outdoors.

'You look stunned, Father,' Mme Poirier said, looking rather concerned as the priest joined her once more on the front porch. 'What on earth have they said to you?'

'They were calling about Jeanette LaPlante's grave—they already knew about it.'

The housekeeper looked surprised but nodded knowingly. 'Marianne must have reported it then. I suppose that makes sense; she was very upset when she left here.'

Marcel frowned at the suggestion. 'Actually, I wish she'd left that to me,' he said. 'It can't be helped now but there's one thing that I find puzzling, Louise. Sergeant Marchand said the police were trying to contact me yesterday afternoon. You didn't mention it. Did they phone or come to the house while I was away?'

'I'd have told you if they had, Father. The police certainly didn't talk to me yesterday. There were no phone calls and the blond woman in the silver car was the only visitor apart from Marianne. I think I told you that.'

'And that's another thing. Who was that woman? Do you think she could have had anything to do with the vandalized grave?'

Mme Poirier shook her head emphatically. 'I'm no detective, Father, but I'd say absolutely not. I suppose she was here around the same time as the vandalism happened but she was neat and clean—not like someone who'd just been messing about in a muddy grave site. I got the impression that she'd just driven up and rung the doorbell. Then she took off as if she didn't have a minute to spare.'

That seemed to make sense but Marcel suddenly felt strangely vulnerable. Perhaps this grave vandalism really was a bizarre warning, he thought. Maybe it was an attempt to scare him off. The police admitted they had some concerns about his safety. Was someone trying to stop him from helping Guy LaPlante? If that was the case, the warning must have come from someone who was trying to harm that unfortunate young man. And that would likely be either Denis LaPlante or Pierre Bouchard—or perhaps the mysterious blond woman in the BMW. Marcel realized now that his safety might depend on whom he decided to trust.

Nineteen

'See what I mean, Father? Someone's lifted the headstone right off the grave and thrown it off to the side. Look, they've broken it right across the middle.' Mme Poirier clucked her tongue in disgust as she pointed out the damage. 'And what a mess after all that rain.'

Marcel bent down to examine the fracture in the stone. 'It's broken right through all right, but I don't see any marks that might have been made by a hammer or heavy instrument,' he said thoughtfully. 'It might have smashed as a result of being thrown down on the ground. Perhaps there was no intention to actually break it.'

'But it was deliberately lifted off the base and thrown aside, wasn't it? And how many people were involved? I doubt if one person could have done it alone.'

Marcel nodded his head in agreement. 'I'd say two or three people worked on this, judging by all the boot marks. They obviously started digging around too. See the way the soil has been disturbed on the sides?' The priest stood back and observed the full length of the grave site. 'This is an awfully narrow plot, Louise,' he said. 'Do you remember the burial taking place. When was it—seven years ago?'

Mme Poirier nodded sadly. 'Yes I do. I was at the funeral and I stood right here when Jeanette was buried. She was the last to be put to rest in this churchyard. Everyone after her went to the new cemetery.'

'So I believe. But her grave seems to have been squeezed in, doesn't it? Was there any concern about not having enough space for another interment in the churchyard?'

'Not that I know of. They buried her here and that was that.'

Marcel shrugged, accepting that no explanation was forthcoming. He realized that nothing more could be done for the moment, and in any case, he needed time to think. 'Let's leave it for the time being, Louise,' he said gently, 'the police are aware of the damage and they've asked us not to touch anything. I'll talk to Marianne in a day or two and we'll see about replacing the headstone. Meanwhile, try not to worry about it. The police are working on the case.'

'I certainly hope so.' Mme Poirier assumed the priest was referring to the case of the vandalized grave and his subtle reference to the murder investigation was completely lost on her. 'I'll get on with my work then, Father,' she said, moving in the direction of the residence. 'Is there anything else you need at the moment?'

'Don't worry about me. You go right ahead and do what you have to do.' Marcel had no intention of telling his housekeeper about the impending arrest yet, especially as the police had given him no information about exactly when and where it would happen. 'I'm going to sit here for a while,' he told her. 'I have a lot of thinking to do and I might be out here for some time.'

The iron park bench at the far end of the churchyard was not very comfortable but it did provide a pleasant view of the village below and Marcel was grateful for its relative seclusion among the tall trees. He needed peace and quiet now. Things seemed to be rushing towards an inexorable climax and this might be his last chance to mull over some of the disturbing information that the police had just given him. It had been such a short telephone conversation but the implications of what Sergeant Marchand had told him were enormous.

The priest folded his arms tightly and stared at the peaceful scene before him. It was hard to believe that a woman had been murdered in this quiet village with its tight-knit population of respectable and upright citizens, and yet it was certain now that a suspect was about to be arrested. It had taken a long time to accumulate all the relevant facts, he thought. It was more than a year now since Fran had drowned and if the arrest was imminent, as Sergeant Marchand said it was, the investigation must have finally yielded sufficient evidence to construct a viable case against the murderer. Had the police managed to build a case to justify the arrest of Guy LaPlante in spite of his many problems? And if so, whose help had they relied on?

Marcel tried to imagine the most logical scenario. He recalled what Gaston Leduc had told him the previous afternoon during the taxi ride from Saint Stephen and how their conversation had forced him to look at the mystery from a different perspective. Some surprising details had come to light as a result of that conversation. In particular, Gaston's suspicion that Guy LaPlante might have somehow pushed his dedicated psychiatrist into the river that day, either deliberately or accidentally, was quite unexpected. But Marcel had to admit that it was a distinct possibility. That scenario seemed to fit into the big picture more clearly than ever.

The priest felt absolutely sure now that it was Guy who had made the emotional confession to murder on that awful Saturday afternoon though he was still puzzled as to why the young man claimed to have murdered his wife. There could be a good explanation for that of course. Guy knew perfectly well that Fran was not his wife but no doubt he was in a traumatic state of mind after her tragic drowning and that was certainly a possible explanation for the bizarre confusion.

The most surprising thing to come out of the conversation with Gaston was the revelation that Pierre Bouchard was actually present when his wife plunged into the St. Croix river. That came as a shock but when all was said and done, Gaston only had Guy LaPlante's word for it, and it was important to keep in mind that Guy's word was unreliable and it should not be taken too seriously.

There was still some possibility of course that the doctor could have been directly responsible for Fran's death but Marcel had serious doubts about that now. Dr. LaFontaine was very clear about the Bouchard's relationship. Despite some noisy disagreements on the job, Pierre and Fran were a professional couple who normally worked well together and deep down they were devoted to each other. Pierre had serious concerns for his wife's safety and it was clear that his only reason for following her to Maplewood Creek was to protect her from any more abuse by Denis and Guy LaPlante. But he would have been outraged if he'd witnessed her drowning at the hands of a disturbed patient and he would have done everything in his power to make sure that blame was placed where it belonged. He would make sure that justice was done. The only problem with that, Marcel thought, is that justice, when applied to such an emotionally disturbed young man, may be very difficult to define.

The story about the homemade wine was very upsetting too because it emphasized the spiteful control that Denis LaPlante had over his son, but it did seem to provide a logical explanation for Fran Bouchard's concerns and her subsequent journey to Maplewood Creek. Gaston was adamant that the stuff was harmless and couldn't possibly have caused Jeanette LaPlante's death but if Guy believed he was somehow to blame for his mother's demise it could well have been the beginning of this whole saga. It wasn't clear how the young man had ended up under psychiatric care in Fredericton but that wasn't particularly relevant now. Regardless of how he came to be at the hospital, if he'd told Fran in a counselling session that he'd poisoned his mother, she would have had a professional obligation to follow it through. And that of course would have brought Denis LaPlante into the picture.

According to Gaston's account, Denis put the idea of poisonous wine into his son's head when they were briefly living together in Fredericton and he seemed to have had a devious and calculating reason for doing so.

By all accounts the obnoxious man was obsessed with obtaining ownership of his late wife's property which he saw as his rightful inheritance, and he must have believed that Guy would give way to blackmail. But the plan obviously backfired. Denis wouldn't have expected the story to travel beyond his own living room, but once Fran became involved, she would have contacted him to see if he could shed any light on the matter. Denis would have hit the roof of course, and he would have done everything in his power to stop his son from talking to the Bouchards. Hence the noisy exchanges in Fran Bouchard's office at the Fredericton Research Hospital.

Of course in one sense it would have been in Denis's interests to have Guy arrested and convicted of poisoning his mother because that would remove him from the scene and Denis would then have access to the valuable property he so desperately wanted. So why was he fighting tooth and nail to stop Fran Bouchard's attempts to resolve the matter? Mme Poirier seemed to think that despite his bullying nature, Denis genuinely cared for his troubled son and if that was so he would not want to see him falsely accused of a crime. Maybe she was right about that but it was more likely that Denis was looking after his own interests. He would have realized that when the story about the homemade wine was examined and found to be false, he'd find himself in serious trouble with the law and he wouldn't want to risk that. Blackmail is an indictable offence punishable by some very severe penalties.

Once the frenetic foursome reached Maplewood Creek things obviously turned out very differently from what they had expected. No doubt Fran Bouchard was intent on discussing her concerns with old Dr. Martin. She would have wanted to get some details about any counselling, treatment or medication that Guy might have received in the past, though Marcel had no idea whether she ever actually obtained that information. But Gaston had described a tumultuous atmosphere in Guy LaPlante's home the morning after they arrived in the village. Pierre wanted his wife to leave the confused patient in Maplewood Creek and return to Fredericton with him. Once Denis arrived on the scene he would have been vigorously trying to persuade Guy to leave these meddling doctors once and for all and go home with his father. It must have been a very bewildering experience for the troubled young man.

The tragic drowning occurred some time during the afternoon of that same day. Someone pushed Fran into the St. Croix river and that would surely have put an end to anyone's preoccupation with homemade wine. The situation would have suddenly become much more serious as they tried to deal with the horrible unexpected death of Pierre's wife. It struck Marcel as being rather odd that the police didn't suspect foul play at the time. Mme Poirier had told him there was a brief inquest some time later which ruled that the drowning was an accidental death and all the villagers, including Marianne Boudreau, simply accepted that without question. Interesting though that Pierre Bouchard signed his own wife's death certificate. Could that be legal?

Marcel was suddenly conscious of the inherent discomfort of the hard iron bench and he shifted his position in an attempt to find a more relaxing pose. Another thought occurred to him as he shuffled about. Gaston had mentioned that Denis LaPlante was in a foul mood on the afternoon of Fran's death as he sat and waited for his taxi at the service station. He was in some discomfort, suffering from a poison ivy rash on his legs and looking as if he carried the weight of the whole world on his shoulders. This seemed to ring a bell with the priest. Where had he heard about poison ivy before? It was from Louise Poirier, he recalled. She'd told him about Father Lemieux's love of fishing and how he made his weekly trip down to the river on his day off. As often as not, she told him, the old priest would come home with rashes on his legs after rambling through patches of poison ivy on the river bank. Perhaps Denis LaPlante had been down there after all on the day Fran Bouchard was drowned.

Whatever happened by the river that day, one thing was certain now. The police were on the point of arresting and charging a murder suspect in the village. The identity of that suspect remained as elusive as ever, and although Marcel felt quite sure that one of the three main players in this on-going drama was the object of police scrutiny, it was not at all certain that the authorities were descending on the right man. Both Pierre and Denis had plenty to gain from Guy's removal from the village and the investigation that had obviously been going on for some time may well have been centered on a search for evidence that could convict him. That troubled young man may well have been the one to cause Fran's death but Marcel had a dreadful fear that the unfortunate fellow would be the one arrested and charged whether he was guilty or not. That cannot be allowed to happen, the priest told himself. Guy LaPlante is psychologically unbalanced and he is not fully responsible for his actions. That must be taken into account if and when he is arrested and charged with murder.

Marcel was shaken from his reverie by the sound of footsteps on the stone pathway behind him. He turned to see Marianne Boudreau awkwardly making her way towards her sister's damaged grave. She had not noticed the priest as he sat there quietly in the shade of tall trees and she was somewhat startled as he called out to her. 'Marianne,' he yelled, 'hold on a minute. I need to talk to you.'

The woman stopped in her tracks and looked across to where the seemingly disembodied voice had emanated from the trees. 'Oh, Father Marcel,' she said as he rose from the bench. 'You gave me quite a shock. I didn't see you down there.' She waited until the priest joined her on the pathway and then mumbled by way of explanation, 'I've just come back to take another look at Jeanette's grave.'

Marcel gently took her arm as she hobbled along, managing with a single crutch now to support her tender knee. 'I'm so sorry about what's happened, Marianne,' he said. 'I still can't make much sense of it, but rest assured, we will replace the headstone as soon as possible. We'll get everything back to normal in a few days.'

'I'm sure we will, Father, but that's not what's bothering me. I'm so angry that someone would do such a thing—such disrespect for the dead and the fact that it's Jeanette's grave makes it such a personal matter.'

'Yes, I can understand that. But it's all been taken in hand now. I believe you reported it to the police yourself?'

'The police?' Marianne looked quite taken aback at the suggestion. 'I've reported it to no one. I thought you would have done that as a matter of course.'

'You mean you didn't report it?' Marcel was suddenly at a loss for words. 'Of course it would normally be my job to do that but when I talked to the police this morning they already knew about it. Louise assumed that you must have contacted the police yourself after you left here yesterday.'

'Certainly not. I went straight from here to Guy's house to tell him what had happened. I've had no contact with the police at all.'

Marcel frowned heavily as they reached Jeanette LaPlante's grave. 'That's very strange,' he said. 'I don't know who else would have called them. Actually, I don't know who else would have even known about it—except the people who did it of course.'

'Well that's the big questions isn't it? Who did all this damage?'

Marcel looked quizzically at the distressed woman. 'Louise said you suspect your brother-in-law, Denis LaPlante. Do you think he might know something about it.'

'It was the first name that came into my head, I must admit, but why he would do such a thing I don't know. He seems to have been bothering Guy over something or other for a long time but he'd have nothing to gain by desecrating his wife's grave.' Marianne painstakingly extracted a tissue from her sleeve and wiped her eyes gently. 'I suppose we should just leave it to the police. They'll be able to figure things out.'

'I'm sure they will.' Marcel hesitated a little before going on. 'There may be much more to this than you think, Marianne,' he said, charily weighing his words. 'You may have to prepare yourself for some more bad news later today. I'm afraid this damage to your sister's grave may be part of a much bigger problem involving your nephew.'

Marcel had tried to choose his words carefully to delicately prepare the dead woman's sister for the worst but apparently his efforts were in vain. She reacted to the priest's words in shock and horror and quickly turned to face him as the two of them stood there before the desecrated grave. 'What are you saying, Father?' she asked in dismay. 'Are you suggesting that Guy vandalized his own mother's grave?'

'No, no, that's not what I'm saying at all, Marianne. I'm simply saying that we have to be ready to hear more from the police about this intrusion. It may be just coincidence that this particular grave has been vandalized, but I don't think so. I think it's been targeted for a particular reason.'

Marianne pulled out her tissues again and pressed them to her eyes. 'I don't understand any of this,' she sobbed. 'First my sister's grave is desecrated and now you tell me someone is trying to harm my nephew. What's going on, Father?'

'That's what we have to find out.' Marcel wanted to tell her more but he resisted the temptation. He remembered Sergeant Marchand's admonition to lie low and say nothing until after the arrest and although he felt sorry for the woman, his greatest fear now was for her unfortunate nephew. 'Tell me Marianne,' he said gently, placing a comforting arm on her shoulder, 'you said you went straight to Guy's house yesterday to tell him what had happened here in the churchyard. How did he react to that news?'

The fretful woman blew her nose loudly as she tried to compose herself. 'It was a dreadful ordeal,' she said miserably. 'Guy was out when I arrived but I have my own key and I let myself in. The storm was moving through the village about then and the thunder and lightening was horrific. It was very intense for a good half hour or more. I was getting worried about Guy being caught in it somewhere. He doesn't take care of himself, you know.'

'And did you have any idea where he was?'

'Well he's been spending a lot of time down by the river lately so I guessed that was where he'd be. I don't know what he's up to—he seems to go down there a lot to sit by the water.'

'You didn't go down there looking for him, did you?'

'Oh no. Eventually he came home soaked to the skin and that's when I told him what had happened. He was very upset about it of course and, strangely enough, his first thought was that his father had something to do with it. We talked about it for a while but in the end we both agreed that it was very unlikely that Denis would do such a dreadful thing to his wife's grave.'

Marcel bit his lip thoughtfully as he took in what Marianne was saying. 'Do you think these trips down to the river have anything to do with Fran's drowning last year?' he asked cautiously. 'I mean, is that still weighing heavily on his mind?'

'It could be, I suppose. He never talks to me about it. That part of his life is still a complete mystery to me. But he's always been fascinated with the rapids down there ever since he was a child. Jeanette took him to see the Niagara river once when he was about ten years old and he never forgot that trip. I think the St. Croix river reminds him of it and I suppose it reminds him of his mother too.'

The roar of a motorcycle engine from the road grabbed their attention and as the startled pair looked across, the unmistakable bulky figure of Denis LaPlante appeared at the main entrance to the churchyard. He stood there for a moment with his hands deep in the pockets of his greasy old jeans and then strode purposefully towards them. Marianne was in no mood for idle chatter with her obstreperous relative. 'I'm out of here,' she said resolutely. 'The last thing I need right now is a wrangle with that fellow.' With a quick turn on her lone crutch she fixed her sites on the back gates and hobbled off towards them with surprising speed and agility.

Denis seemed to be uncharacteristically docile as he approached the priest. 'What's up with her then?' he asked cagily as he watched his estranged sister-in-law disappear into the laneway beyond the church property. 'I suppose she's pissed off with me as usual.'

'I think she is a bit, Denis.' Marcel nodded towards Jeanette LaPlante's grave. 'She's terribly upset about this damage and who can blame her?'

Denis shook his head in surprise as he observed the mess. 'It's Jeanette's grave I've come to talk to you about, Reverend, but I wasn't expecting a mess like this. What the hell's going on?'

'You've heard about the vandalism, then? Was it you who reported it to the police?'

Denis reacted with a sardonic expression on his face as if the priest were completely out of his mind. 'What are you talking about, man?' he said scornfully. 'It was the police who informed me about it.'

'Really? They called you about the damage to your wife's grave?'

'I got a registered letter this morning telling me that they're going to dig up Jeanette's body. That's why I'm here. I want you to put a stop to it.'

Twenty

Marcel heard the words but he struggled to take them in. This news was totally unexpected. Why on earth would the police want to exhume Jeanette LaPlante's body and how would that help them with their case against Fran Bouchard's murderer? It didn't seem to make a lot of sense. 'I can't believe it,' he said incredulously, staring at the disturbed grave in front of him. 'Is that what this is all about?'

'You tell me, Reverend.' Denis sighed in frustration at the priest's apparent unawareness. 'Are you saying you didn't know anything about it?' he hissed. 'Surely the police would have to ask your permission before taking up a grave on church premises. I came here to see if you could stop this crazy project from happening. This is my wife's body we're talking about.'

Marcel shook his head apprehensively. 'This is very troubling, Denis,' he said. 'The police haven't told me anything about an exhumation and you're right—they should at least let me know what's going on. I've been away for a couple of days though and I understand the police have been trying to contact me on an urgent matter. I suppose they might have wanted to talk to me about your wife's grave. But from a legal point of view, I don't think the police would need my permission to exhume a body.'

'But you're the one in charge of church property, aren't you? Can't you prevent them from disturbing people's graves?'

'Not if it's part of a police investigation. They must have got permission from the government department dealing with these matters and there's nothing I can do about it. If they inform me at all, it would only be as a courtesy. As I say, I'm sure the police don't need any permission from me.'

Denis seemed annoyed and disappointed with this news, but with some obvious effort he managed to maintain his composure as if he realized his normal belligerent attitude would get him nowhere. 'Well I'm not going to take this nonsense lying down,' he said stubbornly. 'What right do they have to go digging up people's graves?'

'I suppose they must have their reasons.' Marcel knew he had to keep this unpredictable man calm. Denis LaPlante was known to be hot-tempered and volatile and although he seemed to be keeping his cool now, he was obviously uptight about the imminent exhumation. There was no way of knowing how he might react if things didn't go his way. The priest had to think fast. 'Why don't we go inside?' he said sympathetically. 'I'll get Mme Poirier to make us some coffee and we can see what this is all about.'

It was an unexpected invitation but the anxious fellow hesitated for only a moment before accepting. 'Well, as I say, that's what I'm here for and I'd appreciate any help you can give me. I can tell you, Reverend, I don't want anyone digging up Jeanette's grave.'

The two men slowly made their way to the priest's residence. It seemed strange to be inviting Denis LaPlante in for coffee and Marcel felt a little on edge about it. After all, he'd tended to avoid this difficult man during his short time in the village and with the many negative comments he'd heard from Marianne and Gaston, and even from Guy himself, the priest couldn't help feeling a bit wary about dealing with him on such a delicate matter. Yet he seemed to be calm enough now and perhaps he should be treated no differently from any parishioner in need of kindness and understanding.

Mme Poirier looked quite shocked as the pair entered the front doors. 'Oh, my goodness, Monsieur LaPlante,' she stammered, staring with wide eyes at the unkempt mechanic. 'It's not often we see you around here.' She hurriedly focussed her attention on Marcel before Denis had a chance to answer. 'Is there anything I can get for you, Father?'

'Coffee would be great, Louise. We'll be in the lounge.' The apprehensive expression on the housekeepers face seemed to be sending a message loud and clear—keep that man's greasy clothes off my furniture—but after a moment's hesitation she scurried off to the kitchen to oblige with a fresh pot of coffee.

'Take a seat, Denis,' Marcel said, going through the motions. 'If you want me to help you'll have to give me a bit more information. I'm sure this letter from the police didn't come as a complete shock—I mean the police don't decide to exhume a body for no reason at all, do they?'

The bulky mechanic was obviously uncomfortable with the priest's probing but he seemed to realize that some kind of explanation was required. 'It's all been a stupid misunderstanding,' he mumbled grudgingly. 'I suppose I'd better tell you about it.'

Marcel had to be careful. He realized that Denis LaPlante would assume the village pastor knew nothing about his son's psychiatric counselling and the ongoing conflict he'd had with Pierre Bouchard and his wife. But it would be better that way, he thought, and there'd be nothing to gain by telling him otherwise. 'Tell me about it,' he said innocently. 'Start from the beginning.'

Denis leaned back in his chair and sighed heavily. 'It was something I said as a joke when my son came to live with me in Fredericton last year,' he said. 'We were supposed to be starting a small business and Guy wasn't coming through with the money he'd promised. I got angry about it and I said some stupid things.'

'I didn't think Guy had any money,' Marcel interrupted. 'I've been giving him small jobs around the church for the last six months to help him make ends meet.'

'I don't suppose he has much cash but it's that house of his. It's worth a lot of money. My wife left it to him and he'd promised to sell it before he moved in with me. We'd agreed to put the proceeds into a new business venture. That never happened though. My sister-in-law talked him out of it, stupid bitch, so it messed everything up for us and it led to a lot of hard feelings between me and my son.'

'And what's this joke you're talking about? What did you say to him?'

Denis raised his eyes to the ceiling, as if he were embarrassed to go on. 'I'd been drinking,' he said, 'and I started bugging him about some wine he and Gaston Leduc made years ago when they were kids. His mother died of a heart attack when he was about sixteen and I stupidly told him it was the homemade wine that killed her. He took his mother's death very hard at the time and he went crazy when I told him it was all his fault. It wasn't true of course and I shouldn't have said it. I know that now. The thing is, he took it all too seriously—I didn't think he'd have taken it so bad.'

Marcel furrowed his brow disapprovingly. 'It's pretty bad though, Denis. I can't believe you'd say such a thing to your son. I think anyone would have reacted strongly to such a dreadful accusation. What did he do about it?'

'Well he packed up and left right then and there. I couldn't stop him. I found out later he lived on the streets for two weeks before someone felt sorry for him and gave him a job and a room in some run-down workshop—some kind of small engine repair shop I think.'

The priest knew what happened next but he feigned ignorance. 'And did that work out for him?' he asked nonchalantly. 'I mean is that where he stayed until he returned to the village?'

'No, he didn't—that's the problem. He seemed to go off the deep end soon after that and he ended up in the psychiatric department in the Fredericton Research Hospital. Those two Bouchard quacks messed him up real good and he's never been the same since.'

'You mean he was receiving psychiatric treatment from Doctor Bouchard?'

'That's what they called it. It was Bouchard's wife who was the main problem though. She was worse than him. Guy stupidly told her he'd poisoned his wife, even though he didn't have a wife, and that silly bitch took it all seriously. Next thing I knew she was giving me a hard time over it and no amount of explaining would get her off my back. I told her it was just a stupid joke but she wouldn't have it. She said she needed to check it out.'

The agitated man's rant was interrupted as the door opened and Mme Poirier entered with fresh coffee. She looked disapprovingly at the hulking visitor perched on her spotless couch before carefully placing the loaded tray on the coffee table. 'Anything else, Father?' she asked quietly, obviously hoping for a negative answer. 'Or is that it?'

The preoccupied priest waved her away. 'It's fine, Louise. 'Thank you.' Marcel waited until the door closed behind his housekeeper before going on. 'What does all this have to do with exhuming your wife's body?' he asked pointedly. 'You're telling me Fran Bouchard knew Guy wasn't married and still she took the story about his imaginary wife seriously. Are you saying she just assumed he was talking about his mother? It seems a bit odd doesn't it?'

Denis snorted derisively. 'I don't know what the hell she thought. I gave her a piece of my mind several times but she never came out and told me what she was trying to do. I know Guy got worse and worse—he didn't know whether he was coming or going. That woman seemed to have some kind of hold on him and the next thing I knew she was taking him back to Maplewood Creek. I went mad about that but there was nothing I could do.'

'What about Pierre Bouchard? Did you talk to him about it?'

'I couldn't talk to him. He gave me a hard time when I started making a nuisance of myself and eventually he had me banned from the hospital. They wouldn't let me anywhere near the place after that.'

Marcel poured out two mugs of coffee and handed one to his cantankerous guest. 'I can see why you'd be angry and frustrated,' he said. 'But was there any talk of exhuming your wife's body at the time? I understand you all ended up at Guy's house when you returned to Maplewood Creek and you had a heated discussion with Pierre Bouchard about the whole thing. What came out of that?'

'No one mentioned digging up the grave when we got back to the village but I was worried about them doing just that. Frances Bouchard, said she just wanted to talk to Dr. Martin about it and check Guy's medical records. I was still trying to tell her she was taking it all too seriously and that husband of hers agreed with me, but he didn't have the balls to make her drop it once and for all.'

'And it was that same afternoon that Fran Bouchard drowned in the St. Croix River, wasn't it? When did you find out about that?'

Denis was clearly uncomfortable with that subject. He placed his still full coffee mug on the table and folded his arms tightly across his chest. 'That's the thing, Reverend,' he mumbled uneasily. 'This is where I need your help. That drowning is really the main reason why I came to talk to you today.'

There was a definite change in Denis's manner now and he twitched nervously as if he were about to make a monumental confession of guilt. Marcel saw a weakness that might possibly reveal some vital new information and he forged boldly ahead. 'What do you mean by that?' he asked firmly. 'What do you know about that tragic death?'

The fretful mechanic didn't answer immediately. He swallowed hard and then looked directly at the priest. 'It was Guy who killed her, Father,' he stammered. 'I got him to admit that to me about three months ago but I have to tell you—it's not his fault. He's a sick man and he doesn't know what he's doing most of the time. I can't hand him over to the police—not my own son. But I think he should give himself up. He needs to be in a safe institution somewhere so he can be properly looked after.'

An awkward and eerie silence followed this unexpected outburst. Marcel felt at a loss for words but the shocking allegation seemed to confirm what he'd feared all along. Everything seemed to be falling into place now. Gaston's suspicions about his long-time friend, as well as Pierre Bouchard's intense involvement with the disturbed young man, only added more credibility to what Denis LaPlante was saying.

It seemed certain now that Guy was about to be arrested, but Marcel needed to hear more. 'I know this must be very difficult for you, Denis,' he said gently. 'I can see your dilemma. But I'm still a bit confused about this business with your wife's grave. Is there some connection between Fran Bouchard's death and your son's home-made wine? I mean, why do the police want to exhume your wife's body? What does that have to do with Fran's drowning?'

The agitated man sat bolt upright on the edge of his chair, his eyes blazing with anger. 'Don't you see, Reverend?' he snapped impatiently. 'That quack must have figured out that Guy killed Fran Bouchard and he's determined to get him nailed for it. I can only hope he's taking Guy's mental condition into account. Bouchard has been working on my son ever since he arrived in the village last March—I know that for a fact—but obviously he can't prove anything so he's resurrected the poison wine story to try and get Guy behind bars that way. If they can concoct some evidence that Guy poisoned his mother, that could be presented as a motive for killing Frances Bouchard who was on to him. Pierre Bouchard must have heard all about that home-made wine from his wife and now he's using that ridiculous story to bring murder charges against my son. That's why he's got the police working on it. Obviously they want to dig Jeanette up to do some kind of phoney testing so they can get my son convicted.'

Marcel frowned sceptically. 'But that doesn't make a whole lot of sense, does it? Wouldn't an exhumation be the best thing, Denis? I mean, if they do forensic testing on your wife's remains it should prove once and for all that she wasn't poisoned and then at least Guy will be in the clear on that charge. The drowning death is another matter and we can deal with that separately. Maybe we should just cooperate with the police for now and let them get on with the exhumation.'

Denis shook his head vehemently. 'I don't trust them,' he spit out scornfully. 'You never know what they can come up with. And in any case, I don't want my wife's grave to be disturbed. That's a very personal thing, you know. Jeanette and I had our differences but I wouldn't want to see her disrespected like that.'

That sentiment hit home with unexpected force. 'Yes, I can understand that,' the priest said with genuine understanding. 'I wouldn't want my wife's grave to be disturbed either.' Marcel suddenly felt some empathy for this rough man's plight and he thought of

Clara's grave respectfully settled in a peaceful Montreal cemetery. He remembered how he had lovingly arranged everything after her funeral and made sure that her grave would always be properly maintained. It would be quite traumatic to have it disturbed now, he thought. And yet if it were absolutely essential—if it would save an innocent man from being unjustly blamed he was sure he'd agree to it.

The priest looked quizzically at his unlikely guest. 'As I say, Denis, I can understand how upsetting this must be for you, but I think we have to put your son's welfare first and we have to do what's best for him. We can't risk having him blamed for something he didn't do, can we? And even if we could prevent the exhumation, I don't see how that would help him?'

The frustrated mechanic struggled to remain calm as he listened to the priest's words. 'Well as I've told you,' he said pointedly, 'I've been trying to convince Guy that he must give himself up and confess to the murder of Fran Bouchard. It's the only way. That would put a stop to this nonsense about Jeanette's grave. If my son is charged with murder I'm sure the courts will take his mental illness into account. The worst that can happen is that he'd be placed in an institution for the criminally insane.'

Marcel was horrified at the thought. 'Guy would die in a place like that,' he said, appalled that such a solution could be mentioned so casually. 'He is not so disturbed that he could be considered criminally insane. I hope it would never come to that.'

'So what do you suggest?'

'Well I agree that confession to the police might be a good idea but I think we should be making a case for accidental drowning. My understanding is that your son felt very affectionate towards Fran Bouchard and it's hard to imagine that he really wished to harm her. It may well have been just a terrible accident. Guy is suffering from a lot of guilt and you may have pushed him too hard. Even though you say he has admitted to causing Fran's death, I don't think he means it.'

'Well that would be up to the police and courts to decide, I suppose. The main thing is that he should give himself up. This has been going on too long.'

There was a brief lull in the conversation as the two men mulled over what had been said. It was obvious that Denis LaPlante had no inkling about the imminent arrest and the priest did not feel at liberty to tell him about it.

Sergeant Marchand had made it quite clear that he expected confidentiality and cooperation and Marcel was sure he'd already crossed the line just by having this meeting with the suspect's father. He didn't want to be accused of jeopardizing police work and in any case, he thought, although he could sympathize with this jittery man's concerns about his wife's grave, there were still one or two things that needed to be explained—like why was he so uptight about Pierre Bouchard's apparent efforts to have Guy charged and convicted, for example, when he himself was trying to persuade his unfortunate son to give himself up? Whether Pierre Bouchard or Denis himself got the ball rolling, the results would be exactly the same. Guy would end up in custody.

Marcel broached the subject carefully. 'You are aware that Guy has been receiving counselling and therapy from Dr. Bouchard over the last six months, aren't you?' he asked casually. 'I think you said you knew about it.'

'I knew about it, sure. Guy told me he was seeing him.'

'And you didn't mind about that?'

'No, why should I?'

'Well, it's just that you told me how angry you were when Fran Bouchard was treating your son up in Fredericton and you made it clear that you had no time for Pierre Bouchard either. You weren't happy at all about his taking over the medical practice in the village, were you? And yet you say you didn't mind when Guy started to have regular counselling sessions with him.'

The heavy man shuffled uneasily in his seat. 'It's not the counselling as such,' he said impatiently. 'It was the home-made wine thing that got me pissed off. That woman was trying to make a case out of nothing and she kept giving me a hard time over it.'

'But you seem to have a lot of animosity towards Pierre Bouchard as well.'

'It's true I don't care for him either but I figured if he's the doctor down here there's nothing I can do about it. Guy needs medical care like anyone else. I didn't make a fuss about him going to Bouchard for counselling at the time and I still don't have a problem with the therapy itself. But things are getting out of hand now. I'm pissed off at the quack for reopening that stupid nonsense about the wine and getting the police to mess about with my wife's grave.'

'Yes, you've made that quite clear, but what did you think would come out of the therapy? You knew that Dr. Bouchard was a psychiatrist, didn't you? Did you think Guy would benefit from a program of psychotherapy?'

'I knew Bouchard was a shrink because I'd dealt with him up in Fredericton but, as I said, I've been trying to get Guy to give himself up and I thought if Bouchard was treating him for mental problems that would all be in his favour if it came to a court case.

They'd have proper records and the courts would be told that my son has a few mental problems. They'd take all that into account.'

Marcel frowned heavily at this heartless approach. 'It sounds to me like you don't really care too much about what happens to your son,' he said. 'Guy needs some support and understanding, regardless of what he's done. Surely you must care about that.'

The mechanic showed signs of being pushed to far. 'Of course I care about him,' he snapped angrily, 'but he needs proper attention in a place that specializes in his kind of problems—a safe and secure place.'

'But it's really just Jeanette's grave that's bothering you now, isn't it? You really don't want your wife's remains to be exhumed, do you? Even if it will get your son off the hook? That's what you seem to be telling me?'

Denis sighed in frustration. 'Of course I'd agree to an exhum—having her dug up, if it would help him but I'm saying if Guy admits to causing Frances Bouchard's death, whether it was accidental or not, there'd be no need to dig up my wife. All Bouchard wants is to get Guy put away and he doesn't care how he does it.'

There was so much more to this saga than Denis LaPlante realized. Pierre Bouchard obviously knew whether Guy had caused his wife's death or not because it would have come out in the counselling sessions. According to Gaston's story, Pierre was actually present when the incident occurred and if that's true, it could lend some credibility to Denis's story.

Denis could be right about the need to find viable proof and evidence. It would be difficult to charge Guy with murder when there were only the two of them present at the murder scene and perhaps Pierre had been trying to extract a confession all along.

Marcel couldn't reveal any of this information to the agitated mechanic who sat there anticipating some kind of helpful solution to his dilemma. He'd find out soon enough though when the police made an arrest and he'd have to deal with it then.

This seemed like a good time to end the awkward meeting anyway and Marcel stood up indicating that enough had been said. 'I'm not sure where all this is leading, Denis,' he said firmly. 'I don't know if I can stop an exhumation at this point and I'm not even sure I want to. But it's pretty clear the police have already done some kind of an assessment at the grave site—they've been poking around and they've broken the head stone in the process. They obviously intend to get on with it and I don't think there's a thing I can do to stop it.'

Denis rose reluctantly from his chair, now looking quite vulnerable and unsure of himself. 'In that case I'll have to see Guy right away,' he mumbled. 'He's going to have to give himself up before it's too late.'

'Have you told him about the letter?'

'I haven't had a chance. I was over here yesterday afternoon but he wasn't home and I couldn't find him anywhere. I checked out Gaston's gas bar—I thought he might have been spending some time there but then that storm blew in and I ended up just getting soaked.' The cumbersome man shuffled uneasily towards the door. 'Anyway I'll tell him about the letter now if I can find him. He's going to be pretty upset about it.'

Marcel opened the front door for his visitor, relieved that he was leaving but feeling slightly sorry for him as well. 'You might try the river if he's not home, Denis,' he said kindly. 'Marianne said he's been spending a lot of time down there recently. But go easy on him—he's going to need all the help and support he can get.'

Twenty-One

Marcel stood at the open door and watched Denis LaPlante as he hurried through the iron gates at the end of the stone pathway and into the roadway beyond. The overgrown bushes partly obscured the priest's view but he could make out the mechanic's bulky frame as he hastily mounted his motorcycle and roared off down the hill. This decisive action, quite ordinary in itself, was a powerful defining moment in the saga of Fran Bouchard's murder. Denis was clearly a man with a mission and it was all too evident now that this was the beginning of the end.

Even as he stood there, still unsure about the wisdom of Denis's plan, Marcel knew that there was no time to lose. Two courses of action were relentlessly unfolding, and though they were occurring independently they were destined to collide in a finale of violence and intimidation. Would this intolerant man be capable of dealing with that? Would he provide his son with proper support and defence through this traumatic ordeal or would he just as soon throw him to the wolves?

The wheels of justice were already in motion and Chief Inspector Boivin and his team could arrive in the village at any moment to execute the arrest of Guy LaPlante. Marcel was determined to be present when that happened. Someone had to provide guidance and support to the unfortunate young man in the midst of all this accusation and blame.

There was a sense of urgency in the air now. The priest hastily slammed the front door behind him and he hurried down the stone pathway towards the main road. He knew where he needed to be now and he had no time to waste in getting there. As he reached the main gates a thought suddenly occurred to him and he stopped dead in his tracks. He turned and looked back at the rows of grave stones extending across the churchyard to the far side of the property and he realized that he couldn't leave without checking the ruined grave site once more. The intrusion on Jeanette LaPlante's grave had taken on a new significance now with the knowledge that the disturbance was no petty vandalism. It was obviously caused by a preliminary assessment for a police-mandated exhumation and it clearly warranted a closer look. With sudden resolve Marcel backtracked to make an assessment of his own.

The grave diggers had been determined all right but it was obvious that they'd decided not to proceed—at least for now. Marcel tried to logically assess the preliminary work that had been done. He could see how it would be necessary to remove the heavy headstone first as its weight would have impeded the removal of the stone frame that encompassed the entire grave. The workers had obviously managed to do that but it was quite evident that they'd carelessly thrown the headstone to the ground, and that would account for why it was broken in two.

They had started to dig around the sides of the grave too, probably as part of their feasibility assessment, but the work was obviously abandoned at that point. Perhaps they realized that this site was extremely narrow and it would be very difficult to exhume a body from it without disturbing the graves on either side. This would be particularly true if the ground was wet. The heavy storm had swept through the village in the late afternoon but any hint of bad weather would have been sufficient to call off such a delicate job. The laws governing a legal exhumation were very strict and any official authorization for such a project would require a guarantee that no damage would be caused to neighbouring grave sites.

Marcel scratched his head as he stared at the damaged grave. Is this exhumation really necessary, he wondered, and do the police really intend to continue their work here? Being a widower himself, Marcel could understand why Denis was so opposed to having his wife's body exhumed and subjected to forensic testing. It would be a traumatic experience for him and a disrespectful intrusion on the deceased. Perhaps he was right in trying to prevent it. After all, it was Fran's death that was at the centre of this murder investigation, not Jeanette's, and it was not clear how this exhumation would contribute any useful evidence to the murder case.

The priest knew he couldn't prevent the police from exhuming Jeanette's body, nor did he want to if it was useful and relevant, but he felt he needed some kind of explanation. After all, he was the pastor here and did have some authority on church property. Chief Inspector Boivin had not informed him about what was going on and that, he thought, was unacceptable.

Marcel glanced at his watch. It was close to noon now and he needed to be on his way to Gaston's gas bar but he couldn't leave yet. Some sort of security had to be provided for the grave. It had to be protected from any further damage until it could be determined whether the exhumation was absolutely necessary. He remembered seeing a length of yellow rope hanging in the garage and he rushed across the churchyard to retrieve it. A handful of sturdy garden stakes and a large piece of plywood provided him with all the materials he needed and after rooting out a wooden mallet and a thick black marker, he quickly headed back to the grave site to complete the job.

Within minutes the site was neatly bordered off with forbidding yellow rope and a prominent sign attached to one of the stakes that read: "Please consult the pastor before undertaking any further work on this grave". The priest stepped back and briefly inspected his work. There, he said to himself, that tells them who's in charge around here. With a slight nod of satisfaction he threw down the mallet on the narrow grass verge and hurriedly got on his way.

The steep hill down to the train station was no problem during a casual walk but it could be an annoying obstacle when one was in a hurry. Marcel walked briskly, ignoring the strain in his legs and intent only on reaching Gaston's place as quickly as possible. He could see the roof of the gas bar beyond the station and he pressed on with ever-increasing urgency, confident that Gaston would be there on this quiet Wednesday afternoon. Business was slow at the best of times and unless the multi-tasked entrepreneur had been called out on a taxi run he'd more than likely be sitting in the forecourt eating his lunch.

As it happened, Gaston was washing down the pumps when the priest staggered breathlessly into his humble premises. He looked up in surprise and hurriedly shut of the water supply to his hose as his visitor approached. 'Father Marcel,' he said pleasantly, 'I didn't expect to see you so soon. Is everything all right?'

'I wish I could say it was.' Marcel pointed to the cramped office at the side of the building. 'We need to talk, Gaston. It's about Guy. Everything seems to be coming to a head now and we need to act before it's too late. I think your friend may be in need of some urgent support and assistance.'

The two men walked briskly across the forecourt and Gaston, taken aback at the sudden urgency, anxiously pushed open the flimsy door to his business quarters. 'What's happened, Father?' he asked apprehensively. 'Have they finally caught up with him?'

Marcel sat down heavily on one of the hard wooden chairs beside the counter. 'You could say that, Gaston,' he said grimly, 'and much sooner than I expected. Even as we speak, the police are on his trail. I think they'll be taking him in this afternoon and I'm concerned that he'll have no one to stand up for him. Can you close shop for a while and come with me? I'm on my way down to his place now. I just want someone to be with him when the police arrive.'

'Well, yes, of course.' Gaston was obviously concerned about these developments and he took on a serious tone as he hurriedly removed his work coat and hung it on the back of the office door. 'I'll do whatever

I can,' he said. 'But are you saying the police are about to arrest him in connection with Fran Bouchard's death. I mean, surely they're not going to charge him with murder after all this time?'

'I really don't know what the charges will be.' Marcel weighed his words carefully. 'I spoke to the police this morning and they told me very little. All I know for sure is that they'll be making an arrest this afternoon. They've made it clear they don't want me involved. I shouldn't really be telling you any of this but I can't just sit back and do nothing. Guy is one of my most needy parishioners and I intend to give him all the support I can.'

Gaston sat down on the only other chair available and began to unlace his work boots. 'What about his dad?' he asked cagily. 'Has anyone told him what's going on?'

'I've just had a long chat with Denis and he doesn't know anything about the impending arrest, but I'm a bit worried about him now—he was in quite a state when he left the parish residence about an hour ago.' Marcel sighed heavily. 'That man is a bit of an anomaly. I don't really trust him but my housekeeper seems to think he genuinely cares about his son despite his aggressive attitude. I can only hope she's right.'

Gaston grimaced. 'I don't know about that,' he said cynically. 'I've always found him to be a bit of a bully. I've never known him to have anything but his own interests at heart. What's he mad about now?'

'Well, apparently the police want to exhume his wife's body for forensic testing and he's is furious about it. I can't say I blame him—it must be quite traumatic for him and he doesn't really understand why that would be necessary. He was hoping I could somehow have it stopped.'

Gaston paled at this news and stared at the priest in disbelief. 'You mean they're still taking that home-made wine thing seriously? I thought Dr. Bouchard's wife had put that story to rest once and for all.'

'Apparently not. I know she took it seriously at the time and I'm assuming she reported it to the police before she left Fredericton. That probably explains what's going on now. The police must believe Fran was murdered because of what she knew about the poisoned wine.'

'But I've told you, Father. That wine was not poisonous. It was completely harmless.'

'Yes, Gaston, I'm sure it was—but I don't think the police believe that. And more to the point, if Guy is still worried about it he obviously has his doubts too. Don't forget it was his guilt feelings about that wine that took him to Fran Bouchard's office in the first place.'

'I know, I know, but that was just Guy's imagination running wild. Surely Dr. Bouchard would be able to explain that to the police.'

'Actually I'm not sure he would. But anyway, rightly or wrongly, I think the police see some connection between the death of Jeanette LaPlante and Fran's drowning. They may be trying to establish a clear motive for her murder and obviously they think a forensic test on Jeanette's remains will help them to provide that.' Marcel paused and thought for a minute. 'Do you see what I mean? If Guy poisoned his mother, even accidentally, and Fran knew about it, the police would think that could be a motive for her murder.'

Gaston put away his work boots and pulled on his shoes. 'It doesn't look good, does it?' he said gloomily. 'I never thought it would come to this.'

'Neither did I but it's something I've been afraid of all along.' The priest stood up and peered through the office window at the medical centre across the road. 'I need to get a few things clear with Dr. Bouchard too', he said thoughtfully. 'I'm still a bit confused about his involvement and what he knows about this imminent arrest. Actually, I was thinking I should ask him to come with us to Guy's house.'

'I know Guy trusts him. Do you think he'd be able to help?'

'Possibly, but Denis is with his son at the moment and he could be a bit of a problem. As you know, he's been at loggerheads with Dr. Bouchard for a long time now and I don't want to stir things up any more than necessary. He's down at Guy's house as we speak telling him about the police plans for an exhumation.'

Gaston opened the door and ushered his visitor out onto the forecourt. 'Actually you're too late anyway, Father,' he said. 'I saw Dr. Bouchard leaving the medical centre just before you arrived.'

Marcel raised his eyebrows enquiringly. 'Really?' he said, intrigued with this small piece of information. 'Was he driving or walking? I mean he wasn't leaving the village, was he?'

'I've no idea where he was going but he left with a blond lady in a flashy BMW. I've seen her around here quite a lot over the past few months. They seemed to be on some urgent business today, judging by the way she squealed the tires out of here.'

Marcel stopped abruptly and looked tight-lipped at his young friend. He'd forgotten about the mysterious blond woman in the BMW but now it seemed that her association with Pierre might be relevant in some way. 'I saw that woman when I was down here last weekend,' he said. 'and my housekeeper tells me she was trying to contact me while I was away. Have you any idea who she is?'

'Not a clue, but I've seen her around here two or three times this week. It's the car that gets my attention—she always parks opposite the gas bar and I can't resist ogling it. What would I give to own a set of wheels like that?'

The priest frowned, showing a hint of impatience. The car was of no interest to him at the moment and he only wanted to determine what this woman's business was and whether it related to Guy LaPlante's troubles. 'Was there anyone else with them?' he asked pointedly. 'I mean, did she arrive alone or with someone else?'

'Come to think of it, there was some big guy in a dark suit sitting in the passenger seat. It was quite funny actually. Dr. Bouchard had to squeeze into the back and he looked very uncomfortable all hunched up with his head jammed against the roof. There's not much of a back seat in a sports car like that, you know.'

Marcel tried to make sense of this unexpected activity. What if Denis was right about Pierre Bouchard's role in the arrest and conviction of Guy LaPlante? What if he'd used psychiatric counselling over the past few months to get Guy to admit to his responsibility for Fran's tragic death? This mysterious blond woman could be a colleague of his—perhaps a specialist like Fran Bouchard who'd be able to extract some sort of confession that might hold up in court. If that was the case, Pierre and this woman must be working with the police and they might well be on their way to Guy's house at this very moment—in fact, if that's where they were headed they would have already arrived.

'What are you thinking, Father? Are we going or not?'

Marcel nodded towards Gaston's grungy vehicle and headed briskly towards it. 'We're going,' he said sharply. 'I could be wrong but I have a bad feeling about this. Can you drive us down there right now, Gaston? We have no time to lose.'

The two men hurriedly jumped into the ramshackle taxi and with a screech of grinding gears Gaston hit the road and headed for the west side of the village. The sense of urgency was palpable now and the young mechanic struggled to make sense of it as he manoeuvred through the narrow village streets. 'What are you expecting to find, Father,' he asked somewhat bewildered at the priest's grim silence. 'Do you think Dr. Bouchard is already down there?'

'He may well be. We'll know soon enough.'

It was a short distance to Guy's place and in only a matter of minutes the priest and his reticent assistant arrived at the plush property by the river. The silver BMW was parked in full view behind Denis LaPlante's motorcycle outside the main entrance and, more ominously, a plate armoured police vehicle waited some distance down the road for its unwilling guest.

Marcel jumped out of the taxi and impatiently slammed the rickety door behind him. 'I knew it,' he said with some disappointment in his voice. 'The police are obviously here already and Pierre and his blond friend have beaten us to it.'

Gaston looked puzzled at the priest's concern. 'But does that really matter?' he asked. 'Surely the more support Guy can get the better things will turn out for him.'

The priest placed a friendly hand on his companion's shoulder. 'That's the problem, Gaston,' he said quietly. 'I hope he'll get the support he needs but I'm afraid Dr. Bouchard may not be on his side. You'll have to prepare yourself for that.' He pointed bravely to the imposing front doors. 'Let's see what's going on in there.'

Marcel was determined to make his presence felt though he was quite unsure about how his bold actions would play themselves out. He marched resolutely down the stone pathway to the impressive entrance with Gaston at his heels. His heart was pounding now but the rush of adrenalin only spurred him on. He tugged confidently at the iron knob protruding from the ornate stonework at the side of the door. The old-fashioned doorbell activated immediately and Marcel could hear the astonishing jangle of bells emanating from the heart of the house. He looked bemusedly at his young friend. 'They can't really miss that, can they?' he said grinning forcefully in an attempt to put Gaston at ease. 'They might not be happy to see us but they can hardly ignore us.'

There was no response to the toll of excessive door bells and after repeating the performance several times, Marcel peered through the ornate frame of coloured glass that surrounded the door, cupping his hands around his face and straining his eyes to see any sign of life within. 'They're obviously not here,' he mumbled, vexed at this unwanted roadblock. 'But they must be around somewhere. Maybe they've gone outside—in the back garden perhaps.'

Gaston pointed to the side of the house and led the way. 'Guy does spend a lot of time outside,' he said confidently. 'He could have been sitting out back when this mob arrived. Follow me, Father—I usually take this pathway through the rose bushes.' Everything was still soaked after the storm and Gaston cautiously pushed his way through the overgrown shrubbery to the neglected garden at the back. He stepped hesitatingly onto the slippery stones of the deserted patio, noting with some bated amusement that the empty beer bottles from his previous visit still littered the otherwise impressive stonework. 'Not here, either,' he said grimly. 'That leaves us with one obvious place to look.'

The priest walked slowly to the edge of the patio and stared at the thick wooded area beyond the bounds of Guy's property. 'You mean the river, I suppose? Marianne said he's been spending all his time down there recently, still brooding over Fran Bouchard's tragic death.'

Gaston nodded in agreement. 'That's right,' he said. 'I'm sure that's where he'll be. He's attracted to that river like a moth to a candle.'

Marcel wondered now if he'd been wise to tell Denis where his son could be found so easily. This furious stretch of the St. Croix river was a dangerous place, especially for an emotionally disturbed young man like Guy LaPlante, and there was no way of knowing how he would react to news about his mother's impending exhumation. And that wasn't the only concern. How would he react to a posse of police officers telling him he was being arrested for murder. Guy was obviously still depressed about Fran Bouchard's death and it was very frightening indeed to imagine what he might do if he happened to be anywhere near the spot where she drowned when his whole world came crashing down. 'We've got to get down there, Gaston' he said with a hint of panic in his voice. 'Come on, let's go. Your old friend desperately needs us.'

Gaston had taken this path down to the river hundreds of times before and he insisted on leading the way. 'There are two trails through the woods,' he explained as he made his way to the bottom of the overgrown garden. 'After all the rain I think we'd better take the wider one, even though it's a bit further away.

You've got to watch out for the poison ivy though. It tends to grow in patches right through the wooded area and along the river bank; you can be in a whole heap of trouble if you don't recognize it. Stick to the trail—that's your best bet.'

Marcel sighed impatiently. 'There are more important things to worry about at the moment,' he mumbled edgily. 'I don't care about the poison ivy—just lead me down to the river by the shortest route.'

The well-worn path to the woods was clearly defined through frequent use but it was wet and muddy in places and the pair had to proceed with caution. As they approached the still soaked trees, the roar of the rapids beyond seemed louder than ever and it was evident that the violent storm of the previous day had swelled the river to unusually high levels. Marcel shuddered at the frightening sound. 'Listen to that roar,' he said anxiously. 'These waters are dangerous at the best of times but after all the rain they'll be treacherous. This is not the best place to be giving Guy bad news about his mother's exhumation and it's definitely not the best place to tell him he's under arrest for murder. I just hope the police know what they're doing.'

Marcel felt an urgent need to pick up the pace now as they entered the woods but Gaston was blocking his way as he cautiously pushed through the sodden undergrowth, poking here and there for poison ivy. Growing frustration was evident in Marcel's voice. 'Let me get past you,' he barked impatiently, 'I want to get to the river right now before it's too late.' He hurriedly squeezed by his companion, brushing against thorny twigs that mercilessly scratched his unprotected hands.

Finally free of obstruction, the priest forged ahead, pushing away overhanging branches and trampling down any foliage that happened to be in his way. The roar of the rapids was his guide now and he tenaciously followed their beckoning call, intent only on finding Guy and offering whatever support he could against the traumatic occurrence that was about to befall him—an experience that might quite literally push him over the edge.

In his haste and panic, Marcel soon strayed from the main trail. He found himself fighting through the thick scrub and shrubbery that encroached on him from both sides, but the determined priest bravely soldiered on, ignoring the sharp unyielding branches that tortured his hands. Suddenly he broke through the foliage to the banks of the river and through sweat-filled eyes he could make out the blurred images of two familiar figures some thirty yards along the river bank.

The bulky frame of Denis LaPlante was unmistakable as he stood there gazing at the thunderous white water that came crashing down onto the rocks below. His vulnerable son was standing close to him and the pair were apparently engaged in deep conversation. Marcel felt strangely comforted by the fact that Denis had placed a friendly hand on his son's shoulder. At least that poor young fellow has his father's support, he thought. Their relationship may have been strained and tumultuous for a long time but at least it seems now that he has family by his side in his hour of need.

Marcel stood motionless for a moment as he absorbed this scene. It would be safe now to tell Denis and Guy about the imminent arrest, he thought, and perhaps the three of them could face the police together. Guy would then at least have the combined support of his father and his pastor before undertaking the sad journey to Saint Stephen where no doubt formal charges would be laid. The priest was about to approach the ill-fated pair when his attention was suddenly drawn to two figures hurriedly emerging from the bushes further up the river. It was the blond woman, accompanied by a powerful looking man in a dark suit whose overall appearance left no doubt about his police credentials. As they moved towards the sad duo on the river bank, a dishevelled Pierre Bouchard also appeared and followed at some distance behind.

The blond woman led the way, marching purposefully towards Guy and his father and as she grew nearer she pulled out an impressive silver police badge which she held high above her head. 'Monsieur LaPlante,' she barked out with intimidating authority, 'I'm Detective Inspector Boivin and this is my colleague, Detective Sergeant Marchand.'

Denis swirled around in surprise, his arm still firmly wrapped around his son's shoulder. 'What the hell…,' he began, but he was sternly cut off as the woman continued.

'Denis LaPlante, I'm arresting you for the murder of your wife, Jeanette LaPlante. You are not obliged to say anything at this time, but anything you do say will be taken down and may be used in evidence against you.'

Twenty-Two

Denis LaPlante's response to the sudden intrusion was swift and violent. 'Get back you bitch,' he snarled, grabbing his frail son from behind in a powerful two-armed grip. 'One step closer and this boy's in the river.'

The aggressive reaction was obviously unexpected. Inspector Boivin was momentarily thrown off guard as the hefty fellow spat out his brutal message and her detective sergeant who had moved forward to initiate the arrest was stopped dead in his tracks. A few seconds of agonizing hesitation followed before the murderous mechanic continued his vicious warning. 'I'm not bluffing,' he bellowed furiously over the roar of white water rushing through the rocks. 'This son of mine has caused me more than enough grief and I'm not above dispatching with him here and now. Get back both of you. I've no intention of being arrested—I'll take the two of us into the river if it comes to that.'

Marcel felt his heart pounding in his chest as he observed this shocking encounter and he realized that he had been totally wrong in his assessment of the dramatic arrest that was now underway. He should have known all along, he told himself. This is not about Guy. It's that dreadful father of his who's being charged with murder. And not for the murder of Fran Bouchard it seems, but for the murder of his wife, Jeannette LaPlante. How could I have been so wrong?

The priest was completely taken aback with this unexpected turn of events but at least it was crystal clear now that Guy LaPlante was nothing but a pawn in this deadly game. There was no doubt about it. He was an innocent victim in urgent need of support and protection.

Denis LaPlante's eyes were focussed intently on the police as he scrutinized them for any sign of movement towards him, but Inspector Boivin and her right hand man were rooted to the spot, obviously unsure of their next move. They were caught between a rock and a hard place and they needed to assess the situation carefully before they could make any further progress. A rash decision on their part now could well lead to disastrous consequences for the pathetic young man passively standing there in his father's unyielding grip.

Marcel was struck by the fact that Guy showed no sign of fear and seemed to be strangely compliant with his insufferable tormenter. He was making no attempt to struggle free, and he stood there placidly, almost as if he had a quiet conviction that his own father would never seriously harm him despite the aggressive threats of violence?

It was Sergeant Marchand who finally upped the ante and tackled the predicament head on. 'Don't be a fool, monsieur,' he said firmly as he regained his composure. 'Your son is not involved in this arrest. Release him immediately and face your responsibilities before this thing leads to something more serious. If any harm comes to that young man you alone will be held accountable.'

Denis scowled menacingly but made no response to this admonition. He only tightened his grasp on Guy's slender frame and looked around wildly as if to see who else he was dealing with. He finally fixed his attention on Pierre Bouchard who was standing some distance away. 'Bouchard,' he roared, 'this is your doing—you and that meddling wife of yours. She never fooled me into thinking she was trying to help my son. She was out to get me any way she could and you know it. But the laugh's on you now, isn't it? If you'd left us alone this wretched son of mine wouldn't be here staring death in the face.'

The frenzied fellow had not yet noticed the priest standing there partly hidden by the trees but that was about to change. With the belligerent rhetoric rising by the minute, Marcel could no longer stop himself from becoming directly involved. He was afraid that Denis LaPlante would lose all control and hurl his son into the swirling waters before anyone had a chance to stop him. A measure of calm dialogue was needed now rather than aggressive confrontation. Despite the police presence, Marcel emerged resolutely from the trees and marched boldly towards the pathetic pair. He was determined to do everything in his power to make sure the enraged mechanic could not carry out his threat. 'Denis,' he called, stretching out a hand of cooperation as he approached, 'listen to what Sergeant Marchand is telling you. There's nothing to be gained by resisting arrest. I know you would never harm your son and Guy knows it too. Stop this stupid charade right now.'

The hefty fellow turned in astonishment, momentarily silenced by the unexpected appearance of the village pastor among his accusers. 'You too, Reverend?' he stammered, the wind rapidly vacating his sails. 'What is this—some kind of conspiracy? Are you all in this together?'

Inspector Boivin was livid at this bold usurping of her authority. She quickly moved forward as if to intercept the priest's approach and the angry expression on her face seemed to indicate a torrent of authoritative scolding was about to follow. Evidently she thought better of it. The tough blond woman was obviously a highly intelligent, quick thinking cop and she saw the window of opportunity that had suddenly presented itself out of the blue. Holding back her chomping sergeant with a firm hand on his shoulder she nodded reluctantly in Marcel's direction. 'Talk to him,' she hissed. 'If you know the guy, get him under control.'

Marcel needed no further bidding. He walked directly to the unhappy twosome and looked the accused murderer in the eyes. 'Denis,' he said, at the same time grabbing Guy firmly by the shoulders, 'what's this all about? Don't use your son as a pawn like this—it'll only make things worse for both of you. You will have a chance to defend yourself and explain your side of the story. Let Guy come with me—I've brought his friend, Gaston, along to help him cope with this terrible ordeal.'

Denis LaPlante's grip relaxed almost imperceptively as he stared defiantly at the priest. 'Get those cops out of here,' he said menacingly. 'I'll let my son go once they've gone.'

'I don't think that will be possible, Denis. They're here to make an arrest and they're not going to leave without you. The best thing you can do now is cooperate with them and find yourself a good lawyer.'

The hulking man laughed derisively. 'Fat lot of good that will do,' he snorted. 'They've got me sewn up. They know I poisoned Jeanette and once they take up her grave they'll prove it once and for all.'

The purpose of the exhumation was abundantly clear now but with such a unequivocal confession from the accused it was suddenly unnecessary. 'You'll have to deal with that,' Marcel told him calmly, 'but surely you don't want your son to come to any harm. Release him to me now. The police are not armed and they'll treat you fairly. There's no escape, Denis. It's the end of the road.'

The unfortunate victim in this debacle stared vacantly into space as he listened in complete silence to this tense negotiation between his father and his pastor. What had appeared from a distance to be quiet cooperation now seemed at close range to be outright trauma and Marcel began to fear for the young man's mental wellbeing. He knew only too well that his troubled parishioner was suffering from multiple psychological disorders and he realized that a traumatic experience like this could have far-reaching consequences. But there was no turning back now.

Marcel continued to pull steadily and firmly on the young man's shoulders while staring all the while into the big man's confused face. 'Let him go, Denis,' he said gently. 'We can work things out.' He sensed he had the upper hand now. Sweat trickled from his burning brow but to his great relief, he felt a steady relaxation of Denis's vice-like grip and he saw his chance to firmly pull the zombie-faced young fellow from his father's grasp. Guy stumbled several feet forward and his determined pastor held him there, convinced now that a peaceful conclusion could be reached.

Marcel was suddenly aware that Gaston had joined him and he gently transferred the traumatized young man to the care of his best friend. 'Stay with him, Gaston,' he told him. 'He's going to need some serious help.' Then turning sharply, he looked to where Dr. Bouchard was standing some distance behind the two officers. 'Pierre,' he called, 'this young man is severely traumatized. We need you here.'

The accused murderer appeared to be crushed and defeated as he stood there looking wildly from side to side but Marcel, still unsure of the man's intentions, continued to solicit his cooperation. 'You've done the right thing, Denis,' he said gently. 'You must face up to your crimes now and seek forgiveness. It's never too late to rebuild a ruined life but justice must be served. I urge you to cooperate with the police. It's the best chance you have.'

This was the moment that Sergeant Marchand had been waiting for. Once the victim had been released he had nothing to lose and he lurched forward like an angry tiger seeking his prey. 'Stay right where you are, monsieur,' he growled with handcuffs at the ready and a grim look of determination on his face. 'You're under arrest, mon ami.'

It was the worst thing he could have done. Inspector Boivin grimaced as she watched the calm and subdued demeanour of her suspect disappearing into thin air. With her long experience she knew immediately that such an aggressive approach would be counterproductive and she made a futile attempt to stop her subordinate's ill-advised asperity with a frantic call of caution. 'Wait,' she began, 'keep him calm . . ..' But it was too late. In an instant of folly, the stage had been set once more for a violent confrontation.

Despite his muscular physique and impressive fitness, the detective sergeant was no match for Denis LaPlante. The heavy mechanic had a hundred pounds advantage and with no time to think about his options he reacted to Jean Marchand's aggressive style in the only way he knew how. As the sergeant approached and attempted to apprehend him, the unwilling suspect seized him by the neck and with two enormous hands he effortlessly threw him to the ground.

It was a moment of intense humiliation and embarrassment for sergeant Marchand. The accused murderer's decisive act of violence had taken the seasoned cop by surprise and he lay still for a moment, dazed and confused, before rising slowly from the ground. He held his neck with both hands as if to reposition his shaken head and looked sheepishly at his superior. 'Damn,' he said, 'How the hell did that happen?' But he received no sympathy from the blond woman. No serious injury had been inflicted and she was not about to indulge in any commiseration.

Inspector Boivin was furious that her underling's incompetence had destroyed the chance of a peaceful arrest and her mindset now was focussed squarely on the object of the police sting. Brushing aside her unfortunate detective sergeant, she rushed forward to confront her quarry—but to no avail. In the few seconds of distraction created by the wild confrontation, Denis LaPlante saw the opportunity to carry out an unlikely but daring escape plan. As the incensed woman approached, he nimbly jumped down from the river bank onto the cluster of large rocks below, then with swirling white water rushing over his feet, he used the rocks as stepping stones to make his way unsteadily into the St. Croix river.

It was a difficult and dangerous fete and Denis crouched warily as he slipped and slithered over the slimy rocks, glancing back occasionally to see if anyone had the nerve to pursue him. He needn't have worried. Inspector Boivin, astonished at this foolhardy attempt to escape, had no intention of risking her own life trying to follow him. She stood there dumbfounded, unsure about her next move, and then beckoned her crest-fallen sergeant to join her at the water's edge. 'There's no escape, monsieur,' the woman yelled frantically. 'You are risking your life in these treacherous waters. Stop where you are and we will give you some assistance to get back.'

The hulking fellow laughed scornfully at this warning. He stood upright, swaying slightly to maintain his balance, and turned triumphantly to face his would-be captors. 'Come and arrest me now if you dare,' he yelled above the roar of the foaming water. 'I know these rocks like the back of my hand and I'll make it to the other side of the river. Another eighty metres and I'll be home free out of your jurisdiction, and there's not a thing you can do about it.'

They were bold words but this perilous drama was rapidly escalating out of control. The absconding suspect was ludicrously unfit for such an ambitious plan and the nervous police inspector began to worry about the implications of a tragic death occurring during the course of a routine arrest. She knew there'd be all hell to pay if this hot-headed buffoon slipped into the river and drowned but she felt powerless to stop him in his foolhardy attempt to escape.

Sergeant Marchand was anxious to do his part in capturing the accused murderer but he was equally stumped about what to do. He stood helplessly on the river bank, hands planted firmly on his hips, and gave the only opinion that seemed to make sense. 'It's a tough one, all right,' he mumbled, 'but we'd be fools to go after him with the river this high. I've never seen the water flowing so fast at this time of the year. If he doesn't come back on his own I'm afraid we've lost him.'

Denis was not about to oblige. After making sure the frustrated police twosome had no intention of giving chase, he gave them a derisive middle-finger salute and then continued his precarious journey to freedom.

Sergeant Marchand made one more desperate attempt to win over the escaping suspect. 'Think about what you are doing, monsieur,' he yelled. 'This river is an international border. Even if you make it to the other side you will be entering the United States illegally and you'll face some very serious charges. Make your way back now while you still can.'

There was no noticeable reaction from the self-confessed murderer. He obviously had no intention of returning and he progressed further and further into the raging river, clinging precariously to protruding rocks and searching for ever more dangerous footholds below the surface.

The rest of the entourage stood helplessly by at the water's edge. They were shocked at the deteriorating situation but they felt powerless to offer any assistance. Gaston had remained close to his traumatized friend while Denis LaPlante performed this crazy bid for freedom, but the shock of it seemed to bring Guy back to life. He suddenly pulled away and began to pace back and forth along the river bank, becoming more agitated as he watched his father's foolish antics. 'Father Marcel,' he called pitiably, 'he'll never make it across the river. We've got to persuade him to come back.'

Marcel quickly joined his needy parishioner and put a supportive arm around the young man's shoulder. He made no attempt to hide his apprehension and annoyance as he turned to Chief Inspector Boivin. 'Surely, Madame, we have to find some way to get to him,' he said anxiously. 'We're going to have another drowning on our hands at this rate. One slip and that man's gone.'

The blond woman shrugged in exasperation. 'No one is going to follow him into the river' she said adamantly. 'It's not worth risking anyone's life to secure an arrest under these circumstances. But don't worry, we'll get him back in due course. Sooner or later we'll have him in custody.'

'I think we need to get him back now before it's too late.'

'I'll set up a request for extradition and in time he'll be sent back. I can contact the U.S. authorities from the van and they'll pick him up as soon as he sets foot on American soil.'

Pierre Bouchard frowned at this optimistic comment. 'That is if he ever does set foot on American soil,' he said cynically. 'I mean that's Marcel's point—the man will never make it. How far do these underwater rocks go? It seems to me there's not much white water once you get past the middle of the river and that can only mean the water is a lot deeper there. I doubt if there'll be any useable stepping stones once he crosses the border.'

Gaston agreed. 'Guy and I have been playing here since we were kids and we know every rock at this point in the river,' he said heatedly. 'We've been out into the river as far as Denis is now but we were never crazy enough to try it under these conditions. The river's running so high right now that most of the footholds are under water anyway.' He shook his head in disbelief as he watched the escaping felon gingerly searching for a solid place to stand. 'And we've never been dumb enough to cross the international border so I've no idea what kind of rocks are beyond that point.'

Twenty-Three

Denis LaPlante somehow managed to inch his way towards the middle of the river, more slowly now but stubbornly determined to keep going. He was waist deep in the raging waters and the fast-flowing current was obviously giving him some trouble, but he managed to make his way to a small collection of flat rocks that might offer him a chance to rest. As his would-be captors watched, he pulled his awkward body onto the flat surface and stood up, swaying back and forth to maintain his balance. This should have been a chance for the big man to pause for a moment and perhaps take stock of his chances, but he was too conscious of the audience watching from the river bank and he couldn't resist taunting the horrified spectators one more time. Turning unsteadily towards them he clenched his fists in defiance and raised his arms above his head, claiming a dubious victory. 'I'm free,' he yelled rebelliously. 'A few more metres and I'll cross the border into the glorious USA.'

This was the final tempting of fate. A sudden swell of white, foaming water swept over the bulky man's feet and he quickly lost his grip on the slippery rocks. After performing a graceless dance in an attempt to keep his balance, the ungainly fellow lurched forward and then slipped back into the raging river. He instinctively grabbed the rocks around him and he frantically fought the powerful current in an attempt to climb out. Once or twice he managed to stretch a leg around the rocks' base and it seemed that he might be able to regain his footing on the flat surface but it was a losing battle. Each valiant attempt to climb up to safety was met by the full force of the rapids and he was swept mercilessly back into the river. It soon became clear that any further attempt to climb out of the water was quite futile and the man had no choice but to admit defeat. This was the end of the road. All he could do now was cling to the rocks and wait to be rescued.

If threats and coercion had failed to persuade Denis LaPlante to give up his foolish quest for freedom, an encounter with death seemed to be enough to convince him that surrender might well be his best option. He was utterly exhausted now and he used his last remaining energy to call for help above the roar of the raging river. 'All right,' he yelled hysterically, 'I give up. Get me out of here and I'll come quietly.'

Inspector Boivin reacted to this plea for help with frightening coldness. 'Don't anyone move,' she barked. 'We are neither equipped nor qualified to undertake a rescue here and I don't want any one of you risking his life to reach that man. We need a professional team to conduct a proper rescue operation.' The woman turned quickly to her associate and placing a firm arm around his shoulders she issued her orders. 'Sergeant Marchand,' she said authoritatively as she quickly steered him towards the trail, 'I want you to get back to the van now and call emergency services. We've no time to lose. Tell them we need everything they've got.'

The tough blond woman watched for a moment as the sergeant hurried off through the woods to do her bidding and then turned back to the river, intent on taking full control of the developing situation. She was too late. Her back had been turned for only a few moments but that was all the time that Guy LaPlante needed to implement his own rescue plan. He was down onto the rocks before anyone had a chance to stop him. 'I have to save him,' he shouted back over his shoulder as if to explain his reckless actions. 'He's my father and I'll not see him drown no matter what he's done.'

The determined young fellow climbed down the steep bank to the water and headed out into the river, intent only on accomplishing his dangerous mission and as Gaston watched in horror, he slowly progressed further and further into the fast-flowing water, stretching out his arms for balance and stooping occasionally to hold on to the larger rocks that were still visible above the surface.

The inspector was beside herself with rage. 'Get back, you fool,' she yelled hysterically. 'You have strict orders to stay out of the river. Get back here immediately or I can't be responsible for your safety.'

Marcel placed a calming hand on the woman's trembling back. 'He'll not heed you, Madame,' he said gently. 'We have to be realistic—that man will drown before a rescue team can get here from Saint Stephen. His only chance of survival rests with us. As Guy just said, we can't watch a man drown regardless of what he's done.'

The woman's face flushed with anger. 'I won't be responsible, monsieur,' she snapped. 'The suspect has deliberately placed himself in danger and he has only himself to blame for the hopeless predicament he finds himself in. His son is foolishly risking his own life in this futile attempt to save him.'

'Perhaps he is, but he's younger and fitter than his overweight father and he knows these rocks better than anyone. It's a risk he has to take.' The priest looked resolutely into the inspector's face. 'And with or without your permission, Madame, I feel compelled to join him.'

The astonished woman, still shaking in frustration at her loss of control, watched as Marcel followed his gutsy young parishioner into the raging river, but she had said her last word. She let the priest go without further objection, contenting herself to stand there stony faced, her arms folded in an expression of downright disapproval.

Marcel clambered awkwardly over the rocks and into the rushing water as he attempted to follow the younger man's lead. He felt his heart pounding now as cold water filled his shoes and the strong current threatened to sweep him off his feet. Common sense urged him to turn back, but he knew that was not an option. As a priest, as a fellow human even, he had a duty to do everything possible to help save the life of a drowning man.

There was an element of profound truth in what Inspector Boivin had stated so strongly, however. No one could deny that Denis was the author of his own looming demise and perhaps it could be argued that he had no right to expect anyone to try and save him. The man had created this dire situation through his own arrogant stupidity and now his foolish actions were threatening to mete out a sort of natural justice. But there was more to it than that. Denis's irresponsibility had placed his son's life in danger as well as his own and if Guy got into difficulty he would need some assistance to return safely to the river bank. If it became a matter of priority on who should be saved first, Marcel knew where his focus of attention would be.

The accused man was seriously floundering now as he clung to the slippery rocks, splashing occasionally as he made more useless attempts to pull himself forward but he had spent his last shreds of energy and uncontrolled panic was taking over. 'Help me, son,' he called weakly as he saw Guy fighting the powerful current in a courageous attempt to reach him. 'I can't hold on much longer.'

Guy was obviously giving little thought to his own safety as he forged ahead through the powerful river. He seemed oblivious to the fact that with one mistake, one slip, he himself would be swept away in the raging waters and he continued to push himself ever closer one step at a time, clinging to protruding rocks and desperately searching for solid footholds on submerged stepping stones. 'Hold on, Papa,' he yelled against the river's roar. 'Don't let go—I'll soon be with you.'

Marcel laboured on bravely as he tried to shorten the distance between himself and Guy. He was no great swimmer himself and it took every ounce of courage he possessed to keep going. But there was no turning back now. He was afraid Guy would over extend himself in this reckless attempt to save his father and he would end up in the water himself. Marcel knew he had to do everything possible to prevent that from happening. 'Take your time,' he warned as he got closer. 'Don't try to do this by yourself, Guy. Your father's weight is far too much for one man. Wait until I reach you. Between the two of us we'll have a chance of pulling him to safety.'

The priest's words were carried away in the wind and if the would-be rescuer heard them at all he paid them no heed. He had reached relative safety on the cluster of flat rocks now and he quickly pulled himself on to them, crawling on hands and knees to where his weakened father was still clinging for dear life. 'Don't give up, Papa,' he pleaded. 'I can help you to climb out.' The young man lay face down on the flat surface and precariously pushed himself forward towards the edge of the slippery rocks. He extended both arms out to his hapless father. 'Grab my hands, Papa, and pull yourself forward,' he said encouragingly. 'Don't panic—you need to take your time.'

There was no obvious response from the fat man. He no longer had the energy to speak and he stared vacantly into his son's face as if traumatized by the seeming inevitability of his fate. His gnarled hands gripped the rocks as if they were welded to them and white water rushed mercilessly over his pathetic face, pushing strands of wet hair over his cheeks and into his gaping mouth. But the penetrating cold had taken its toll; he no longer had the energy to reach out to the rescuing hands that seemed so tantalizingly close and Guy, frustrated by his father's inaction, pushed himself even further forward in a desperate attempt to reach him.

'Wait until I get there, Guy,' Marcel yelled again as the young man slipped into an even more perilous position. The anxious priest tried to move more quickly through the gushing water, crouching awkwardly in an attempt to steady himself. 'I'll be with you in just a few moments. Don't try to hold him by yourself against the force of the river. Wait a few more seconds and I'll be there. We can do this together.'

Guy turned his panic-stricken face towards his approaching mentor. 'Then hurry, Father,' he sobbed. 'He can't help himself anymore. If we don't bring him in now we're going to lose him.'

The young man's words were like a final confirmation of the inevitable and Denis LaPlante reacted to them with one last desperate attempt to save himself. Mustering up the very last dregs of energy in his bulky body he pried his hands away from the rocks and grabbed his son's slender arms. It was a mindless act of desperation but it destroyed his only chance of rescue in one fell swoop. The weight of the man's enormous body was far beyond Guy's ability to hold it and in an instant the younger man was cruelly dragged over the slippery rocks and into the raging river.

Marcel watched in horror as the two men struggled violently in the deep water. The swift current captured them immediately and they would have been swept away in a flash but for the few protruding rocks that were still visible around them. Guy was perilously weighed down by the big man's powerful grasp and he fought frantically for breath as he was dragged in and out of the rampant rapids. Somehow he managed to wrench one arm free and he thrashed about in a desperate attempt to keep his head above the surface while his free hand groped for a firm hold in the cluster of sharp rocks around him. It seemed like an impossible task. Each time he came close to succeeding, the weight of Denis's writhing body mercilessly dragged him away and he was pulled back under the foaming white waters.

It was a matter of life and death now and Marcel was beyond any concerns for his own safety. He forced himself forward, half swimming and half dragging himself from one slippery rock to another, frantically trying to reach the struggling pair. He felt for footholds but they were no longer there and with alarming suddenness he too was struggling for breath as the powerful current threatened to drag him away. He tried to call out. 'Hold on, Guy. Don't give up,' he managed to yell, but any further calling was cruelly stopped as a thunderous swell of water swept over him and dragged him below the surface with frightful force.

The priest fought furiously for breath and as his head rose once more above the surface he witnessed the final scene of this dreadful saga. Guy, still hampered by his father's iron grip, was suddenly dragged into the powerful current and the two drowning men sank heavily under the foaming white water. One grasping hand appeared briefly above the surface as they were swept away, then that too disappeared and only the swirling waters and the relentless roar of the river remained.

Marcel realized he had reached the cluster of rocks where Denis had shown his last act of defiance. It was a relatively solid place and the only spot to take refuge against the powerful current. He painfully dragged himself onto the flat surface and lay face down, breathing heavily as he tried to catch his breath. He'd witnessed the final demise of Guy LaPlante and his wretched father and it was a bitter conclusion for him to accept. 'My God,' he sputtered angrily, 'we should have been able to save them. We could have prevented this tragedy if we'd all worked together from the start.' He was exhausted now but he forced himself to look down the river once more for any sign of the young man he'd so desperately wanted to save. 'Guy,' he moaned, 'why did you do it? You've sacrificed your own life in a foolish attempt to save your worthless father. You didn't deserve to die like this.'

Marcel had to save himself now but he lay motionless on the rocks, unable to find the energy he needed to make his way back to the river bank. He thought he heard his name being called but the roar of flowing water prevented him from hearing clearly. At first, it was as if he'd merely imagined it but suddenly he was aware of his rescuer's presence. A firm hand fell on his shoulder and a familiar friendly voice called again. 'Marcel, there's nothing more you can do. You're all in. Let me help you back across these treacherous rocks.'

The exhausted priest turned his head to look up at his benefactor. His vision was blurred through water-filled eyes and by the wet hair that draped across them but he could make out the familiar silhouette against the glare of the afternoon sun. 'Pierre,' he said incredulously. 'It's you.'

'Of course it's me. Who the hell else would it be?'

Twenty-Four

'Let's face it, Father. It was a foolish thing to do.' Superintendent Marc Laroque didn't mince his words as he reviewed the events that had taken place in Maplewood Creek the previous week and he spoke with an air of authority as he met with Marcel Dion and Pierre Bouchard. 'We're delighted of course that you're both alive, but we could easily have lost four lives instead of two. If that had happened, it would have been a direct result of your failure to follow police directions.'

Marcel nodded in agreement but didn't look entirely convinced. 'I understand what you are saying, superintendent, and I realize that safety procedures have been developed through long and sometimes painful experience. I respect that. But you must understand that in my profession it's sometimes necessary to think outside the box. I simply couldn't imagine standing there while a drowning man calls for help and not lifting a finger to help him, even if it did put my own life at risk.'

Marc Laroque was not about to yield on the point he was making. 'Many people think that way,' he said forcefully, 'and I'm telling you they are wrong if it puts another life in jeopardy. I know it's difficult to think coherently in a time of crisis and it's tempting to just follow one's instincts. I've seen it happen many times. When people are trapped in a burning building, for example, parents want to rush in to save their children or someone wants to rescue an elderly relative. We can't let them do it. They are not equipped to succeed and they'd almost certainly die in the process if they tried.'

'A burning building? That might be a little different…'

'But that's the position you were in, Father Dion. If you'd drowned along with Denis LaPlante and his son you would have ended up as a dead hero and what use would you be then? No use at all.' The superintendent sat back in his chair and interlocked his fingers across his ample middle. 'Inspector Boivin was absolutely right to forbid any foolish rescue attempts under the circumstances,' he said sombrely. 'You ignored that warning and let me tell you, Father, you're extremely lucky to be alive.'

'I have to accept that of course,' the priest continued, 'but the thing is, I've sweated blood this past few weeks trying to work out what was going on with Guy LaPlante and I was determined to be there for him if and when he needed me. As things turned out I think my worst fears were confirmed. That young man's father was charged with murder yet it seems that Guy's needs were totally neglected throughout the investigation.'

'No, no, that's not true at all.' Pierre Bouchard coughed uneasily. 'I know it needs explaining. . . '

Marcel looked at his doctor friend sitting beside him. 'I'm not entirely sure what your role has been in all this, Pierre,' he said. 'I think you have a lot of explaining to do, but I'm beginning to understand that you were trying to continue the work begun by your late wife. I mean, once I realized that Denis was being charged with murder it became clear to me that Guy had been unfairly implicated all along and I'm guessing that you took up your wife's cause to protect him.'

'It was a bit more complicated than that.' Pierre raised his eyebrows meaningfully. 'We'll talk about it,' he said. 'I know you were kept in the dark and I apologize for that. It was quite a complex project really and now that it's over I think you have a right to an explanation.'

Marcel nodded. 'I think you're right,' he agreed, 'but as I say, whatever was going on, Guy seems to have been a victim during this past few weeks. That unfortunate young man put his life on the line trying to save his father, regardless of his crimes. He waded into that river without a second thought for his own safety and there was no way I was going to let him go alone. I knew Denis had no chance once he started floundering in the water but I was determined to get Guy back to safety and I'm devastated that I failed.' The priest glanced from one man to the other and then added angrily, 'I have to say, I think with better cooperation and communication things could have turned out very differently. We lost two lives needlessly because we didn't share information and we didn't work together.'

Superintendent Laroque shook his head unconvinced but he didn't respond to Marcel's argument. Instead he turned his attention to Pierre. 'I have to say this, Dr. Bouchard. We appreciate all the help you have given us in this investigation but the agreement was that you would follow Chief Inspector Boivin's orders in anything relating to the case. You didn't follow her instructions during the attempted arrest and I think you too risked your life in a misguided attempt to help your friend here. I can understand your desire to assist Father Dion, but I can only tell you what I've said to him—you took a big risk and you're lucky to be alive.'

Pierre smiled weakly. 'Yes, I think we've both been suitably reprimanded about that,' he said, 'but as Marcel has explained, we did what we felt we had to do. We are the two main caregivers in the village and I'm afraid we are both incorrigibly service oriented. When someone's life is in danger our natural instinct is to get out there and give some assistance.'

Pierre folded his arms and sighed heavily as if he needed to get things off his mind. 'I appreciate the difficulty you are facing, superintendent, given that the case ended so tragically,' he said patiently, 'and I know you have to complete your report based on the facts. I don't envy you on that score, but right now I think Marcel has a right to know what's been going on. As I've said, I think he deserves some kind of explanation.'

Superintendent Laroque didn't reply immediately. He picked up a sheaf of papers from his desk and leafed through them, finally selecting one near the bottom of the pile. 'I'm aware of that,' he mumbled nonchalantly. 'That's one reason why I wanted to meet with the two of you today.'

Marcel looked up somewhat puzzled. 'I'm intrigued,' he said. 'What do I need to hear? Am I missing something?'

'I'm afraid you became involved in this case inadvertently, Father.' The superintendent softened his tone, giving the impression that he was being reluctantly apologetic. 'But once you started meddling, if I can call it that, we had to keep you under a watchful eye.' He peered over his glasses and added empathetically, 'No one is really blaming you—it wasn't your fault. I know you were just trying to do your job.'

'A watchful eye…? I don't understand.'

'Well let me start from the beginning. This case has been on the books one way or another for more than seven years now and no one expected it to end the way it did. We planned well and you're right, we should have been able to avoid those tragic drownings. I think mistakes were made and that will be made clear in the reports.'

'When you say seven years, are you referring to Jeanette LaPlante's death? It's seven years since she died.'

'That's correct. It was your predecessor, Father Lemieux, who first approached the police after Mme LaPlante's death. The death certificate indicated that she had died of natural causes and the body was released for burial with no concerns. Some time later the priest told us he had reason to believe she'd been murdered, so we had to follow it through. We investigated it thoroughly at the time but we couldn't find a shred of evidence for any foul play. All we really had was the priest's suspicions and in the end we simply had to file the case for future reference. We were ready to reopen the case if any solid evidence ever came to light.'

'And of course it did.'

'Yes, it did eventually. Last September Dr. Bouchard's wife contacted us. As you know, she was a psychiatrist up in Fredericton and Guy LaPlante was a patient of hers. She wasn't very specific at first but she believed that the police needed to investigate a possible murder case in Maplewood Creek. She was referring to Mme LaPlante's death. But Dr. Bouchard can tell you more about that—he was directly involved.'

'Not that directly, actually.' Pierre shuffled for a more comfortable position on the hard chair. 'In fact I didn't have a clue what was going on at that point. I knew Fran had a new patient who'd been referred to her by a family doctor in the area and the case seemed to be occupying an inordinate amount of her time. As the superintendent says, it was Guy LaPlante. I didn't know it then, but he was suffering from a severe psychological disorder which caused him to assume the personality of his father.'

Marcel gasped at this revelation. 'What do you mean?' he asked incredulously. 'Are you saying Guy thought he was his father?'

'Not exactly. But he couldn't face up to what his father had done. He felt guilty on behalf of his father, if you like, and he went so far as to blame himself for his father's crime.'

'So Guy knew about that then? He knew what Denis had done?'

'Not until recently. As I'm sure you know, Denis and Guy were living together in Fredericton last year. Apparently Denis flew into a violent rage one night while he was drunk and he revealed some disturbing information about the death of his wife, Jeanette.

Anyway, after he'd calmed down, he realized that he'd said too much so he tried to convince his son that it was all his fault.'

'You mean the home-made wine thing?'

'That's right. In fact we know now that Denis poisoned that home-made wine before his wife drank it.'

'I thought as much—and Guy must have found out about that?'

'Well Denis more or less told him when he was ranting and raging and that's what set Guy off. By the time he was under Fran's care he was telling her that he'd poisoned his wife. He was assuming his father's personality, you see. Of course it took Fran five minutes to find out that Guy didn't have a wife, and she suspected immediately that he was suffering from some kind of bizarre illusion. Fran was an expert in that kind of thing. She'd dealt with one or two similar cases before and she'd published a paper about them. It was right up her street and she just couldn't let go of it.'

Marcel nodded thoughtfully. 'And that's what led her to Denis LaPlante?'

'It did. Many psychiatrists would have simply put it down to a wild imagination that had gone totally out of control but Fran was more astute than that. She knew Guy was covering for someone. She knew he was assuming someone else's personality and taking on that person's guilt. And it didn't take her long to discover who that someone was.'

Marcel knew this part of the story as a result of his conversation with Dr. René LaFontaine. 'And that opened a whole new can of worms,' he said knowingly. 'I understand Denis LaPlante made quite a nuisance of himself at the hospital in Fredericton where you both worked.'

'Yes he did and it was getting worse and worse all the time. That's when I became involved. Fran had questioned Denis about his wife's death and he must have feared that she was on to him. He started making loud, disruptive scenes in her office and eventually we had to ban him from the place altogether.'

Superintendent Laroque nodded earnestly. 'It was at that point that Fran Bouchard called us and told us about her suspicions. We explained to her that we'd already investigated the case but we'd be prepared to reopen it if she had some hard evidence to support her suspicions. . .'

Pierre interrupted. 'She did tell me that she'd contacted the police in Saint Stephen,' he agreed. 'I wanted her to leave it at that but it was no use—she couldn't let go. She was worried that Denis would worm his way out of it and convince the police that it was all his son's fault and she couldn't accept that. Guy was a sick man and quite unable to defend himself but I thought she should have left all that in the hands of the police.'

'And Fran disagreed?'

'That's right. The next thing I knew she was making arrangements to take Guy home to his aunt's house in Maplewood Creek. She was very secretive about it all too and she wouldn't give me any details. I found that infuriating. I discovered later that she had planned to interview Dr. Martin about Jeanette LaPlante's death certificate in the hopes of finding some discrepancies that might point a finger at her husband.'

'Did she ever do that?'

'She never had a chance. That bastard pushed her into the river to get her off his back. I know I should have been more vigilant in protecting her but he caught me off guard. I really wasn't expecting that.'

Superintendent Laroque waved his finger in disagreement. 'Now that was never proved, Dr. Bouchard. I know you've always believed that Denis LaPlante was responsible for your wife's death but as you well know, we found no viable evidence to support that claim. I don't think we are in a position to make statements like that.'

'Officially, perhaps. But as you know, superintendent, I would never have agreed to help you with the investigation if I hadn't been convinced of it. That conviction has dominated my every move since I arrived in the village.'

Things were beginning to make more sense now and Marcel stroked his chin thoughtfully. 'Gaston told me you were involved in a rescue attempt, Pierre. Did you actually see what happened that afternoon? I mean, if you saw anything at all that involved Denis LaPlante wouldn't you have been a key witness? Surely he could have been charged on that basis.'

'It wasn't as obvious as that. You may have heard that we had a big shouting match on Guy's front door step that day and in the end Denis and I left the house in a furious mood. I don't know where he went but I went to have a word with Dr. Martin. Fran had contacted him on the phone a few times so he knew what was going on. I spent a couple of hours with him during the afternoon and he showed me the records pertaining to Mme LaPlante's death—that's what Fran was interested in. That was the whole point of her trip down from Fredericton.'

'Yes, but how did you end up at the river that afternoon?'

Pierre recollected his thoughts for a moment before answering. 'I discovered some very disturbing things in Dr. Martin's records and reports,' he said cautiously. 'I decided to take a short walk to mull things over and I simply followed the trail that led me down to the water. I had assumed that Fran and Guy were still in the house but suddenly, and purely by accident, I came across them at the river. I arrived just in time to see Guy fooling about on the rocks. I saw him slip off into the water. Fran was standing back by the trees when she was suddenly pushed violently from behind. Someone had sneaked up though the bushes and pushed her with such force that she was literally flung into the river. I only got a glimpse of the heavy-set man who pushed her but I'm sure it was Denis LaPlante. I heard him making off through the woods.' Pierre paused, obviously upset at the memory. 'It was terrible,' he said sadly. 'I ran up and clambered over the rocks as fast as I could and Guy and I tried to save her but we didn't stand a chance. She was just swept away by that powerful current.'

'I've heard something about that, Pierre. I'm so sorry—it must have been terrible.'

'It changed my life, I can tell you.'

'And I believe it had a traumatic effect on Guy too.'

'He went totally to pieces. The following few days were absolutely horrendous for me so I really had no time for him. I had to decide what to do. I knew that Denis LaPlante was responsible for Fran's death and I was determined to bring him to justice but it was difficult to make a case. I didn't actually get a good view of him, you see. The police had nothing to go on.'

Superintendent Laroque leaned forward on his desk. 'That's right,' he said firmly. 'Regardless of what we believe privately, there was no evidence that could stand up in court. The inquest ruled it as a tragic accident and we had to accept that.' He adjusted his glasses to read the paper he held in his hands. 'But this is something entirely different,' he went on. 'Dr. Bouchard believed the medical records and the death certificate of Jeanette LaPlante indicated that her death may not have been from natural causes after all. He convinced us to reopen the case. This is an extract from Doctor Martin's report at the time of Jeanette LaPlante's death. It's this document that got the case against Denis LaPlante rolling.'

Marcel looked puzzled. 'Wouldn't you have had access to that report seven years ago when Father Lemieux first expressed his suspicions about Jeanette's death?'

'We did, of course, and in hind sight we should have had all the medical records reviewed by someone else. But Dr. Martin was a fully qualified physician and his report said the woman died of a heart attack. We accepted that as a professional and legal opinion.'

Pierre scowled. 'Dr. Martin was shamefully incompetent,' he said derisively. 'He should have suspected that Jeanette had been poisoned and that could have been confirmed very easily by a comprehensive post mortem examination. I told him as much when I met with him that day and I think it scared the living daylights out of him. He decided there and then to retire from his medical practice and he left the village the following week. As far as I know he's been living in Florida ever since.'

'So are you saying you came to Maplewood Creek to find evidence for Jeanette's murder rather than Fran's?' Marcel shrugged questioningly. 'Is that what this is all about?'

'That's exactly why I came. I knew I couldn't prove Denis LaPlante murdered my wife but I was damned sure we could get him for poisoning his own wife. The police were sceptical at first but they were eager to get some real evidence that would stand up in court. Inspector Boivin was assigned to the case and the superintendent agreed to let me work alongside her in an attempt to get Guy on our side. The medical records were valuable as far as they went, you see, but they weren't really sufficient—we needed a witness as well. I felt that if I could work with Guy and stabilize his mental condition he would be able to tell me what he knew about his mother's death. With time and patience and some proper psychiatric help I felt he could be a viable witness in court.'

Superintendent Laroque's expression indicated some serious doubt. 'You were more optimistic about that than we were,' he said. 'A defence lawyer would have done everything possible to discredit him. What we really needed was permission to exhume the body so that some proper forensic testing could be done. It took us a long time to get that permission but we knew if the tests were positive it would prove foul play beyond any doubt. Once that was done witness information from Guy, if he was willing to testify, would simply support the evidence. That probably would have been sufficient to convict Denis LaPlante.'

The priest nodded as the big picture began to emerge and he turned to his friend with a cautious smile. 'I can see now why you took advantage of the vacant position at the medical centre. You had a definite plan with clear objectives and you needed a position where no one would suspect you were doing police work. What better position than village doctor—you could work with Guy on a regular basis and keep the police up to date on his progress. I suppose you were quite confident that no one would suspect a thing.'

Pierre laughed. 'You could put it like that I suppose but things didn't work out exactly as planned. After a few days I began to feel that I belonged in Maplewood Creek. Your friendship meant a lot to me—it still does—and I realized that when the police work was all finished I wouldn't want to go back to the stress and strain of the big city hospital. I was well accepted by the whole community and it seemed to me that being a general practitioner in a small village would suit me very well. I thought it would be a good way for me to find the inner peace I needed after Fran's death.'

'But you still had to get on with your main project—I mean working with Guy LaPlante?'

'Of course. That fitted in very well with the general practice though and things were progressing smoothly until one day everything changed.'

'What happened?'

'You got involved. That threw a wrench in the works and Inspector Boivin and I were hard pressed trying to keep one step ahead of you. I was sworn to secrecy of course and I couldn't tell you what was going on. There was some concern about your safety too. Then things got quite complicated over the last couple of weeks when you suddenly confronted me at the golf course.'

Superintendent Laroque seemed to relax a little and he smiled as he concurred with Pierre's explanation. 'I'm afraid he's right, Father,' he said. 'We were hoping to make the arrest after we'd exhumed the body, but when you went off to Fredericton last week and talked to Dr. LaFontaine about the case we knew we had to bring things to a head right away. Then that storm came in and caused us some more problems. We had to put the exhumation on hold.'

'That's something that puzzled me. How did you know I'd been to Fredericton? Did someone follow me up there?'

Pierre grinned impishly. 'René called me,' he said. 'As soon as you'd gone he realized he'd said far too much and he called me immediately. He wasn't sure about what you were up to and he couldn't even be sure you were a real priest. He knew there was an investigation going on down here but he wasn't in on any of the details and he just wanted to be sure he hadn't complicated things. I had to tell inspector Boivin of course. She hit the roof and that's when she tried to contact you.'

Marcel shrugged his shoulders in mock defiance. 'I did what I thought was necessary,' he said. 'Guy was my only concern. Come hell or high water I was determined to be there for him if he needed me.' The priest paused for a moment as he pondered his own words. 'But you know,' he said, turning to Pierre once more, 'there's still a lot I don't understand. There are still one or two things you'll have to explain.'

'Such as?'

'Well for one thing, why did you tell me you'd been in that old confessional box we used to have in the church?'

'Oh, that…'

Pierre was about to provide an explanation but the superintendent interrupted with a wave of his hand. 'Look,' he said, glancing at his watch, 'I've said everything I have to say for the moment. We'll need to talk again over the next few weeks but I think that's it for now. You're both free to go.'

The meeting was suddenly over and the three men gathered their things and dispersed to go their separate ways. Marcel made his way out of the police administrative building to the high street, followed closely by his friend. 'We can tie up the loose ends on our own,' Pierre said, pulling up his collar against the brisk wind. 'I realize there are a few more things that need an explanation. Will you be playing golf this Monday?'

'I wouldn't miss it.'

'Good. We can talk then.'

Twenty-Five

Pierre Bouchard drove rather too swiftly into the unpaved parking lot at Maplewood Creek golf club, throwing up dust and pebbles into the cool morning air. He alighted from his car and slammed the driver's door, grinning when he noticed his golf partner was already waiting for him. 'I thought you'd have ordered the coffee by now,' he said jovially as he walked across the gravelled surface. 'Bad as it is, I think we've become dependent on it now, especially on these cool October mornings.'

Marcel was sitting on the wooden steps leading up to the main entrance of the club house, and he rose as the doctor approached. 'Well it should be good and strong by now,' he smiled. 'We'll soon find out.'

Much had happened over the previous two or three weeks and the priest felt somewhat apprehensive as he tried to normalize his friendship with the village doctor. He was relieved of course that the tragic saga seemed to be finally over. The meeting with superintendent Laroque had provided answers to many of the nagging questions that had preoccupied him for so long, but he grieved for the sad young man who had died so needlessly. Guy LaPlante had been at the centre of the whole investigation and there was no doubt now that he'd been an innocent victim all along. Marcel needed to talk about that.

The small talk was at first uncomfortable and contrived as the two men sat down at one of the rickety tables in the club house diner, but the conversation soon turned to matters that remained prominent in both their minds.

'Well, things are a little different from the last time we were here,' Pierre said, taking a quick sip of the foul black coffee. 'I'm afraid I behaved rather badly.'

'Not at all.' The priest fumbled with his paper cup, turning it slowly as he recalled the unpleasant exchange they'd had. 'I think I caught you unaware,' he said calmly. 'I did rather put you on the spot and knowing what I know now, I think I asked you some questions that you couldn't possibly have answered.'

'Well that's true enough. I must admit I was surprised when you started asking me about Guy. I knew you'd taken him under your wing and you'd been helping him with odd jobs, but I didn't think you had linked him to Fran's death. That came as a bit of a shock. Of course I realized right away what had happened.'

'What do you mean?'

Pierre hesitated a moment as if on shaky ground. 'Well he confessed to you, didn't he? He confessed to murder.'

'Confessed?' The priest raised admonishing eyebrows. 'That's something I can't really talk about.'

'Yes, I understand that but the fact is, Guy told me he was going to do it. When you started to question me about his possible guilt I knew right away that that's what must have happened.'

Marcel was surprised and somewhat irritated to hear this. 'Guy told you that?' he asked tersely. 'He actually told you he was going to confession to confess to murder?'

The doctor nodded. 'It was about three months ago,' he said. 'Guy was still fretting over Fran's death and he seemed to be getting worse despite the intensive counselling I was giving him. But more and more he kept confusing Fran's drowning with his own mother's death. As I explained in our meeting with Superintendent Laroque, Guy was assuming his father's guilt and in one of our counselling sessions he broke down completely. He rushed out of my office saying that he was going to the church to confess to murder.'

'Do you mean he was blaming himself for Fran's death?'

'No, not at all. As far as he was concerned, Fran's drowning was an accident. He was blaming himself for his mother's death, taking on Denis's guilt, but he seemed to have an overwhelming need to confess that he'd killed his wife as if that would somehow get his father off the hook.'

The priest furrowed his brow as he listened to Pierre's account of the young man's troubling confusion. 'But that means you've been aware of my involvement for some time,' he said. 'Didn't you just say you were shocked to find out about that when we were here two weeks ago?'

'No, no—that's the strange thing about it. I never believed that Guy had actually followed through with that plan, you see. I thought it was simply a moment of emotional crisis and he was just sounding off—it's not unusual with that kind of patient. As I say, he rushed out of my surgery that afternoon in a terrible state saying he was going to find the priest and confess to murder. I really didn't take him seriously at first but it began to bother me some time later. I was afraid he might actually go through with it so I went over to your residence to warn you about what was going on.'

'I don't remember that.'

'You weren't there. It was Saturday afternoon and your housekeeper said you were over in the church for confessions. That really panicked me because I definitely didn't want Guy to be making confessions to murder so I hurried over to the church to see if I could find him. There was no sign of him. There was no sign of you either. I knocked on the confessional door to get your attention and I even went into the penitent's side to see if I could talk to you there. You weren't in there. The place was completely empty and I can tell you, I was very relieved about that.'

Marcel stared at his friend as the truth dawned on him. 'You were looking for me in the confessional box? That's why you told me you'd been in there, isn't it? Have you any idea how that confused me? Only one penitent ever made use of that wretched confessional and there you were telling me it was you. What did you think I was going to make of that?'

'I didn't know anything about that, I'm afraid. I just assumed you were there hearing confessions every Saturday afternoon. I should have explained.'

'So what did you do when you couldn't find Guy?'

'Well I just assumed that he'd gone home directly from the surgery, and the flap about going to confession was just a blustery tantrum caused by his chronic frustrations. There was no point in telling you any of this at the time and I just put it to the back of my mind. It was only when you confronted me a couple of weeks ago that I realized Guy must have found you on that Saturday afternoon after all and carried out his bizarre plan—he confessed to murder. It was the worst thing he could have done. It was only then that I realized what you must have been going through.'

The priest shook his head as he thought about the mental turmoil he'd endured over the previous two or three weeks. 'If only you'd been able to explain all that when I asked you about it,' he said wistfully. 'It would have saved me a great deal of mental anguish.'

'I wanted to tell you but the investigation was just reaching a climax at that point and we had Denis LaPlante under round-the-clock surveillance. I couldn't risk jeopardizing that. I could understand your predicament though. You'd mentioned Celine Hubert and I remembered that I'd been to her house just a few days before. She'd been laughing about the uncomfortable conditions in the confessional when she was growing up and I joked about it with her. I told her I had sore knees for a week after kneeling on that hard wooden kneeler. It wasn't true of course, but I realized that it must have been a bit confusing for you when she told you I'd said that. Unfortunately, I couldn't really explain.'

'No, I see that now. I wish you had though; as I say it would have saved me some anxiety and quite possibly it would have saved me the trip up to Fredericton too. I was facing a frustrating dilemma after talking to you that day and I needed some professional advice on what to do.'

'Is that why you talked to René LaFontaine?'

'Oh no, that was completely unplanned. I went to Fredericton to stay with a colleague of mine and to have a chat with the bishop. It was a spur-of-the-moment decision to visit the hospital. As it was close by I went to see if they could give me any information about Guy. But it was only after meeting with Dr. LaFontaine that I discovered Fran was Guy's psychiatrist and, more to the point, I found out that she was actually your wife. Before that I couldn't figure out who she was. People in the village were aware of the drowning accident but they seemed to be a bit confused about Fran's identity. Most of them assumed she was somehow emotionally attached to Guy. They thought she was his wife or his girlfriend.'

Pierre's face reddened slightly and he struggled to maintain his composure. 'That incensed me no end,' he said pointedly, striking the table with the palm of his hand. 'I didn't blame Guy so much because he didn't know any better, but Fran should have put a stop to that nonsense right from the start.'

'It must have been very upsetting for you,' Marcel said kindly.

'It was absolutely infuriating. Fran thought it was amusing to have a patient fantasizing about her and pretending that she was his wife. She believed it was all part of the healing process and maybe she was right. She was an expert on these things. But she didn't give a damn about my feelings. She knew full well that it was embarrassing and humiliating for me yet she allowed the charade to continue.'

'Was it because you were so angry that you followed her down to Maplewood Creek?'

'The only reason I followed her down here was to try and keep things in proper perspective but in hindsight, maybe I shouldn't have bothered. It just led to that terrible row we had at Guy's house. Everything came to a head that afternoon. Denis LaPlante got me all riled up and I told Fran I wanted her to return to Fredericton with me immediately. When she refused I stormed off in an absolute fury.'

Marcel stared at his friend for a moment, trying to assess the angry turmoil that still raged in his mind. It was obvious that the memories of that dreadful day were still very painful for him. But Pierre was revealing a vulnerability that he'd never shown before and Marcel realized that his worst fears were about to be confirmed.

'You told Superintendent Laroque that you and Denis LaPlante left Guy's house about the same time, didn't you?' the priest asked quietly. 'I know you went to talk with Dr. Martin but you didn't say where Denis went.'

'I've no idea where he went. I'd just answered the door to Mme Boudreau and Gaston Leduc when he arrived, yelling and screaming. We had a bit of a shouting match and as I say I stormed off to Dr. Martin's place. Denis LaPlante went marching off up the road complaining belligerently about everyone and everything.'

'And that was the last time you saw him that day, wasn't it?'

'Yes, I suppose it was.'

'Let me ask you something, Pierre. Do you really believe Denis came down to the water later in the afternoon?' The priest looked intently at his friend. 'I mean do you really believe it was Denis LaPlante who pushed your wife into the St. Croix river that day?'

Pierre stared into his coffee, avoiding the priest's steady gaze. When he looked up his tear-filled eyes were guilty and pleading. 'You know, don't you?' he whispered. 'You know what really happened?'

'It was you who pushed Fran into the river, wasn't it?'

The doctor's voice was barely audible when he replied. 'I loved her so much—I never intended to harm her... How did you know?'

'I've suspected it for some time, Pierre, but I became convinced of it after our meeting with Superintendent Laroque.'

'I must have said something...'

'You weren't very believable. You talked about getting a glimpse of Denis LaPlante, the heavy-set man hiding in the bushes, how he was escaping through the woods. But I know for a fact that Denis wasn't there. I know the police found no evidence of it—no footprints, no trodden undergrowth. In fact I know that Denis was sitting angrily in Gaston Leduc's service station waiting for transport back to Saint Stephen's when Fran was thrown into the water. He never left that chair until his taxi arrived—there's a reliable witness for that.'

Pierre leaned heavily on the table, supporting his head in his hands. 'I'm glad you know, Marcel,' he said quietly. 'I've wanted to tell you more than anyone and it's a relief to be able to talk about it. But you must believe me, I never meant to harm her.'

'I couldn't imagine you wanting to harm anyone. You've dedicated your whole life to helping and caring for others. How could such a terrible thing have happened? What did happen exactly?'

The distraught doctor sighed heavily as he tried to explain. 'As I told you, I came across them unexpectedly,' he murmured sadly. 'Fran was standing there with her back to me as I came through the woods and reached the river. She was watching Guy fooling about on the rocks as if she didn't have a care in the world and that annoyed me intensely. I was already feeling very angry with her but to see her socializing with this severely disturbed patient infuriated me all over again. Without thinking, I angrily shoved her from behind, but I must have pushed much harder than I intended. To my absolute horror she went hurtling into the water.' Pierre paused and covered his face with his hands. 'She couldn't swim, you know,' he said with muffled voice. 'In fact she was terrified of fast-flowing water. I was totally shocked with what I had done and I jumped onto the rocks and into the river immediately in a frantic attempt to save her. Guy did his best too, but we had no chance. I climbed out and ran along the river bank trying to keep her in sight but it was no use. She was gone. It took us a full two hours to recover her body.'

Marcel leaned forward, placing a comforting hand on Pierre's shoulder. 'I understand what you are saying, Pierre,' he said gently. 'You lost control for one fleeting moment. I can't imagine how dreadful you must feel about that, but I know you are no murderer. You didn't plan Fran's death in cold blood. You are no Denis LaPlante, but you must face the fact that you made a culpable error of judgement. You allowed yourself a moment of violence that led to terrible consequences and you must accept responsibility for that.'

'I know that's true. I blamed that dreadful man for Fran's death. It was his crime that caused Guy's tortuous psychiatric condition and it was because of him that Fran came down here from Fredericton in the first place. None of this would have happened if it weren't for Denis LaPlante. It was all too easy to pin the blame on that man.'

Marcel nodded, understanding what his friend meant. 'And you'd just discovered incriminating evidence pertaining to Jeanette LaPlante's death, hadn't you? It was the perfect opportunity for you to make sure Denis paid the price. You knew you could persuade the police to build a case against him and you even offered your services to help Guy become a viable witness. But it's obvious what you did, Pierre. You diverted attention from your own criminal act by focussing all the attention on Denis LaPlante's crime. It was a devious strategy but strangely enough it seems to have worked. I'm sure the police don't suspect a thing.'

Pierre sat back in his chair and folded his arms tightly across his chest. 'Is that so bad, Marcel?' he asked pleadingly. 'The inquest ruled that Fran's death was accidental. I know it was my aggressive act that led to her death but in my heart I can only think of it as a dreadful accident. I never for one second intended to harm her. As far as the police are concerned that incident is settled and as you say, there is no criminal case to be made. But I suffer daily for her loss. Fran was everything to me and I've lost her forever. That is my permanent punishment. Why should I do anything more?'

'Because of what you did to Guy? Didn't you just use him as a pawn to achieve the conviction of his father? Didn't you use him to cover up your own criminal negligence?'

'You may think I used him, but in fact I cared very much for that young man's welfare. I did my very best to treat his condition and in the end I achieved some positive results. By the time the arrest was underway, Guy was clear about his father's guilt and he was able to detach himself from it. That was remarkable progress. Fran could never have done any better than that.'

'That may be true but you would have made him a witness in the trial of his own father, wouldn't you? What would that have done to him? There's every reason to believe it would have unravelled all the progress he'd made.'

'No, in the end I realized that Superintendent Laroque was right. We could never have used Guy as a witness in court—that would never have worked. That's why the police moved to have Jeanette LaPlante's body exhumed. Guy knew his father was going to be arrested but he made it clear he would never stand as a witness against him.'

Marcel nodded sadly. 'He was faithful to the end, wasn't he? In spite of everything, that unfortunate young man could not give up on his father, even to the point of sacrificing his own life in a futile attempt to save him from drowning. He was an inspiration to us all.'

'He was indeed.' Pierre looked intently at the priest as if to receive direction and advice, or perhaps absolution. 'I've made my confession to you, Marcel,' he said. 'I've bared my soul and I've been as honest and candid as I can be. But where do I go from here? I need your help and advice.'

Marcel did not reply immediately. He sat with his elbows leaning on the table and his chin resting on clasped hands. He recalled the conflicting advice given by his pragmatic colleague, Gérard Rousseau, and his superior, Bishop Giguère. There was merit to both points of view, he thought, and after giving a great deal of consideration to each of them, he was convinced that a middle ground must be found. In any case, he was on his own now. This decision was his alone and he had to act according to his deepest beliefs and convictions. The priest finally spoke with confidence and self assurance. 'I'll not judge you, Pierre,' he said firmly. 'Your conscience is your guide now and you must do what you believe is right. You've spoken to me as a friend and professional colleague many times before, but this is the first time you have confided in me as your pastor. You have confessed your failing and I take that very seriously. I'll say only this—you are a good man; you've done some wonderful work in the village and these simple people respect you enormously. I won't tell you what to do but I have every confidence that you'll do the right thing.'

There seemed to be nothing else to say and the two men sat there in silence for a while as they pondered these final words. Marcel realized that their friendship would never be the same again, but like never before he felt he'd achieved the essential function of his priesthood. His was not to judge, but to lead his parishioners to take responsibility for their own actions. His penitents, if they could be called that, must have the courage of their own convictions and they must do what they themselves believe is right. He knew that now. This dreadful saga had reached its final conclusion and despite the frustrations, fears and pains it had brought, Marcel realized his priesthood had come of age because of it. He was eager to continue his work with the people of Maplewood Creek with newly-found strength and conviction, and he was determined to be a source of comfort and compassion for them. Whether Pierre could continue his work in the village remained to be seen.

A cool morning breeze swept over the open fairways as the two men left the club house and maple trees, still clinging to the last leaves of autumn, swayed gently back and forth along the fringes of the course. The peaceful scene had its own unique charm, tranquil and inviting, and it typified the very essence of this village that had become so dear.

Golf was no longer on the cards this morning. There was much thinking to do and important decisions had to be made. Marcel grasped his friend's hand and shook it warmly. 'Take care, my friend,' he said with genuine concern. 'No doubt we'll be in touch.'

The gentle words seemed to bond with a reverberating chord that still lingered in the doctor's memory. Perhaps it was that pleasant March afternoon when the two of them had first arrived in Maplewood Creek, apprehensive and fearful about embarking on a new life.

Pierre looked at his pastor and smiled. 'In a village this size?' he said. 'How can we avoid it?'

About the Author

Jon Brownridge was born in Leeds, England. His early life, schooling, and upbringing took place in this city, but he was privileged to receive a high-quality secondary education at Cheswardine Hall, Shropshire. Here he found, not only an opportunity for academic excellence, but a love of adventure, achievement, and independence as well.

Jon qualified as a secondary school teacher through the University of London Institute of Education, and after teaching in England for five years he took up a teaching position in Toronto, Canada. Through the University of Toronto he earned an M.Ed. degree and then a doctorate in the Philosophy of Education. The final fifteen years of his career in Education were spent as a school principal in Toronto.

Printed in Dunstable, United Kingdom